CHANGE OF MISSION

Also by

Award Winning Author

Ralph R. "Rick" Steinke

***

In the Jake Fortina Series:

Major Jake Fortina and the Tier One Threat

Jake Fortina and the Roman Conspiracy

***

Next Mission: US Defense Attaché to France

PRAISE FOR
CHANGE OF MISSION

"Fast-paced and with more hair-raising twists and turns than a Calabrian road, this is the best Jake Fortina novel yet.

In this latest installment, after surviving a brutal assassination attempt in the opening moments, Military Attaché to the US Embassy in Rome, Jake Fortina makes the tough but selfless decision to retire from service to dedicate his life to his wife Sara--a formidable Italian Carabinieri officer in her own right--with an eye toward starting a family. Their dangerous past, however, has other plans.

Steinke expertly gathers story threads from his two previous novels and tightens them like the strangling wire of a mafia garotte. Iranian hitmen, Russian oligarchs, and the dreaded 'Ndrangheta mafia of southern Italy all have reasons to see Jake and Sara dead. Steinke's mastery of plotting shines brightly as these plans kick into high gear. It's a front row seat alongside an author whose real-life experience and expertise inform every nail-biting moment, and a deep connection to the politics, the history, and social/military/criminal landscape his characters travel.

Aptly titled *Change of Mission*, the novel's focus zeros in on a kidnapping in the remote Aspromonte mountain massif to become Steinke's most intimate story yet. Not only does Steinke deliver the military, espionage, and law Italian enforcement realism we've come to expect, but human truths about love, loyalty, and especially the power of faith that make this a book not to be missed. Once you grab a copy, *Change of Mission* will grab you, and you won't be able to put it down!"

—**Michael Frost Beckner**, author, the *Spy Game* novels (motion picture of the same name, 2001), Hollywood screenwriter, and executive producer

"Change of Mission by Rick Steinke continues the exceptional journey of the Jake Fortina series and may be Steinke's best installment yet. Like its predecessors, "Tier One Threat" and "Roman Conspiracy," this novel immediately immerses readers in gripping drama, action, and adventure. Each book in the series feels like a film trilogy in the making, and I eagerly anticipate seeing it on the big screen. This is a remarkable book by a talented author, and I am excited to see what lies ahead for Jake and Sara!"

—**Command Sergeant Major** (US Army, Ret) **Daniel Pinion**, multiple deployment Iraq War veteran and award-winning author of *Chop that Sh*t Up, Leadership and Life Lessons Learned While In The Military*

"Rick Steinke's third book in the Jake Fortina series confirms and, if possible, given his two previous Jake Fortina books, improves upon the exceptional quality of Steinke's narrative ability and story-telling skills. The book masterfully weaves together different narrative threads such as geopolitics, international intrigue, and organized crime. Everything personal and professional about Jake Fortina's history converges—like a cluster bomb— in a crescendo in the story's climactic finish. This book is not only for geopolitical thriller lovers, but I highly recommend it to all readers!"

—**Major General** (Italian Carabinieri, Ret) **Sebastiano Comitini**, former Commander, Carabinieri Special Intervention Group (GIS) and Commander, 2d Carabinieri Mobile Brigade

"Change of Mission by Ralph R. "Rick" Steinke delivers a compelling and detailed exploration of transnational organized crime. Set in Italy, this thriller pits Jake Fortina and his multinational team, including a US Army sergeant and a Ukrainian colonel working alongside the Italian Carabinieri, against the formidable 'Ndrangheta. Rick's deep understanding of the operations and impacts of global crime syndicates is evident throughout the narrative. He expertly weaves together credible and intricate plot lines that highlight the connections and conflicts among different international groups, including disruptive Iranian elements. His precise and knowledgeable writing captures the complexity of combating transnational crime, making Change of Mission an insightful and engaging read for anyone fascinated by the real-world intricacies of international law enforcement pitted against organized crime."

—**Stephen Noguera**, NCIS Special Agent (Ret), former NCIS Chair and Deputy Program Director of the Countering Transnational Organized Crime (CTOC) Program at the George C. Marshall European Center for Security Studies

"An exciting, engaging, and interesting read! The narrative, in addition to being captivating, is made light and easy thanks to the short chapters, which are a breeze to read. Rick Steinke's work is very professional and his attention to detail is exquisite. He is gifted with a real talent for this kind of story! A beautiful story and action thriller worthy of a future film adaptation."

—**Lieutenant General** (Italian Army, Ret) **Gianni Marizza**; former Deputy Commander, Multinational Corps, Iraq, and former Director, Institute for High Defense Studies, Italy

"Ian Flemming's tenth of eleven novels, *On Her Majesty's Secret Service* gave the world James Bond, a newly married man who loses his bride to the gunfire of his enemies. All readers of Flemming's works continue to wonder "what if?" Bond had saved his wife. What would his legacy have been?

In Rick Steinke's on-going Jake Fortina military attaché global thriller saga, *Change of Mission*, the military Bond-like qualities of Fortina are joined together with the equally gifted law enforcement and martial talents of his own bride, Sara Simonetti-Fortina. As with Flemming's novels, Steinke's latest book is stitched together with militarily precision and well-crafted lines of action and suspense that are pressed into each chapter, bounded by pivoting problems that are confronted chapter by chapter. What Bond could have done, Fortina does because of the aid of his Italian bride and two military teammates, a US Army sergeant, and a Ukrainian colonel.

This is another engaging and page-turning story by Rick Steinke. Ian Flemming would be proud, and James Bond would be envious! Highly recommended."

—**Dennis Mansfield**, author of the historical science fiction trilogy, *To Trust In What We Cannot See.*

CHANGE OF MISSION:

A JAKE FORTINA SERIES NOVEL

RALPH R. "RICK" STEINKE

Change of Mission: A Jake Fortina Series Novel

By Ralph R. "Rick" Steinke

Copyright 2024 by Ralph R. "Rick" Steinke

Paperback

ISBN: 979-8-9880754-0-0

Hardcover

ISBN: 979-8-9880754-1-7

All rights reserved. No part of this publication may be reproduced, stored in a retrieval system, or transmitted in any form or by any means electronic, mechanical, photocopy, recording, or any other now known or developed in the future, except for brief quotations in printed reviews, without the proper permission of the author.

Published by: Steinwald Productions, LLC (A Rick Steinke writing and publishing company)

AUTHOR'S NOTE

THE VIEWS EXPRESSED in this publication are those of the author and do not necessarily reflect the official policy or position of the US Department of Defense or the US government.

While this book references historical facts, events, and names, this is a work of fiction. Except for those individuals obviously referenced in history, all the characters—even though some names may be the same as or approximate living individuals—are completely fictitious, as are some commercial businesses.

DEDICATION

To Susan, my best friend, the love of my life, loving mother to our children, and wonderful *abuela* to our grandchildren.

ACRONYMS

AC-130	"A" stands for attack; "C" stands for cargo. It is a US Air Force cargo aircraft that has been armed and modified to make it an attack aircraft
AK-47	*Avtomat Kalishnikova* (Russian assault rifle, 1947)
BDU	Battle Dress Uniform (US Army)
Carbs	English abbreviation for Carabinieri, an independent branch of the Italian armed forces, with a national and local law enforcement mission
ENDEX	End of exercise
EUROPOL	European Union Agency for Law Enforcement Cooperation
GIS	*Gruppo Intervento Speciale* (Italian); Special Intervention Group (English)
ID	Identification or identity card
NVGs	Night vision goggles
Ret.	Retired
U2S	A high-altitude intelligence, surveillance and reconnaissance (ISR) aircraft that flies 24/7/365.

"It took me years to realize. And maybe I can save you the trouble. But...in the book of every soldier's life, the military is a chapter. That's it. Some people think it's the whole book. No, it's part of you. It never, never leaves you. But it's not...not the whole story."

—Ike Fletcher, (*Mending the Line,* 2022 Motion Picture)

"A fool will lose tomorrow, reaching back for yesterday."

—Dionne Warwick, "I'll Never Love This Way Again" (song lyrics, 1979)

CHAPTER 1

The Escape

JAKE FORTINA, SARA SIMONETTI-FORTINA, and their two Italian Carabinieri escorts walked hurriedly along the *Passetto di Borgo,* the Vatican's 800-year-old emergency secret route used by popes to flee threats to them and the Vatican. Several minutes prior, Jake and Sara were attending a Catholic mass inside St. Peter's Basilica when two Carabinieri police officers approached them and warned them that their lives were in imminent danger. With the help of the two Carabinieri officers and a Vatican Swiss Guard, they were quickly escorted through a massive 250-year-old door and onto an elevated secret passageway.

"What's next?" Jake asked as the foursome continued to walk quickly but calmly.

"You know Sergeant Manuel Alvarez, correct?" responded the Carabinieri sergeant who seemed to Jake to be in charge.

"I do," replied Jake.

"He's the one who alerted us. He received a phone call from a Ukrainian contact about the threat."

Hennadiy Kovalenko? pondered Fortina.

"What was the Ukrainian's name?" asked Fortina.

"My partner and I don't know. But I'm willing to bet someone much higher in our chain of command does," replied the sergeant. "Our orders were to get you out of the Basilica and to safety as soon as possible. We were directed to bring you this way. When we reach the *Castel Sant'Angelo* (Saint Angelo Castle), we will walk through it and exit to the street, where you will meet a motorized Carabinieri escort. There will be three Carabinieri patrol cars parked curbside."

The *Castel Sant'Angelo*, originally built as a mausoleum for Roman Emperor Hadrian in AD 139 and converted into a castle in the tenth century, had a secret passageway connecting to the Vatican. Construction on it began in 1277 and was completed by Pope Nicholas III. In the late fifteenth century, Pope Alexander VI (Rodrigo Borgia, a Spaniard) resided there. Many decades later, it served as a prison. Today, *Castel Sant'Angelo* is a major Roman landmark. Situated on the banks of the Tiber River, it's a museum featuring suits of armor.

"Just to be clear," continued the officer, setting a brisk pace, "when we clear the passageway and go through the castle, the three Carabinieri vehicles will be stationed along the curb, ready to go. You will both jump in the backseat of the middle vehicle. There will be escort vehicles in the front and back."

"Where are we going?" asked Jake.

"To the Pio IX," replied the officer. "It's a very nice Italian military hotel and conference facility converted from old Papal Army barracks built under Pope Pius IX's direction." (Pope Pius IX served from 1846-1878, the longest-verified Papal reign.)

Jake turned toward Sara with an inquisitive look.

"The Pio IX is a *foresteria*," replied Sara. "The nicest in the country. I'll tell you more later."

Jake was aware that the term *foresteria* denoted a place of temporary lodging reserved for Italian military service members and their families and that there were several such places throughout Italy.

"Why there?" Sara asked the Carabinieri officer.

"I'm not *sure* why, but that is where we've been directed to take you," the sergeant replied.

"Why not to our private residence?" asked Jake, knowing the question was somewhat rhetorical.

"I don't know," responded the sergeant. "Those were the orders we were given."

"Our place of residence might be compromised," suggested Sara.

"That is quite possible," Jake agreed.

The foursome entered the *Castel Sant'Angelo* through the Vatican escape passageway and exited the castle curbside, per the Carabinieri officer's instruction. Immediately spotting the three dark blue Alfa Romeo 159s, CARABINIERI emblazoned in white letters on both sides, they headed for the middle patrol car. Just before their arrival at the car, a Carabinieri officer jumped out of the front right passenger seat and opened the back door. Jake, then Sara, slid into the back seat. The Carabinieri officer shut the door, and within seconds, the three vehicles, with sirens blaring, pulled away from the curb.

They headed westbound in the center lane on the three-lane, one-way road toward the *Piazza* (Plaza) *Pia*. Despite their sirens, the heavy traffic ahead of them did not allow their speeds to exceed 20 miles per hour. Traveling about fifty yards, the lead vehicle took a fusillade of fire. The shots were coming from the stone bridge connecting their road to the *Piazza*, about 70 yards ahead.

The lead patrol car's front-seat passenger immediately assessed that the fires were coming from three shooters at the vehicle's 11 o'clock. They had emerged from a white van parked in an officially designated parking area on the east side of the bridge and had the Carabinieri vehicles in their sights.

The lead driver instinctively decided continuing would only put him, his partner, and follow-on vehicles closer to the shooters. He stopped the car, intending to exit and take up a firing position. As he did, two 7.62 mm rounds struck the driver of the lead patrol car. One struck his neck and the other his chest. He died instantly. Another bullet grazed his partner's left shoulder. But the wounded *appuntato* (sergeant) was mobile and able to function as he exited the vehicle to crouch behind the right front tire.

He put the wheel well and the Alpha Romeo's engine block between him and the shooters. Without raising his head, he reached over the hood and returned fire with his service-issued Beretta model 92, 9 mm pistol. The officer knew his fire would not be accurate, but he also knew the shooters would realize that they were receiving return fire.

At the first sound of gunfire, Jake, unarmed, immediately unlocked his seatbelt, unlocked Sara's seatbelt, grabbed Sara by her left arm, and pulled her down to the seat. Jake covered Sara with his body.

Because the three-patrol-car-team had short notice for the mission and where to assemble, the Carabinieri were without their more lethal M4 carbines or Heckler & Koch MP5 submachine guns. Other than providing momentary cover fire, a 9 mm pistol was no match for the AK-47 fire coming from the bridge.

The lead Carabinieri officer providing the heroic return fire did his job. Just as the three shooters got their heads down, Jake yelled from the back seat.

"*Torna indietro!*" (Turn back!)

He didn't have to. The driver slammed the vehicle in reverse at the same moment Jake shouted his directive. The third vehicle's driver, his training also kicking in, threw his vehicle in reverse, anticipating the second vehicle's need to back up.

After backing up forty yards on what was, fortunately, a lightly trafficked road, they quickly turned right and headed down the two-lane *Borgo Sant'Angelo* against traffic, their sirens still blaring. Once they cleared the corner building, they removed themselves from direct observation—and fire—by the three shooters. Because the Carabinieri officers' main mission was to protect their American and Italian passengers, the drivers were left with no choice but to leave their two stranded partners—with one, unbeknownst to them, dead in the lead vehicle—to their own devices and training.

The assailants observed the maneuvers of the second and third vehicles. They jumped in their van and drove off. The courageous, wounded Carabinieri officer from the original lead vehicle lived to see another day. Several Carabinieri patrol cars in the city center heard the distress call relayed by the third vehicle, and help sped to the officers left behind.

Jake and Sara both sat back up. Jake, unarmed, looked at Sara and squeezed her left hand. Sara's right hand squeezed the handle of her Beretta PX4 Storm subcompact pistol. She took it everywhere, including to church.

"We're not out of the woods yet, Sara, but have you pissed off anybody lately?" Jake queried innocently, trying to add some levity after a brush with death.

"No more than usual," she smiled slightly. "I was going to ask you the same thing!"

Jake grinned.

Jake prayed silently for the two *Carabinie*ri officers left behind and thanked God for removing Sara and her fellow Carabinieri officers from harm's way.

CHAPTER 2

The Italian Dolomite Mountains: Three Months Prior

"HOW THE HELL DID YOU FIND ME?" a surprised Enzo asked the Ruskey who had called him.

A 'Ndrangheta Mafia *camorrista di sgarro* rank (corporal) hitman, Enzo was one of the local "go to" 'Ndrangheta soldiers in the northern Italian Alpine city and province of Bolzano (Bozen for local German speakers). Enzo had worked with the Russian in torturing an unfortunate Myanmar Army colonel who got caught trying to carry an electronic bug into a conference of like-minded aspiring autocrats and fascists in the Dolomite mountains. Enzo finished the torture job by grinding up the dead colonel's body in a woodchipper, per the cold-blooded instructions of the Russian now on the phone.

"What? Did you think your organization was the only one that has friends in this area?" replied Nikolai.

Nikolai, nicknamed "the torturer" and a former employee of the Warner Group, a paramilitary group considered the private Army of Vasily Puchta, had tortured civilians in Syria. He was later recruited to join the Wolfpack, a similar but much smaller and better-paid paramilitary group that served the megalomaniac interests of Anatoly Roman Volkov, a.k.a. "the Wolf." Volkov was Russia's second most wealthy and powerful oligarch behind Puchta. Volkov was now sitting in a Roman prison, about to face charges for conspiracy to detonate a suitcase nuclear weapon on Italian soil. With his former senior boss in prison and his former "Wolfpack" organization in disarray, Nikolai, after laying low for a few months, needed work.

Some three months prior, Nikolai was fortunate to have avoided the combined US and Italian military assault on the Farm, from where the Wolfpack had directed their illicit operations and where they were housed. When the shooting by the US-Italy Task Force started, Nikolai stayed hunkered down in the Farm's makeshift barracks. The task force's sharpshooters slaughtered the Farm's drunk five-man reaction team in less than five seconds.

Luckily for Nikolai, the task force's mission was to seize the suitcase nuke from the Farm's guarded safe, not to assault and wipe out the inhabitants of the small compound.

Nikolai waited an additional ten minutes after the firing subsided, and he heard the last task force vehicle drive off before finally emerging from the barracks. All he saw were dead bodies. He—and two of his Pack buddies who also hid out during the shooting—took the chance to escape the Farm before the Carabinieri cleanup squads came in. He'd been laying low ever since.

"So, what do you want?" Enzo asked.

"I'm looking for work," replied Nikolai. "And so is a friend of mine. He goes by 'Cyberkid.' He's a social media genius. I believe you could use *his* talents, too."

CHAPTER 3

I Hope I Survive This

AURELIO ROMEO ENDED THE PHONE CALL. His mafia *Capo* was not happy with the report. Not only had Romeo's two men failed their assassination mission inside the Basilica, but his three-man backup team had also failed to kill the American and Italian officers as they departed the *Castel Sant'Angelo*.

A *santista* ("saintist") in the 'Ndrangheta (roughly meaning "manly virtue") Mafia organization, one of the largest, wealthiest, and most powerful transnational organized crime organizations on the planet, Romeo had worked hard to get to this station in his criminal life. It had taken fourteen years, working through the Lower Society and ranks of *picciotto, camorrista, and camorrista di sgarro*, but, as a *santista*, he had reached the initial rung of the 'Ndrangheta's "Major Society." Since the 1960s, when the 'Ndrangheta began to expand, the ranks of *santista* had swelled, but it still meant he had more responsibilities and expectations to meet, and the consequences of mistakes were more severe.

The 'Ndrangheta, based mainly in Italy's Calabria region, the southernmost region on the Italian peninsula reaching all the way to the toe of the Italian "boot," evolved from the late 1700s, eventually congealing in the late 1800s in the region's prison system, before spilling out into the public. The shadow organization wasn't publicly written about until 1888 when a newspaper in the deeply southern Italian town of Palmi wrote about increasingly common "razor slashings" to the face and "ritual knife duals."

In Palmi's bars and brothels, gang members fought with clubs and knives. Much like the Sicilian *Cosa Nostra* Mafia and the Naples-based *Camorra* Mafia, the fights' losers, or those arrested by local police, refused to give up the names of those who hurt them. The Sicilian and Neapolitan-based tradition of *omerta*, a code of silence protecting criminal activity as well as refusal to give evidence to authorities, was metastasizing in Calabria, too.

The original Sicilian Mafia and the Naples-based Camorra Mafia groups, however, established their roots and began to take shape in the early to mid-1800s. 'Ndrangheta was the third (and final) of the three major Italian Mafia organizations to coalesce in Italy's turbulent nineteenth century, a century when Italy also unified its several regions and islands into a single sovereign country.

In the early 2000s, however, there were 200 to 300—maybe more—'Ndrangheta members who held the rank of *santista*. By 2013, the 'Ndrangheta Mafia had grown so large that a Swiss research group assessed that it made more money than Deutsche Bank and McDonald's put together, with annual revenues of over 60 billion dollars.

Now, I'm somebody, thought Romeo after receiving his most recent *fiore* (flower), a 'Ndrangheta-specific award used to signify a promotion.

Romeo had proven to his mafia bosses that he possessed the most important trait of all for becoming a successful, mid-level mafia boss, or any successful mafia member, for that matter: *loyalty*. He had proven his loyalty multiple times, first as an Italian government tax-evader, then as an unhesitating thief, extortionist, maimer, and, finally, killer. But now, he had failed. *His* plan had failed. *His* men had failed to kill the

American Army officer and Italian Carabinieri officer as they were coming out of St. Peter's Basilica.

It was a good plan, he thought. *Our plastic composite daggers evaded the magnetometers outside the Basilica. We were ready. They didn't stand a chance.*

But at the eleventh hour, somebody had tipped off the Carabinieri before Romeo's men could get to their two human targets inside the church. The Carabinieri police officers had responded swiftly, removing the American and Italian from harm's way.

Romeo had gone so far as to anticipate *that* contingency as well, figuring that if the two were tipped off or something went wrong inside of the church, they would either be given refuge in the Vatican or try to escape the Vatican via the *Passetto di Borgo*. For the former contingency, he would have continued to surveil the Vatican, the US Embassy, and the couple's gated community and waited them out. But as to the latter—the escape through the secret passageway—Romeo had an armed, three-man team ready. They were the reserve force, ready to move at a phone call, to be positioned where and when Romeo needed them in the city to ambush the American-Italian couple.

When one of Romeo's lookouts spotted the three Carabinieri patrol cars as they pulled up to park at the *Castel Sant'Angelo* to await their American and Italian passengers, the three shooters were immediately notified.

My plan was brilliant, he thought. *The bastard Carabinieri forces probably thought a stupid mafioso like me would not know about that secret passageway, let alone plan for that contingency, but I did.*

Romeo then thought of how his men had botched the ambush. They had effectively stopped the lead vehicle, but they had also killed a Carabinieri officer with nothing to show for it.

Switching from a feeling of pride to fear, Romeo knew his boss would be angry.

He's going to be disgusted with me, he thought. *I hope I survive this.*

CHAPTER 4

The Pio IX Military Officers' Hotel

"ARE YOU A VERONA FAN?" Sara asked the male clerk, who was wearing a crisp white shirt and shiny black vest, standing behind the hotel's check-in desk.

As she pushed her Italian military identification card across the top of the mahogany check-in counter, the clerk turned his gaze away from the television. It was high on the wall near the check-in desk and currently featured an Italian *Serie A* (major league) soccer match between Hellas Verona and Milan.

"I am!" he replied. His first thought of the stunning, perpetually tanned Sara Simonetti-Fortina was that she must be a trophy wife of one of the Italian Army's senior generals. Then he looked down at Sara's ID card.

Wow, she is the most beautiful Carabinieri officer I've seen, and I've seen some pretty ones, he thought. He smiled broadly at Sara.

"Good for you!" replied Sara. "So am I. At least Verona is having a better year than normal, no?"

"Yes, they are *Signora*," he replied, "although Milan has been giving them fits tonight."

"No problem," replied Sara casually, "they usually play better in the second half anyway."

"Yes, they do," affirmed the clerk. "How can I help you?"

"Listen, our room is a bit cramped. Would it be possible to

get an upgrade?"

The room wasn't exactly *cramped*. The problem was that it had separate twin beds, which was not exactly the sleeping arrangement Sara and Jake were looking for. They were both grateful that the Carabinieri had removed them from mortal threats a few hours earlier, and Sara thought that the decision to put them up in the Pio IX military gated compound near the center of Rome, a compound that held the finest Italian officers' temporary quarters in the country, as well as a plush, marbled dining room, was a brilliant move.

Inside Pio IX's 15-foot-high external cement walls and 12-foot-high electronically controlled entry gate, with 24-hour guards to protect the top generals of the Italian Army who held official meetings and conferences there, as well as met there socially, Sara knew she and Jake would be well-protected. That is, until Italian authorities had more time to assess the threat and determine what to do with them both.

"Let me check, ma'am," said the clerk. "I'll be right back."

"Gooooal!" yelled Sara as the man passed through a door to the back office. The man immediately reappeared through the door with a big smile on his face. After watching the television replay, he smiled at Sara again and disappeared.

After about three minutes, he reappeared.

"Yes, ma'am. We have three general officers' rooms available with king-size beds, and none have been reserved. You may certainly occupy one, at least for the next few days."

"That should be more than enough time," replied Sara. "*Molte grazie.*" She turned to leave before remembering, and turning back to the clerk, she asked, "By the way, could I happen to buy a bottle of prosecco here?"

"Don't worry, ma'am," he replied. "The refrigerators in all the senior officers' rooms are stocked with plenty of prosecco, wine, beer, whiskey, and soft drinks."

"Thanks again," replied Sara.

Well, now, she thought, a wicked little smile spreading across her face. *Jake and I are going to have* fun *tonight.*

CHAPTER 5

The Crimine

IT WAS A MAJOR MEETING OF THE *CRIMINE*. Some fifty or sixty years earlier, before the 'Ndrangheta outgrew the Sicilian Mafia and the Neapolitan Camorra, the *Crimine* (also referred to as the *Santa* or saint) would have consisted of four people. It was the foursome's job to advise the *Capo Crimine*—the Godfather—the most revered and feared *mafioso* who stood at the top of the 'Ndrangheta pyramid. Now, much like a corporate board, and due to the 'Ndrangheta's breathtaking economic and territorial expansion since the 1960s, there were twelve *Crimine* (pronounced Crim-me-nay) members. Naturally, some underling *mafiosi* privately referred to the board as the twelve apostles.

The *Crimine* was gathered to talk about what to do about an American Army lieutenant colonel and an Italian Carabinieri lieutenant colonel and, moreover, what action to recommend to the *Capo Crimine* for his approval. There were a handful of 'Ndrangheta members who had infiltrated the Carabinieri, and they had vigilantly kept their ears to the ground. Rumors had swirled about what had happened in a private compound located southeast of Rome several months prior and who was involved. One corrupt Carabinieri officer and two corrupt Italian government officials had corroborated that Fortina and Simonetti-Fortina were involved in the arrest of Brigadier General Cadorna and that they were both *likely*—although unproven—to have been involved in the task force raid on the Farm.

The Wolf and Boris Stepanov paid the 'Ndrangheta handsomely to support the Wolf and his Wolfpack. That support included whatever items or services were needed to accomplish their illicit activities inside and beyond Italy's borders. The 'Ndrangheta provided building materials, vehicles, massive lead safes, woodchippers, computers, and construction contracts for the Farm. And they expected much greater business ahead. But now, with the Wolf incarcerated, that source of business was almost all gone.

The mafia members who had infiltrated Italy's national government were not the only source of information or intelligence for the 'Ndrangheta. There were also a dozen or so corrupt Italian government officials who had connections to the 'Ndrangheta. Underwritten by hefty bribes, the government officials' crimes ranged from looking the other way to full-out cooperation with the 'Ndrangheta whenever the risk was not too great or at least worth the payoff.

Even worse than the abrupt loss of business, several members of the *Crimine* were also angered that one of the 'Ndrangheta's most prized Italian government-connected collaborators, Italian Army Brigadier General Constantino Cadorna, had been rolled up in an alleged conspiracy to supply an American far-right militia group with AK-47s. Cadorna had held a senior logistics position in the Italian Armed Forces, perfect for helping the mafia siphon off Italian military equipment and weapons. Several *Crimine* members wanted to devise a way to free the Italian general for what they—with their mafia "moral" calculus—perceived to be "unjust" charges.

The 'Ndrangheta also wanted revenge—in the words of the 'Ndrangheta leadership, "justice"—for the loss of business from the Wolf. They were deciding how that justice would be meted out against the "excessively bold" American and Italian officers.

CHAPTER 6

Taking Stock

AFTER THE DOOR TO THEIR NEW ROOM CLOSED, Jake and Sara turned to each other and embraced. The day's brushes with death, the subsequent adrenaline, and the joy of still breathing overtook them. Neither spoke. Not with words. Not at first. Tears sliding down his face, Jake slowly raised his hands to stroke Sara's hair back from her eyes. He found tears there, too.

They stared at each other for a few moments, remembering their many brushes with death over the last four years. Fate and God had brought them back together and helped them survive. Silently, as they stared into each other's eyes, they sent up a prayer for their lives and their love.

Sara pulled Jake's shirt up and traced her hands across the warm skin of his back, reassuring herself that he was in one piece. It wasn't enough. "I must see you," she whispered.

At her words, the dam broke. Need washed over them. Caught up in the violence of its current, they pulled clothes from their bodies. They couldn't tell whose hands were whose.

Finally naked, chests heaving as though they'd run a mile, their bodies collided in passion. Lips found lips. Jake and Sara both grunted and moaned. Hands were everywhere at once. Bodies pressed tightly together.

Jake grasped Sara around the waist and lifted her to him, his lips never leaving hers. Sara wrapped her legs around Jake's torso as he walked them to the king-sized bed. Jake lowered them to the mattress, and they spent their need, passion, and adrenaline on finding their pleasure together.

Later, when they were temporarily spent, they took turns showering and washing their underclothes in the bathroom. Sara washed first and Jake second. When he came out of the large ensuite wearing the big fluffy robe, he found chilled prosecco waiting for him in a fluted glass.

"What's this, *Cara Mia*?" He grinned.

"You wish for round two, yes?" Sara jauntily raised her eyebrow.

"*Si*," Jake intoned. "Always." He took the glass from her and downed it in one go. Smirking, he took the glass from her hand and set it down.

"So soon?" Sara laughed as Jake lowered his face to hers.

"*Si*," he whispered against her lips. He pulled the belt on her robe loose as she pulled his.

They did not find sleep until the wee hours of the morning.

Later, after waking up and celebrating their continued existence on the Earth by getting lost in each other again, they went down to breakfast in the beautifully appointed dining room of Pio IX.

As they waited for their cappuccinos and croissants, they remembered trailing an Iranian terrorist through Italy. It had nearly cost them their lives.

Sara waited until the waiter placed their order on the white linen-clothed table. In the center was a perfect pink carnation in a small, white porcelain flute.

Thinking of the prior day's narrow escape from serious injury or death and remembering the passion from the night before, Sara couldn't pass up the opportunity to tease Jake just a little. She feigned a concerned look.

"You know, Jake, we need to stop this habit of laying on top of each other like that," began Sara.

Successfully resisting the reflex to spit it out, Jake instead choked on his cappuccino. His mind raced to the night prior. Had he done something Sara was not pleased about? He hesitated. Seeing Jake's hesitation and perplexed look, Sara knew her tease had found its target.

"*Excuse* me?" responded Jake, slightly cocking his head to the side.

"Well, I laid on top of you—what was it, almost four years ago on top of that cliff—and you did me a similar favor yesterday afternoon in that patrol car."

Sara smiled broadly. Jake's countenance changed as his mental light bulb came on. Jake thought fondly and with gratitude of four years prior, when Sara had moved quickly to cover him—and the lighted cell phone he had in his hand—after shots had been fired at the couple. They had been kneeling at the top of a cliff overlooking three terrorists and their boat below.

"Well, I would agree, *Cara Mia*. We do need to stop getting ourselves in situations like that." Jake chuckled. "But if it were to happen again, I'd be right there, laying on top of you."

"Likewise, good lookin'," Sara smiled.

Jake and Sara enjoyed a few seconds of blissful silence, knowing their love for each other was as strong as ever.

Sighing with deep satisfaction, Sara continued, "I have a meeting with a couple of senior Carabinieri officers this morning." They ate a couple of bites of their breakfast.

"How do you think that will go?" asked Jake, pondering the unexpected circumstances they now found themselves in.

"I'm sure we'll talk about the threat to me, and possibly you, if they know anything. I expect we'll also chat about our stay here. I don't expect it will last that long, and of course, they can't force me—and certainly not you—to stay here. But it's nice they decided to give us a mini vacation."

Sara took a bite of her croissant and paused, considering.

"There are a lot of Carabinieri officers in the country who

are living under some kind of threat, and I'm just one of them."

Jake nodded, looking at Sara.

"Well, I know I'm preaching to the choir, as we say in the US, but we must be smart about this. I think it's fortuitous that we live in a gated apartment complex. That will help mitigate the threat. But, as you know, we're going to have to be extra alert during our comings and goings or whenever we are out and about in the city. Constant situational awareness has always been the nature of our chosen professions, *Cara Mia*, but from this point forward, our vigilance will need to be even more heightened."

"I know, I know," Sara responded. "It might cramp our impromptu nights out on the town."

"Or not." Jake smiled. "Maybe impromptu is the way to go? Keeps the bad guys on their toes. No?"

"You do have a point," she replied, smiling broadly as she finished her cappuccino.

"By the way," Jake said as he leaned across the table and took her hand resting on the table, "I love you, and I loved our impromptu party last night." He grinned conspiratorially.

"I love you, too," replied Sara, returning his grin. "And by the way, our party last night was not so impromptu."

Jake's grin turned wanton. *God, how I do love this woman*, he thought.

***

When he got back to the room, Jake tried to call his boss, the US Army Attaché to Italy, Colonel Marion Seaton. With Seaton and Fortina both from Michigan, the two officers had something in common. But Jake understood that no matter how much a supervisor and subordinate might have in common, it was respect—*professional* and *personal*, to be sure—that mattered most. And Fortina, the West Point graduate, had plenty of respect for Seaton, the Michigan State University and Army ROTC (Reserve Officer Training Corps) graduate. That mutual respect is what underpinned their entire relationship.

Seaton did not answer his cell phone. He then called Seaton's office phone, getting Seaton's civilian office assistant on the line. She was the wife of a former senior US diplomat in the embassy who had retired in Rome. A US citizen, she held a high-level security clearance and was equally fluent in English and Italian.

"He left the office saying he was headed downtown, to your location," she said.

Jake was not surprised. It was just like Colonel Seaton to clear his calendar to personally check on one of his subordinates' well-being, especially after a harrowing day.

Twenty minutes after that, the internal call button on the landline phone in Jake and Sara's room lit up. Then the phone rang.

"*Pronto* (ready)," responded Jake, using the standard telephone greeting for Italy.

"Sir, this is Giuseppe from the front desk. A US Army colonel—a Colonel Seaton, Marion—from the US Embassy just walked in. He said he'd like to see you."

It was common for Europeans to speak a person's last name first, with a slight pause before saying the first name.

Jake didn't hesitate.

"Sure thing," he responded. "Please let him know I'll be there in a few minutes."

Jake quickly put on his shoes and straightened up the room in the event the two came back to the room for a more secure place to chat. However, Jake also knew the Pio IX hotel common areas were plenty big for the two to have a private conversation.

As Jake approached the front desk check-in area, he saw

Colonel Seaton seated in a plush black leather chair, dressed in business casual attire—a dark blue sport coat over a light blue button-down shirt with the collar open and black slacks and black leather loafers. Jake came out of the room wearing the same shirt and suit pants he'd had on the day prior to his precipitous departure from the Vatican church service, minus the suit coat and tie.

Ever the resourceful travelers, he and Sara had washed their underclothes in the bathroom the evening prior and hung the intimate items up to dry. A glass of prosecco later, and they got lost in round two of their passion. They both wanted to have children. Sara was acutely aware of the optimal days to conceive. Stressful day be damned. She was not about to let the opportunity go by.

As Jake approached Colonel Seaton, the US Embassy Rome Army Attaché and ever the gentleman, Seaton stood. Jake stuck out his hand to shake Seaton's, but Jake was surprised to get a hug from his boss instead.

"How are you, Jake?" asked Seaton, releasing him. "I was worried about you and Sara."

"She's fine, and I'm fine. We had a little excitement yesterday, but it's all good." Jake motioned around the lobby. "Can't beat these five-star accommodations, eh, sir?" he said to change the subject quickly.

"No kidding," Seaton replied. "Gosh, I thought the Fort Myer's Officers' Club and quarters back in Washington DC were pretty darn nice, but this is a step up. I wouldn't blame you if you and Sara decided to have an extended stay here."

Seaton chuckled, and Fortina smiled.

"I hear, ya,' sir," Fortina replied. "But we don't think that will be necessary."

"Speaking of that," Seaton motioned toward the library, "let's take a walk and find a private place where we can chat," replied Seaton.

CHAPTER 7

Big Changes?

JAKE AND COLONEL SEATON FINISHED THEIR TALK in Pio IX's vacant library. After Jake said goodbye to Seaton, he headed out to the dining room, where he spotted a lovely lady sitting in a common area not far from the bar. She was enjoying a glass of freshly pressed orange juice.

"Mind if I join you, ma'am?" asked Jake.

"Well, you look like a fairly nice guy," the lady replied. "But you should know I'm married to this good-looking Yank. He might not be too happy about this."

"Don't worry, I can handle him," Jake replied coyly.

"Well...if you insist, sure," Sara laughed. "But you're buying."

"What will it be?" Jake asked.

"An espresso, black," she stated definitively as the waiter approached.

Jake signaled him and ordered two black espressos.

"So, Mister Poker Face," Sara half-teased, "how did your meeting go?"

"I'm not sure," replied Jake.

Sara heard the anxiety in Jake's voice. Something about his talk with Colonel Seaton had unsettled him.

"But," he added, "the colonel asked how you were. I told him we were both OK."

"Thanks." She reached across the table and squeezed his

hand. "What is it that you're not sure about?"

"Wait, Sara. How was *your* meeting with your general and colonel?"

"You go first, Jake. I asked first."

"OK," replied Jake. He took a moment to gather his thoughts. "Well, the meeting was a bit odd. Colonel Seaton said there had been some pressure from a US Senator who thought I crossed the line of acceptable duties for a military attaché by participating in that raid with the task force. This senator…" Jake paused again, considering the possible implications. Sara squeezed his hand, and Jake continued, "Apparently, he sits on the US Senate's Armed Services and Foreign Relations Committees." Jake frowned. "I'm not sure how he found out about my presence at the task force's raid, but he did. He said a military attaché had no business engaging in activities like that, and I should be returned from duty here to the United States." Jake's frown deepened.

"Even though there was an outcome that positively affected the national security of your country and mine?" responded Sara.

Jake nodded unhappily, "Yep."

"Wow," Jake could hear the mild shock in Sara's voice. "My question sounded ridiculously sterile, given what we both did." Her voice rose slightly in volume and disbelief. "We were involved in stopping a Russian madman from carrying out his horrific objectives." She gestured expansively. "Who knows how many American and Italian lives were saved? And this senator is worried about attaché protocol?" Sara's voice dripped with disdain.

"Apparently, *what* we *did* doesn't matter," responded Jake. "My sense is that there might be more to this," he sighed in frustration as his gaze wandered to his empty espresso cup, "but I can't quite put my finger on it."

"Does a senator have the power to force the US Department of Defense to bring you—us—" she hesitated for the barest moment, "back to the United States?"

Jake met Sara's eyes. "I'm afraid so. Recently, a senator from Alabama held up the promotions of over 200 of our most senior officers—generals and admirals—for months because he did not like the military services' approach to handling abortions for our US servicewomen."

"What are your thoughts about that?" asked Sara tentatively.

"The policy on abortions?" answered Jake.

"No. This senator is possibly making you end your—our—" she amended, "tour early and forcing you to accept a transfer back to the US."

"I'm not sure yet, Sara. It's too fresh in my mind." Resolved, he took her hand in his, "But I can tell you this: if it comes to pass, it's my inclination to follow you and your service to Italy, wherever it takes us, and not the other way around. We can talk more about this later, of course. But that's where my heart is."

"Wait. What?" Sara was momentarily speechless. Tears threatened. "You mean...your heart is telling you to follow *me* in my Carabinieri assignments? Like...you might *leave* the US Army?" Incredulous was the only word that could possibly describe the tone of Sara's question.

"Yes. I will follow you in *your* assignments, Sara, for as long as you stay with the Carabinieri and *long* thereafter, for whatever it is *we* agree to do together."

Jake saw the tears well up in Sara's eyes. She took his other hand in hers, and they sat there for a few seconds, just looking into each other's eyes. In their three years of marriage, a scenario like this was something Jake and Sara had never discussed. But as military professionals on their own career paths, they had understood the day would someday come.

Somewhat traditional—even old-fashioned—Sara thought

that it would be her place to let Jake's military career lead the way for them both. Especially since she very much wanted to have—and raise—a child. But Jake's thoughts on the matter brightened the warm glow already burning in Sara's heart.

I can't believe this man would choose me and my career over his, Sara marveled.

CHAPTER 8

At The Yearly German Embassy Reception: One Month Prior

THE IRANIAN ARMY LIEUTENANT COLONEL was aware of the American-Italian couple's every move. But Babak Rahimi did not want to risk looking at them directly. Fortunately for Rahimi, he didn't need to. He had just learned from official Italian diplomatic announcements—and from the Attaché Guidebook produced by Italy's Foreign Ministry—that the American Army officer Jake Fortina had been assigned to Rome. At the October 3rd German Reunification Day celebration in the German Embassy, he didn't know he would find the American officer and his Italian wife there. Rahimi understood this would be a rare opportunity to confirm their presence in Rome to his bosses back in Tehran.

The Iranian Army lieutenant colonel's entry to the German Embassy event was easy. He was officially invited to the event by the German Ambassador to Italy. After World War II, in 1952, the new Federal Republic of Germany formally established diplomatic relations with Iran. In fact, Germany's diplomacy—no matter the German form of government—with Iran dated back to the 1800s. Italy, too, had formal diplomatic relations with Tehran.

The United States, on the other hand, had no formal diplomatic relations with Iran. For nearly five months since April

7, 1980, the Iranian regime had held sixty-six US citizens hostage. Pakistan served as Iran's "protecting power" (an international diplomacy term; a protecting power "monitors and safeguards the interests of the parties to a conflict and their nationals") in the United States. Switzerland served as the United States' protecting power in Iran.

"Yuri, I need your help, my friend," said Lieutenant Colonel Rahimi to his Russian military attaché counterpart. "We need to take a selfie."

"I understand, my friend," replied the Russian officer.

Rahimi did not need to explain further. The two military attachés had decided to work together after their first couple of meetings over a coffee at some side-street, hole-in-the-wall Roman café.

Observing that US Army Lieutenant Colonel Jake Fortina and his wife, Italian Carabinieri officer Sara Simonetti-Fortina, were in animated conversation with a Ukrainian officer, Lieutenant Colonel Rahimi, without fanfare and as efficiently as possible, took the selfie. Taking less than two seconds to ensure Fortina and Simonetti were in the photo's background, he lowered the camera and checked the results. Bingo.

CHAPTER 9

Fake News

THE "CYBERKID" COULDN'T BELIEVE HIS GOOD FORTUNE. After Nikolai "the torturer" introduced him to Enzo, an 'Ndrangheta Mafia operative with whom Nikolai had worked in torturing a confession from a Myanmar colonel, the Cyberkid was vetted to see if his cyber and social media talents might be of use to the 'Ndrangheta. It quickly became obvious to 'Ndrangheta leaders that the Kid could become quite useful to the 'Ndrangheta's massive organized crime and money laundering businesses throughout the world, but especially in Italy.

The Cyberkid's verbal contract with the largest Italian Mafia organization was straightforward.

"You do what we tell you and produce good results, and we pay you just fine. However, if you ever cross us, we will give you three choices for your severance package: a short shuffle—while wearing some highly fashionable, Gucci-designed cement boots—off a high cliff overlooking the Mediterranean Sea; be drugged, sealed in a steel barrel, and pushed off the same cliff—and hopefully for you—to never wake up inside that barrel, or take a leisurely but short swim in a vat of acid. Most people choose the first option."

The Cyberkid nodded in understanding.

He had no intention of doing anything other than what his 'Ndrangheta handler told him to do. His intentions and activities that followed them, under the specific guidance of his handler and the handler's senior echelon mafia leadership, were working remarkably well.

The Cyberkid had released—convincing enough for many people—cyber bots and bogies into the local Italian social media biosphere, creating the false narrative that Italian Army Brigadier General Cadorna was the victim of a "politically induced entrapment" by the Carabinieri "deep state." It was right out of the Cyberkid's playbook for advancing the agenda of the ultimate Republican Party nominee in the 2016 US presidential election. While most Italians questioned the false theories about the general's apprehension, a sizable enough minority lapped it up like it was the Holy Truth. This further lent fuel to the fire for many Italian government officials who were on the 'Ndrangheta payroll to publicly question Cadorna's arrest.

"How are you able to do this so convincingly?" the mafia handler asked the Cyberkid.

"The first thing you do is create doubt," declared the Kid. "Then you flood the cyberspace with anything—any bullshit—that twists, shades, calls into question, or outright *denies the truth*. You then give voice to those influential or prominent people, especially those who are capable of believing—and, just as importantly—repeating their own lies over and over again, who support your false theory and narrative. It's quite simple."

CHAPTER 10

We Found Them: One Month Earlier

"MR. VICE-PRIME MINISTER, WE FOUND THEM," declared Omar Daghestani, Iran's Minister of Intelligence.

The Vice-Prime Minister was the top man in the Iranian government who knew of—and directed— Iran's clandestine efforts to develop and deploy a virus stronger than the Spanish Flu against the United States, Israel, and Jews located around the world. The 1918–1920 influenza, which swept through the trenches and beyond during the final months of World War I, was, per capita, ten times more deadly than the Covid virus. But the nefarious Iranian plot was stopped through the dogged, combined efforts of the US, French, British, and Italian governments, a US Seal Team, and the resourcefulness and bravery of a US Army military attaché and his female Carabinieri accomplice on the ground. For the preceding four years, the Iranian Vice-Prime Minister wanted the couple—especially the American—to be located and killed.

"Where are they?" replied the Vice-Prime Minister.

"In Rome," replied Daghestani.

"How do we know that?"

"We have photo confirmation from our military attaché there," responded Intelligence Minister Daghestani.

The Vice-Minister nodded.

"Are our objectives still the same concerning those two individuals?" asked Daghestani.

"Not completely, no," replied the Vice-Minister. "I don't think it's wise for us to kill the Carabinieri officer. We still have good and long-standing diplomatic relations with the Italian government. If we harm her in Italy, it will be like crapping on Rome's doorstep. That does not make good business sense. As to the American, I want him dead. But we must not leave any trace that it was us who killed him. It has been four years since the American foiled our efforts to develop the most lethal virus—and, of course, its vaccine for our people—since the merciless Spanish Flu. His death in Italy should not make the Americans nor the Italians think of us first, and we need to use that fact to our advantage. But eliminating him in Italy will play to our advantage. I'm sure a US military attaché has a host of adversaries in Rome who would like to do him professional or even physical harm and embarrass the United States as much as possible."

CHAPTER 11

Extraordinary Security Measures?

"THE QUESTION IS, DO WE RECOMMEND any extraordinary security measures in protecting Lieutenant Colonel Simonetti-Fortina?" asked the two-star Carabinieri general.

"By temporarily moving her to the Pio IX officers' residence, she is out of sight and physically protected from whoever her assailants were. But this is a short-term solution. As to the longer term, I'm not sure we can or should do more. Our Carabinieri philosophy has always been to live among the people in our villages, towns, and cities across Italy, to be seen by the people locally, and to provide daily local reassurances that we are there for every citizen. To place someone in a special protective security status does the opposite. Besides, how many of us do not have the crosshairs of multiple crime organizations and criminals already upon us?"

It was a fair, if rhetorical, question. Over the previous decades, the Carabinieri Corps had lost many officers in the line of duty. In 2019, without knowing the specifics of each case, 2,033 officers were injured, according to Carabinieri statistics. That was out of an overall force of 110,000 Carabinieri.

Over the previous decades, perhaps the most famous Carabinieri officer to have been assassinated was General Carlo Alberto Dalla Chiesa, along with his 32-year-old bride of less than two months, Emanuela Setti Carraro, and their bodyguard, Domenico Russo. Dalla Chiesa was the Deputy Commander of the entire Italian Carabinieri Corps when he met his end at the hands of gunmen on the narrow streets of Palermo, Sicily, in September 1982.

While he had expressed personal trepidations about being physically exposed in the heart of Sicilian Mafia country, Dalla Chiesa had been leading the charge in breaking the Sicilian Mafia's back, and he believed he could not do that by sitting behind a desk in Rome. So, he volunteered to relocate to the center of the Sicilian Mafia's territory.

The one-star general and colonel in the room nodded in agreement. They understood that it was their place to not only "live among the people in our villages, towns, and cities across Italy" but to continue the fight—sometimes under warlike conditions—against Italy's major mafia organizations, namely, the 'Ndrangheta, Neapolitan, and Sicilian Mafias.

They understood the ceaseless, relentless nature of the fight for peace and justice. It had been part of Italy's cultural and national landscape for almost two centuries.

More recently, in 2017, members of the Carabinieri arrested the legendary 'Ndrangheta Mafia boss Giuseppe Giorgi, known as *The Goat*. In early 2020, hundreds of Carabinieri, working with Italy's financial police—the *Guardia di Finanza*—arrested nearly 100 people in Sicily who, led by two local mafia clans, had systematically pillaged European Union investment funds destined for the people and state of Italy.

In December 2019, the Carabinieri arrested more than 300 members of the 'Ndrangheta, considered by the Carabinieri to be the most vicious of the infamous mafia groups. But for any of the senior Carabinieri officers in the room, it was unthinkable to consider some special physical security treatment other than their training, equipment, tactics and procedures, culture, and personal vigilance provided them.

"I don't think Simonetti seeks or would want any type of special treatment," said the colonel, who had known Sara for several years. "In fact, I believe she would chafe at it. The sooner she gets out of the Pio IX, and the sooner things get back to as normal as is physically possible in her Carabinieri life, the happier she will be."

"I agree," responded the major general. "We will recommend no further additional physical security measures. Fortunately, she does live in a gated community with the American and that will also help mitigate any threats out there."

CHAPTER 12

The Chapel

WITH JAKE AT HER SIDE, Sara held his hand and prayed. They sat in the pews at Rome's *Divina Sapienza* (Divine Wisdom) Chapel. Upon waking that morning, only two days after the 'Ndrangheta attack on them at the Vatican, Sara felt the need to seek the chapel for prayer. She knew she could pray anywhere, anytime. But today, she decided to act on what she felt was God's urging.

Only three others had made the easy and discrete 900-yard walk from the Pio IX foresteria, the joint Italian Ministry of Defense, and the Italian Armed Forces' officers' club, hotel, conference center, and temporary quarters.

The chapel also functioned as a place of respite and reflection for the thousands of university students attending the Sapienza University of Rome (often called "Sapienza" or the University of Rome). The university's enrollment made it one of the largest universities in Europe. Founded in 1303, it is also one of the world's oldest.

As Sara sat in this holy place, her prayers were simple. She thanked God that she and Jake had survived the second attack on them in four years. She prayed also for a "healthy child." Being in her late thirties, Sara understood the physiological challenges of having a child increased with each passing year. But she felt, deeply, that she and Jake were ready to welcome a child to their world.

CHAPTER 13

Leaks And Less Security

AS CLASSIFIED INFORMATION LEAKS GO, it's not always clear who—or how, either carelessly or deliberately—leaked the secret information. But in this case, the Russian oligarch, a.k.a. "the Wolf," was incarcerated on charges of importing a weapon of mass destruction, conspiring to detonate said weapon in Italian territorial waters, money laundering, extortion, and a host of lesser crimes since the Carabinieri raid on his Spanish Steps neighborhood apartment, was thrilled that someone did leak the information.

A corrupt Italian politician, using the 'Ndrangheta network, got the message to the Wolf that the US Army Lieutenant Colonel Jake Fortina had played "a leading role" in crushing the Wolf's plans to threaten Italy and the North Atlantic Treaty Organization (NATO) with a nuclear weapon. Like Vasily Puchta, the Russian President whom the Wolf had planned to overthrow, the Wolf could never let anyone cross him and get away with it. Doing so would weaken his standing and reputation as a man never to be trifled with, certainly not without consequences. He understood that vanquishing his political and media opponents—through staged "accidental" deaths or blatant, out-in-the-open direct assassinations—is what had kept Vasily Puchta in the Kremlin going on 25 years. The American had to go.

Delivering the order to kill Jake Fortina for a tidy sum of

$15 million was not hard. The 'Ndrangheta knew the multi-billionaire Wolf had bottomless financial pockets—not to mention Swiss bank accounts—so the 'Ndrangheta had pressed for a hefty $25 million in compensation. But the Wolf stood fast at $15 million, thinking, *I have principles, even in prison.*

The sum made it clear to the 'Ndrangheta that the Wolf wanted the American dead in the worst way. And they had plenty of actively scheming and well-connected inmates in the prison. Much like in the late 1800s, when the 'Ndrangheta coalesced and evolved in southern Italy's prisons, its criminal reach to the outside world was strong, with a functioning chain of command inside as well as outside the local prison system. With Italian prisons rated the third most overcrowded of fifteen countries in Western Europe, that certainly did not hinder 'Ndrangheta from communicating almost as freely as if they were standing in an Italian village square.

And when the onslaught of Covid hit Italy hard in the late winter of 2020—and the morgues began to fill to capacity—prison riots, for fear of overcrowded conditions and the easy spread of the disease, began to erupt across the Italian peninsula. By March 11, 2020, fourteen prisoners had died during the riots, and hundreds of prison officers were injured. Relatives of mafia prisoners began protesting immediately. Many of the mafias' top leaders, some already in poor health, were released. The 'Ndrangheta was well-positioned to take advantage of the lowered security standards and even the chaos that ensued. They never stopped pressing for that advantage to keep their intra-prison communications as strong as ever.

CHAPTER 14

Back Home

JAKE AND SARA SURVEYED THE AREA before turning off the busy *via Cassia* toward the electronic gate of their apartment complex. The *Centro Residenziale Avila*, located due north of Rome just off Rome's *Grande Raccordo Annulare* (ring road) on the very busy *via Cassia*, one of Rome's original roads (originating circa 240 BC), was once home to the deposed King of Afghanistan. The US Embassy allowed a handful of its US employees to live there because of the Centro's added security features. Nonetheless, one could never be too safe, especially when there was already a target on one's back.

"Home, sweet home," said Jake as the gate rolled open.

"Indeed, it is," replied Sara.

It had been five days since the attack on the couple at St. Peter's Basilica. Sara's Carabinieri colleagues had warned them and removed them from the "X." After surviving the same-day, subsequently harrowing attempted ambush, they were hidden for a few days in Rome's Pio IX Officers Club and Hotel. The high-walled facility had excellent security measures. Now, they were back home, ready to re-establish their daily lives and routines as a US military attaché and Italian law enforcement officer in one of the world's great cities.

"Where do we go from here?" asked Sara as Jake wheeled the car down to the subterranean garage and parked.

"Well, wherever we go, we do so carefully," Jake sighed,

rubbing his hand over his face. "I know we've both been in a vigilant mode most of our adult lives, but now, we need to be even more vigilant."

"Of course," Sara replied in resignation, "you are right. Definitely more vigilant."

"But we've got this, *Cara Mia*," Jake said as he grasped her hand, lifted it to his lips, and kissed it gently. "You and me. Together."

"I know. I know we do," Sara smiled. They both undid their seatbelts and exited the vehicle.

In their previous days in the Pio IX hotel, they'd discussed who their enemies might be and who might want either one or both dead. There were several contenders for the top of that short list. Surviving members of the Wolfpack, who Jake and Sara suspected had survived the Joint US-Italy Task Force raid on the Farm, were on it.

The mafia, too, was a prime contender. And, truth be told, Sara and Jake also considered the Iranians. Since their successful takedown of an Iranian plot to infect hundreds of thousands—if not millions—of Americans and Jews around the world, rumors had been swirling among the world's prominent intelligence agencies as to who was at the forefront of US and Italian efforts to stop the Iranian threat.

They discussed the possibilities again as they headed into their apartment.

CHAPTER 15

Change Of Mission

JAKE WAS FEELING ANXIOUS. It was not a feeling he was used to, especially when waiting outside Colonel Marion Seaton's office. Seaton had called Jake for a meeting but did not inform Jake of the agenda. Their meetings were rarely contentious or difficult and never fraught. But this morning felt different, and Jake was not quite sure why.

"C'mon in, Jake," said the US Army colonel upon opening the door. "Have a seat."

Jake sat down on the couch and across the coffee table from his boss. Seaton was comfortably ensconced in his well-worn brown leather swivel chair.

"What's up, sir?" asked Jake.

"Jake, do you remember a while back when I mentioned that some US Senator from Mississippi apparently wanted you to be pulled off attaché duty for going on that raid of the Wolf's Farm?"

"I do," answered Jake.

"Well, it's all bullshit, but this has gone to the next phase."

"And what phase is that?" asked Jake.

"The army is pulling you out of Rome and sending you back to Washington DC."

The finality of the colonel's tone and words gave Jake pause. He leaned back on the couch and nodded. Jake understood he had stretched the limits—smashed through them, actually—of what activities a US military attaché assigned to a US Embassy was authorized to do, and being part of a joint US-Italian armed military operation on the soil of the host country was not one of them.

But I'd do it again in a heartbeat, he thought.

"To do what?" responded Jake.

"That's not clear yet," responded Seaton. "For the interim, you'll be assigned to Headquarters, Department of the Army G-3/5/7 Strategic Operations Directorate, in the Pentagon. I'm not sure what your exact job or title will be yet, but I'm sure the army will want to take advantage of your extensive international military security cooperation experience and expertise once you get there."

Damn, that sounds ridiculously sugar-coated, thought Seaton. *This politically induced reassignment is a crock of crap, and Jake and I both know it.*

Jake again gave an affirmative nod, looked Colonel Seaton in the eyes, and remained silent.

What neither Jake nor Seaton knew was that Mississippi's US Senator James Brock, who served on the US Senate's Foreign Relations Committee as well as Armed Services Committee, had also learned that Jake had complained about LTC Beauregard Bragg and his racist ideologies. It was Brock who had strongly pushed for Bragg—from Brock's home state of Mississippi—to be assigned to Rome. When Bragg had been rolled up by the US Army Criminal Investigation Division for US domestic conspiracy charges, Brock was embarrassed by it. Bragg had been "Brock's man in Italy," or so Brock liked to think. Eliminating any visible or living remnants of the embarrassing and ugly affair was Brock's way of dealing with it, and Jake Fortina was one of the remnants that had to be eliminated from the scene.

"Look, Jake, this is not right, and you and I both know it. But our hands are tied. As you also know, civilian oversight of our US Armed Forces is an American tradition dating back to George Washington and the First Continental Congress. It's the right thing for our democracy. But occasionally, politicians abuse their power. And while I don't know all the details, I'm pretty sure Brock is being overly heavy-handed here."

Jake was still in listening mode.

Jake thought of an Alabama-elected US Senator, who, because he disagreed with the US Department of Defense's policy on abortions for military service members, had single-handedly blocked the promotions of the most senior generals and admirals in the US Armed Forces for months. It was becoming a major national security challenge—even threat—but nobody seemed to be able to do anything about the senator's actions. Finally, after months, the Alabama senator had relented in some specific cases.

"Our senior military leadership has very little room to maneuver in this regard. You remember the Lieutenant Colonel (Alexander) Vindman case, right?" asked Seaton.

"Yep. The guy got screwed," replied Jake.

Seaton considered the former Ukraine expert who served on the National Security Council at the White House. Vindman had spoken truth to power concerning a phone call between the US and Ukrainian Presidents. He revealed that the US president threatened to hold back US military aid to Ukraine pending Ukraine's investigation of a US citizen's activities in Ukraine. The civilian in question had connections to a primary political opponent of the then-sitting president. After Vindman had the temerity to speak out, the president's administration went after Vindman, terminating his promotion potential to colonel. Vindman ended up resigning.

"He did get screwed, no doubt," replied Seaton.

Both men were quiet for another moment. Jake looked up from the coffee table.

"What does my timeline look like, sir?" asked Jake.

"The army pushed to have you out of here in 45 days, and we pushed back," replied Seaton.

Both Jake and Seaton knew that from a standing start, given all the things that had to happen with a major move from Europe—the publication and receipt of official army orders, the screening and shipping of household effects, shipping or selling a car, the closing of local rental contracts, finding a place to live at the other end, turning over his duties to someone else, etc.—those 45 days constituted a short, pressure-packed, and stress-inducing timeline.

What about Sara? Thought Jake. *Sure, we alluded to this possibility a while back, but now what?*

"What did the army say after you pushed back?" asked Jake.

"We asked for 90 days to have you transferred back to the US. But the army came back with a maximum of 60. Unfortunately, there is not a heck of a lot we can do about that. This frustrates me as much as it does you, Jake."

"Got it," replied Jake. "I'll deal with it."

"I know you will," replied Seaton.

***

Forty-eight hours later, Jake was back in Colonel Seaton's office. Jake and Sara had a long talk about Jake's being abruptly reassigned to the United States. In Jake's mind, it was clear what his course of action was going to be, and Sara fully agreed with him.

"Sir, first of all, thanks for getting me the 60 days instead of the 45 so that Sara and I have a bit more breathing room time to get our stuff together," began Jake.

"No sweat, Jake," replied Seaton. "We really wanted the ninety days, but we had no room to maneuver."

"I understand, sir," replied Jake.

"Speaking of room to maneuver," continued Jake. "I'm submitting my retirement papers today, effective in 60 days or as soon as the army approves them. I'm not going back to the US. I'm asking for a "European out" (the term used for when military members seek to retire in place, and in this case, Europe). I will take whatever final leave days are owed to me and use them here in Italy."

"Can't say I'm shocked," said Seaton. "There is a time when we all must do exactly what you're about to do. When that point comes—and how we get there—is different for everybody. Some people never really see it coming. But my experience is that most—but not all—people *know* when that time is."

"Roger that, sir," responded Jake.

"But I will add this," said Seaton. "You have performed one hell of a service to our national security and our fellow citizens. Your retirement will be our army's and nation's loss. Full stop."

"Thank you, sir," replied Jake.

"If I could ask," continued Seaton, "What do you plan on doing with the rest of your life?"

"Besides being a good husband to my beautiful bride, I'm not one hundred percent sure. I just know that it's time for a change of mission," answered Jake.

CHAPTER 16

The Orders

AURELIO ROMEO SAT ON THE PARK BENCH in Rome's verdant Villa Borghese Gardens. He shifted his position on the slatted blue wooden bench. He had been told by his mafia boss someone would meet him at the bench. He had no idea who the person would be because that's exactly how the 'Ndrangheta Mafia played the game. Were Romeo to get arrested for murder or attempted murder, he truly would not know who the person was that delivered the order to kill his intended victim. That provided the 'Ndrangheta with plausible deniability, an element crucial to most major crimes the massive mafia organization conducted.

After his duo of hand-picked mafia assassins failed to kill or seriously wound Jake Fortina and Sara Simonetti-Fortina inside St. Peter's Basilica, and Romeo's backup team of shooters had also failed to kill the American and Italian officers in an ambush, Romeo knew he was standing on thin ice. The fact that he was sitting out in the open on a park bench while observing an occasional passerby made him feel slightly more comfortable. It was better than meeting someone in a dark alley. At least this way, he figured he'd have plenty of warning if his life was in imminent danger.

If they are going to kill me at close range, it won't be here, out in the open, he thought.

That somewhat positive thought quickly turned into an

anxious one.

But one of their sharpshooters could take me out with a rifle from long range, he thought.

That thought had Romeo subtly scanning 360 degrees around him for the third time since he'd arrived at the park bench.

Spotting a large clump of trees about 150 yards away, *the shooter could be in there*, he thought.

He attempted to steady his mind by focusing on his mission and the meeting at hand.

Whoever this person is, he is late, came the next rambling thought.

Only three people were in sight: a happy young teen-aged boy walking with his happier girlfriend, arm-in-arm, in a grassy meadow centered in Romeo's field of vision, about forty yards away, and an elderly lady with a cane approaching him from his right, about thirty yards away. Having looked to his left for a minute, he was surprised when he heard a deep feminine voice beside him.

"May I sit down?" she asked. "It's been a long walk."

"Of course," replied Romeo, sliding over to the left side of the bench to give the lady room to sit down.

But I'll have to ask her to leave when my contact arrives, he thought.

The lady sat down, *rather close,* thought Romeo.

"It's a beautiful morning, isn't it?" asked the lady.

"Yes, it is," responded Romeo. "Quite beautiful."

The lady knew Romeo from the mugshot photo she'd seen the day prior. To confirm she had the right man, she was told he would have "a Calabrian accent." Romeo's few words confirmed she had found her mark. She turned and looked Romeo in the eyes.

Up close, Romeo could now see that the woman was fifteen or twenty years younger than her hair color portrayed. He returned her brief stare—the only moment she would allow it for the rest of the conversation—and quickly observed beautiful dark eyes with olive-toned skin covered in light-colored makeup to maintain her elderly ruse. In those brief moments before she continued, her sensual perfume overwhelmed him, and Romeo knew the woman did not need her cane.

"I understand you have a beautiful family," commented the lady.

Romeo's mind snapped back to the present moment. He was stunned by the mysterious lady's comment.

How does she know I have a family? He anxiously pondered.

The disguised lady had homed in on the last vestige of anything Romeo truly cared for in this world. The mafia was the fateful "profession" into which he was practically born. But his wife and two daughters constituted his entire world.

The lady sat silent, turning her head to look straight ahead, and giving Romeo time to formulate an answer.

He finally managed to eke one out.

"My family *is* beautiful," he replied.

"And your *other* family wants to keep it that way," said the lady in a deliberate and ominous tone, obviously referring to the 'Ndrangheta Mafia "family."

The lady handed him a piece of paper. It was a bit larger than a standard business card. "Captain Pietro Bondanella" was hand-written, in near-perfect block letters, on the plain white card.

Romeo stared at the name on the card.

"You got it?" asked the lady, still looking straight ahead from the park bench.

"Si," responded Romeo.

The lady reached over, took the card from Romeo's hand, flipped it over, and handed it back to Romeo.

"Locate this Carabinieri officer, kill him, and leave no trace of the body," read the message on the back.

Romeo stared at the card. The lady again let several more seconds pass by. When it was clear that Romeo understood, she again took the paper card back.

Romeo was stunned at how beautiful, lithe, and sensual the lady's tan hands and long fingers were. From her side profile, he could now see just how beautiful she was.

The lady pulled out a small Bic lighter, lit the card on fire, and stomped the smoldering ashes in the dirt.

Her 'Ndrangheta handlers were taking no chances that Romeo might have changed his spots and might be wearing an electronic bug. They also wanted to leave no trace of who delivered the message. Plausible deniability and misdirection were a part of almost all "major" 'Ndrangheta operations.

The lady handed Romeo a second card.

"All will be forgiven when you finish the job. You have four weeks."

Again, after giving Romeo a few seconds to absorb the information, she took the card, lit it on fire, dropped it in the dirt at her feet, and ground its black and delicate ashes to dust with the soles of her brown leather, old lady lace-up shoes.

The lady looked straight ahead, off into the distance. She paused. Still staring straight ahead, she spoke.

"Don't let your beautiful family end up like those ashes I just stomped out."

The lady got up and slowly walked away, retaining her credible demeanor as an elderly woman in need of a cane.

Romeo leaned back on the bench and looked up at the bright blue Roman sky as the cards' words sunk in. He let out a long sigh.

I cannot fail, he thought.

CHAPTER 17

Three Weeks Later: Good News

IN A WORLD WHERE RECENT NEWS HAD BEEN MOSTLY BAD, Jake was happy to receive some good news. After sharing it with Sara, he wanted his boss to be the first professional colleague at the embassy to know the news.

"Sir, I wanted to let you know my retirement has been approved, effective the last day of next month," said Fortina.

"Wow, Jake, you mean the Department of the Army approved your retirement some two weeks after you submitted the paperwork? That's like some kind of record, isn't it?" replied Colonel Seaton.

"I think they want to get rid of me in the worst kind of way," chuckled Fortina.

"Sadly, Jake, you and I know there is some truth to that. The pressure from that Mississippi senator's staffers to get you safely retired has been unrelenting. Just like Alex Vindman, getting you out faster solves somebody's problem...but it does nothing for the United States Army. But it's out of sight, out of mind for the politician."

"No doubt about that, sir. And it sucks to be leaving in this way, but I'm at peace with my unexpected early departure. And more importantly, so is Sara. While I believe she would have come with me to the US, I also believe it's much better for both of us if I take a European out and stay in the neighborhood, so to speak."

"Well, I haven't had to reach the retirement point yet, Jake, but I, too, know that day is not far off. And for sure, my bride will be very involved when we come to that decision point,' replied Seaton.

"Totally understand," said Jake. "By the way, I'd like to take my last days of leave I have here in Rome before I punch out, if that's doable. Until then, of course, if there is anything you need me for, I'll be in the office doing run-of-the-mill attaché stuff and prepping for my retirement, but I'm ready and available for anything else you might need me for."

"Jake, I want you to take most of your remaining time in the army to focus on taking care of your personal business so that you can go through a proper transition over to the civilian side. But there is one thing I could use your help on."

"Say the word, sir."

"The Commanding General of the NATO Intelligence, Surveillance, and Reconnaissance Force, Brigadier General Andrew Clark, is running a big NATO exercise in Sigonella, down in Sicily, in three weeks. He had a guy with your international and Southern European military relations expertise—but not your counterterrorism expertise—to help with the exercise. That person recently had to drop out of the exercise, and there are no other US military officers in Italy, let alone in Europe, with your background. General Clark and his staff are scrambling to find somebody to replace the person who dropped out. I've known Clark for several years and would like to help him out. You'd serve in an advisory role as well as a mentoring and play-acting role during the exercise. It would be for a solid six days, Sunday through Friday. After that, I wouldn't care if you went fishing every day. Besides, at that point, you will only have a week or two before you officially retire."

"I know General Clark, too," replied Jake.

"Wait. What? You *know* 'Spoo'?" responded Seaton, now using the general's callsign, one that Air Force (and other US military) pilots retain for their entire careers and longer.

"I do," replied Jake, smiling.

"How the...how do you know him, Jake?" asked Seaton.

"The Marshall Center. When I was there for one year getting my master's degree, Clark was there as the Air Force Chair and Program Director for Central Asia, as a lieutenant colonel. After the Air Force sent him to the Army War College for a year, the Air Force sent him to the Marshall Center in Germany. His one year at the Marshall Center was intended to broaden his understanding of internationally combined US military operations, as well as increase his geo-strategic and political-military expertise. The Marshall Center is a very international, civil-military organization. Turns out, the Air Force was thinking ahead—or just got lucky," said Jake, laughing, "because that's exactly the kind of NATO organization Brigadier General Clark now commands. While at the Marshall Center, Spoo and I drank our fair share of Scotch together, too. That was not terrible preparation for the NATO assignment, either."

Seaton laughed out loud. Fortina chuckled with him.

"So does that mean your answer is a 'yes,' Jake?" asked Seaton.

"No, sir," replied Jake. "It means it's a hell yes."

CHAPTER 18

Surveillance

LIFE IS BETTER NOW, THOUGHT THE CARABINIERI CAPTAIN. *Since I stopped working for that crazy, corrupt general, life has been much better.*

Indeed, for Captain Pietro Bondanella, life *was* better. Since the Italian general—Bondanella's former boss—had been arrested, Bondanella had been reassigned to an administrative position within the Italian Carabinieri General Headquarters. The Carabinieri Headquarters, located at *Viale Romania* 45 and in an upscale part of Rome, north of the verdant *Villa Borghese* Park and not far from Rome's *Parioli* quarter, was in a neighborhood far too expensive for the Carabinieri captain to afford. A 900-square-foot, one-bedroom apartment located northwest of Rome's city limits was the most he could afford. But it required a 45-minute one-way daily commute in and out of the city. That's if he left early in the morning. If he left after 7:20 a.m., it could take him two hours by car.

But the captain's new position allowed him to spend much more time with his beautiful Veronese wife Carla and their cutie-pie, eighteen-month-old daughter than being a general's aide-de-camp. In that role, Bondanella had to be available to the Italian general officer twenty-four hours per day, seven days per week. And the overbearing general had made sure Bondanella *was* available, occasionally testing—at times cruelly playing with—Bondanella's responsiveness. Bondanella always gave 100 percent in his duty performance to keep the general from tormenting him further. Out of the half-dozen or so senior military officers he'd met in his ten years of Carabinieri service, Bondanella respected the wayward general the least.

In a few weeks, Bondanella would appear before an Italian military tribunal to present his side of a conversation he'd overheard between his former boss, Italian Army Brigadier General Constantino Cadorna, and US Army Lieutenant Colonel Beauregard Bragg. The conversation had been about Bragg requesting—and Cadorna agreeing to supply—the American and his US militia organizations with AK-47 automatic rifles and ammunition. Because this conversation occurred *before* Italian law enforcement officials later caught Cadorna on tape making a similar deal, the young captain's personal testimony would be crucial for the Italian government prosecutor's overall conspiracy and illegal weapons charges against Cadorna.

However, Bondanella's new duty assignment was beginning to allow the thirty-two-year-old captain to feel a bit too relaxed. Never thinking that a Carabinieri junior officer would be surveilled, especially while being in his home territory on Italian soil rather than some far-flung place of conflict like Kabul, Afghanistan, where he once served, Bondanella began to get sloppy and make mistakes with his personal security.

The worst mistakes involved doing everything by habit: leaving his apartment at the same time every morning, getting home in roughly the same fifteen to twenty-minute time window every night, taking the same mode of transportation every day, and even habitually grabbing a sandwich for lunch from a mom-and-pop café located near the Carabinieri Headquarters every afternoon. He liked going to the café because the shop's owners got to know him personally, in a city that could be quite impersonal. And the *mafioso* hitman Aurelio Romeo liked it, too. He liked it a lot. It made surveilling Bondanella's every move entirely too easy.

Bondanella might as well be a human statue, thought Romeo as he considered the ways he could kill the Carabinieri captain and make him disappear forever.

CHAPTER 19

A Gift From Allah

IRANIAN VICE-PRIME MINISTER ABDISHER DABIRI was beside himself with joy. He masterminded the original plot to decimate Jewish populations around the world with a more virulent strain of the Spanish Flu. The most extreme and powerful anti-Americans and anti-Semites in the Iranian government helped him execute his plans. While the plot did not fit perfectly with Iran's long-standing goal to "push Israel into the sea," if the damned American Army officer and his female Italian accomplice hadn't foiled it, millions of Jews and Americans would have died, thought Dabiri enraged.

But now, *Allah has given us a gift*, he thought.

Iran's Military Attaché to Italy, Lieutenant Colonel Babak Rahimi, was already considered a hero by Dabiri and his Iranian government lieutenants. Rahimi had discovered the presence of the American officer and Italian officer in Rome, and he had provided a photo to prove it.

Dabiri decided that the American had to be killed.

"Lieutenant Colonel Rahimi has negotiated a deal to have the Italian Mafia pay us 10 million dollars to kill him!" recounted Dabiri to his Intelligence Minister, Omar Daghestani. "That can only be a gift from Allah!"

The 'Ndrangheta, wishing to keep their "hands clean," decided to take $5 million off the top and subcontract the hit to the Iranians for $10 million after they accepted the Wolf's $15 million offer to kill the American.

Dabiri found the major terms of the death deal more than agreeable. First, the Iranians were to kill the American, where was immaterial. Second, there could be absolutely no connection to the Wolf or the 'Ndrangheta Mafia, who brokered the contract deal. Third, the 'Ndrangheta would provide "absolutely no assistance—zero—to Iran" in performing the hit. 'Ndrangheta's *Crimine*, its executive board of a dozen senior *mafiosi* who advised the *Capo Crimine*—the Godfather—had insisted that there be "absolutely no" 'Ndrangheta fingerprints" on the operation.

This was especially necessary because their target was a senior *American* Army officer.

"We piss off the Italian government and law enforcement almost every day," the Godfather had said, laughing, "but we don't want to start a new war with American law enforcement."

While Dabiri praised Allah for what he thought was a bargain of a deal, enriching him and "two or three" of his closest deputies, he did not realize that the 'Ndrangheta Mafia leadership had taken a tidy commission of $5 million—from the Wolf's original deal of $15 million—for themselves. Furthermore, to protect their interests, the 'Ndrangheta had negotiated with the Wolf, still awaiting trial in prison, that they would "subcontract the job" and that "there can be no guarantees" as to the American officer's demise. This provided some insurance that the Wolf would not come after the 'Ndrangheta in the event the Iranians failed.

But was it *enough* insurance?

CHAPTER 20

Time To Move

FOR JAKE AND SARA, CHANGING THEIR HOME'S LOCATION was inevitable. With Jake soon retiring and no longer an official part of the US Embassy community in Rome, a US Embassy-provided or endorsed apartment in Rome was no longer possible.

Still, it's unexpected when retirement and the need to change professional direction sneaks up on you, thought Jake.

"This new apartment is quite a bit smaller than our previous one," said Sara, "but its proximity to the Carabinieri Headquarters in downtown Rome is much better than our embassy apartment."

"I agree," confirmed Jake. "No great view of the Roman hillsides, but it does have a gated entry off the street."

With Jake retiring, Jake and Sara realized the elevated real estate prices in Rome, coupled with Sara's livable but middle-class salary as a Carabinieri officer and Jake's military retirement pay (about 43 percent of his base pay as a US Army lieutenant colonel with 21 years of service), required them to make some difficult housing tradeoffs in one of the most desirable cities in Europe.

The apartment's location, at 51 *via Giovanni Arrivabene*, north by northwest of the city's center and about a quarter of a mile west of the *Corso di Francia*, a major north–south artery running into the heart of Rome, provided good access to the city and Carabinieri Headquarters. That was very important for Sara, whose place of work was also near the heart of Rome. But it was much less important for Jake, who would retire in a few short weeks with only a vague idea of what he might do with the rest of his life. The 1200-square-foot, two-bedroom apartment, which Jake and Sara purchased for $575 per square foot in this part of Rome, was the first home purchase for both Sara and Jake.

The apartment was in a clean neighborhood of stone or stucco-facade buildings that housed apartments of varying sizes. The tallest buildings in the neighborhood were no more than six or seven stories high, giving the area more of a suburban than a big city feel, even though they were well within Rome's city limits.

They chose the third-floor apartment in their five-floored building because of the additional security it provided by being higher off the ground than the bottom two floors and, therefore, theoretically, was less accessible to intruders.

In only a couple of weeks, they would leave their *via Cassia* residence. Sara was excited to move into her new digs. Looking out about 150 yards from the balcony to the south, Sara could see the *Scuola Primaria Franceso Mengotti* (the Francesco Mengotti primary school).

Hopefully, our son or daughter will someday attend that school, thought Sara.

It was more of a hope or prayer than a thought. Sara very much wanted to have a child, as did Jake, but Sara was concerned that time was running out.

CHAPTER 21

The Handler And The Truthmaker

AZAR ZADEHA WAS ANXIOUS TO MEET HER NEWLY AS-SIGNED "OPERATOR." Iranian government officials thought her to be the perfect "handler" for the dozen or so secret agents Iran had in Italy. As a woman, she was not the first person that Italians would think of as Iran's lead handler and espionage agent in Italy.

Half of her assigned agents—all with fake identification cards and falsified passports—had made their way over the Mediterranean Sea from Libya to the Italian Island of Lampedusa. During the illegal—and precarious—journey, they mixed in well with Moroccans, Syrians, Libyans, and others who sought a new life in Italy and wealthy Europe beyond it. The other half of the Iranian agents were in Italy legally. With her cover as an Iran Air employee, Zadeha understood she had to be careful. But her confidence was boosted whenever she reminded herself that she did not fit the male stereotype of an Iranian or Hezbollah terrorist and, therefore, was not on the radar of Italian counter-espionage officials.

Zadeha had been informed that her newly assigned operator was ruthless. Not only had he quietly dispatched two Iranian journalists and one thirty-something, anti-Iranian government lady who had been gaining too much influence—influence that was directed *against* the Iranian government—on social media, but her newly assigned operator was also known to have tortured protestors and even children in a secret prison outside of Tehran.

Kamran Masoumi "is among the most depraved and effective assassins and torturers in the business," Iran's Minister of Intelligence had told Zadeha during her briefing. "That is why I love him so much. His results speak for themselves," continued the Minister, as if speaking about some banal business operation. "And now, he's needed for this critical mission. He's perfect for the job."

He had become so effective at torturing false confessions out of people that he had earned the twisted nickname of "the Truthmaker." As far as the Iranian government was conveniently concerned, if anybody confessed to and signed any transgression against the Iranian government or its laws, the confession was deemed "the truth." And their punishment was thereby justified.

On February 21, 2023, a CNN Special Report entitled "How Iran Used a Network of Secret Torture Centers to Crush an Uprising" appeared on the news wires. And Kamran Masoumi, Zadeha's newly assigned operator, had relished every moment of his participation in those depraved and perverted torture sessions of innocent men and women. "When necessary," according to Masoumi, he had also directed his evil psychological warfare against children.

On March 16, 2023, Amnesty International reported that even Iranian government *child* detainees had been "subjected to flogging, electric shocks, and sexual violence in a brutal protest crackdown" directed at mostly young Iranians who wanted more of what the United States and Western democracies had: more freedom and liberty, and a better and more promising way of life. The orgy of brutality against Iranian protestors was directed from the very top ranks of the Iranian government, supported by the twin pillars of Iran's intelligence and security forces.

***

Not only would the 'Ndrangheta Mafia pay the Iranian government handsomely for killing the American, but doing so would also exact revenge on the American Army officer who foiled Iran's plan to infect, *en shâ Allah*, hundreds of thousands, even millions of Americans and Jews with a virus ten times more lethal than the devastating Spanish Flu of 1918–1920.

CHAPTER 22

The Exercise

AS HE SAT OUTSIDE THE US AIR FORCE BRIGADIER GENERAL'S OFFICE, Jake was happy. He couldn't imagine a better professional conclusion to his twenty-one years of active US Army service. It was early Sunday afternoon. According to official plans, the large NATO, around-the-clock exercise based out of Sigonella, Sicily, would commence at 7 a.m. on Monday and finish "no later than midnight" on Thursday. Jake had already been clued in on his roles for the exercise. Multiple NATO partner countries, including Canada, Estonia, France, Germany, Greece, Italy, the Netherlands, Norway, Spain, the United States, and several others, and from the ranks of soldier, sailor, and airman through general officer and admiral, would participate in the exercise.

On Friday morning, the day after the exercise was scheduled to conclude, multiple "after-action reviews" would take place, honestly and seriously assessing how the NATO Intelligence, Surveillance, and Reconnaissance Force performed and, more importantly, where it needed improvement to be combat-ready, and, just as importantly, how it needed to improve peacetime deterrence and monitoring operations.

It sounds so stinkin' cliché, thought Jake. *But this is my last chance to give back as an active-duty Army officer.*

Jake was happy Colonel Seaton had asked him to participate in the exercise despite the myriad administrative, logistic, and even medical tasks required by Jake's retirement and transition from active duty to civilian life. *Only two weeks left to serve,* Jake thought. He both lamented the loss and was excited about his change of mission.

The general's door opened.

"Hey, Jake, long time no see!" began General Clark.

"It has been quite a while, sir," responded Jake, meeting the general's extended hand with his to shake warmly, as old friends.

"C'mon in and have a seat," said Clark. "Care for a cup of coffee? Espresso?"

"I'd love an espresso," replied Jake.

"How do you take it?" asked Clark.

"Black," responded Jake.

"Perfect," answered Clark.

Jake had known Brigadier General Clark to be a humble and self-effacing leader, so seeing him dismiss his aide, the Turkish Sergeant Major (a senior rank not uncommon in NATO's ranks), and make the espresso himself did not surprise Jake.

Jake had tremendous respect for Clark. Clark had accumulated almost 1,400 hours of combat flight time over Afghanistan, Bosnia, Kosovo, and Iraq, as well as a total of over 4,000 hours in the U2S and AC-130U aircraft. As a captain and pilot of an AC-130 Spectre gunship (armed with a 25mm Gatling gun, rapid-fire 40mm Bofors cannon, and a 105mm howitzer), the University of Wisconsin Air Force ROTC graduate had taken the initiative to scramble his crew and aircraft to support a US ground force that was fighting for its life in Iraq. For that operation and for the critical air support that Clark's aircraft and crew had provided in an extremely hostile environment, Clark was awarded the US Air Force's Distinguished Flying Cross with a "V" device for valor.

After asking each other about their families, General Clark

got down to business.

"Jake, I really appreciate you coming down from Rome to help us with this exercise," said Clark.

"I wouldn't have it any other way," responded Fortina.

"You know, Jake, I asked Colonel Seaton if I could borrow you for this exercise," replied Clark. "There are few US officers in the European theater that have your international military background and none who have your overall international background and counterterrorism background."

"Colonel Seaton didn't mention that you'd asked for me specifically," chuckled Fortina. "Well, I hope I don't jack this up then, sir."

"Haha, I know you better than that," answered Clark. "I didn't want Colonel Seaton to know that I knew you. Didn't want Colonel Seaton to feel pressured to send you down here, either. But I'm super glad you volunteered to come down to Sicily for this. I need your help making sure this exercise is as realistic and as efficient as possible. I want to interject several events and scenarios that will force my entire team to react to unforeseen contingencies, and maybe a couple that are foreseen, just to make sure our standard operating procedures are as sound as they can be. The bottom line is that I want this entire international NATO team to be more mission-ready for crises after the exercise is complete than before it began."

"Got it, sir," replied Fortina. "I'll do my best."

"Of that, I have no doubt," replied the US Air Force brigadier general.

CHAPTER 23

Old Roman Roads

I LOVE THESE OLD ROMAN ROADS, thought the 'Ndrangheta *soldato* ("soldier," the second lowest ranking member of the mafia). *They make my job easy!*

The *via Cassia* was one of the ancient, original roads of Rome. However, unlike many other Roman roads throughout Europe that had become overgrown and known only to locals or curious, history-minded tourists, this road had seen continuous use for over 2000 years. Its composition has changed a few times within the last three hundred years, with the most recent change being to asphalt pavement, which is common in several European countries. The two-way road could never be expanded because of encroaching urban infrastructure from both sides. This forced all vehicles into single, opposing lanes. The *via Cassia*—running roughly north–south through the northern half of Rome—made for a perfect combination of daily, bumper-to-bumper traffic jams within the Eternal City.

The mafia soldier's two partners added redundancy to his mission. Each partner was a *picciotto* (the lowest mafia rank). One was posted across the street and about two blocks farther north, with another seated on a bench on the same side of the street as the first soldier but another five blocks up the road. The 'Ndrangheta bosses were fully committed to kidnapping their target, and redundant lookouts were well worth the time and effort.

After weeks of surveilling the US Army and Italian carabinieri officers, the mafia trio was able to confirm the old beat-up car they drove through the streets of Rome. The car had become a joke among the three hitmen.

"You'd think those two officers could afford a better vehicle than that clown car!" joked one of the lookouts about the dented and scratched-up, inexpensive Fiat that Jake and Sara had chosen for the turbulent streets of Rome. On Roman roads, accepted distances between vehicles were measured by inches instead of feet. That was better than in Rome's southern neighbor, Naples, where acceptable distances between vehicles were measured in *millimeters*. Softly "bumping" a vehicle while parallel parking your vehicle in a tight spot was considered by many Romans and Neapolitans to be an acceptable practice.

The three *mafiosi* each mocked the couple in their own way.

Usually, it was the American who would drive the old car that had its fair share of blemishes and scratches on it, but occasionally, his wife could be seen in it, too. Unbeknownst to the three criminals, Jake and Sara saw no sense in taking a newer or better model vehicle through the car-unfriendly streets of Rome, where bumps and dings between cars and their drivers were as easily accepted—albeit often after much loud profanity and horn honking by the afflicted drivers—as they were given. These frequent scrapes between vehicles, rarely reported to police, were understood by Romans to be the price of driving in the crowded Eternal City.

On this day, the three lookouts were looking for a specific driver. They wanted to confirm that the driver passed by during roughly the same half-hour window that the watching trio had grown accustomed to observing.

The first mafia member to spot the car and its driver confirmed their arrival to his two teammates. It was easy to do so without raising suspicion among local residents. He simply spoke into his cell phone, as if Facetiming with a child or grandchild. Except his two killer partners were the ones at the other end.

"Traffic is busy today," he said.

That verified that the car they had been targeting had just passed by the first lookout. While the traffic was indeed bumper-to-bumper, "traffic is busy" was not the true meaning of the lookout's message. The other two lookouts also confirmed they had sighted their target car, as well as, more importantly, its driver. There was no doubt. The mission would be on the next time the three lookouts would stand on the sides of the busy *via Cassia*, in slightly different locations from where they were hanging out today.

CHAPTER 24

Time To Visit A Doctor

SARA SOMONETTI-FORTINA FELT UNCOMFORTABLE. It was a different, queasy kind of feeling, one that she had not experienced before. Having never had the virus, she wondered, *is this how COVID starts?*

It had been over a year since her last COVID vaccine. But the virus was again beginning to surge in Rome, and this was clearly in her mind. Her period was several days late, adding to the concern and intrigue about her odd feelings. Her fever was slight, and so was her headache, but that was it in terms of flu-like symptoms. She did not have the sniffles, and her sense of smell was intact.

With Jake gone off to Sicily, *it's time to visit a doctor*, thought Sara.

She decided to check in with her longtime friend, who had also become Sara's personal doctor since Sara's arrival in Rome. Her friend and classmate at the Italian Military Academy in Modena, the good doctor, was accepted into medical school upon her commissioning as a second lieutenant in the Italian Army. After graduation, she joined the ranks of medical professionals in the Italian Army. Now, she was a civilian doctor living in Rome. Only minutes into the phone call, her heavily booked doctor friend, in a country with a shortage of physicians, agreed to see Sara within 48 hours.

On the day of her visit, Sara couldn't wait any longer. She

needed to find out. Was she pregnant?

Observing the results of her in-home pregnancy test, Sara's heart almost leaped out of her chest. She couldn't stop staring at the test's faint but definitely positive result. Her hope turned into a prayer that the results were true as indicated.

Thank God, she thought, *that today I'm also feeling much better.*

Sara's slightly elevated temperature and headache had gone away. Nonetheless, she decided to press on with seeing her female doctor friend. The in-home pregnancy test results seemed too good to be true.

Arriving at her friend's office early and taking another test soon after arrival, Sara's friend and doctor returned smiling widely, her whole face glowing.

"Sara, there is no doubt about it, girl! You are pregnant! About six weeks."

All the months of trying and all of Sara's prayers for her heart's biggest desire were answered.

I know this is just the beginning of our journey in having this child, thought Sara. *But please, dear God, let this child be a healthy one.*

Sara's heart was soaring.

I will tell Jake face-to-face on Friday evening when he returns from Sicily! She resolved.

CHAPTER 25

The Hit

AURELIO ROMEO HAD THOUGHT LONG AND HARD about how to kill the Carabinieri captain and get rid of his body. Romeo was not a big reader or watcher of the news, so he had little reason to know why he was given the mission to "kill the captain and make him disappear." Besides, the captain had yet to be mentioned in the handful of news stories about the wayward Carabinieri general whose conspiracy trial would begin in five weeks. Romeo knew only that his mission was to kill the captain, get rid of the body, and ensure it would never be discovered again. Of the original four-week deadline he was given to complete the job, only five days remained.

With each passing day, he became increasingly concerned—and sleepless—that the Carabinieri captain might suddenly go away on vacation with his family or perhaps have a loved one or close friend die and, therefore, be expected to attend that person's funeral in some far-flung place in Italy. That would make Romeo's job—and the requirement to meet the deadline—much harder. After eighteen days of intense observation, Romeo had gotten to know the captain's habits and the timing of his comings and goings around Rome quite well. A few more days were not going to add much to his knowledge about the Carabinieri officer's daily routine.

Thank God, the captain has been very routine in his daily activities, thought the 'Ndrangheta mid-level operator, desperately wanting to redeem himself after he failed to have the American-Italian military couple killed.

His options for the best kill and snatch locations had been reduced to two: near Captain Bondanella's favorite lunch place, about five blocks from the Carabinieri Headquarters in Rome, or outside the captain's apartment, from which Bondanella departed for work each morning and returned to each evening. While a bold murder and snatching of the body just a few blocks from the Carabinieri Headquarters would have made Romeo a hero—*even a legend*, he liked to think—among his mafia peers and leaders, he understood that such a midday hit in the relatively busy streets of downtown Rome, while possible, was fraught with challenges in terms of the second part of his mission: *making the captain disappear.*

Killing the captain was the first challenge. But to Romeo, making the captain vanish into thin air was only marginally less important than the first part. Of course, a corpse could not testify in court against Brigadier General Cadorna, but a corpse could provide clues to Carabinieri investigators that could greatly damage not only Romeo but also the 'Ndrangheta organization. The fact that the health and perhaps even lives of Romeo's family members depended on Romeo accomplishing his mission also weighed heavily upon him.

I will not kill Bondanella in his home, thought Romeo. *The presence of the captain's wife would make the operation far too risky and messy, especially if I must kill her, too. If she doesn't die, she will surely notify police authorities at the first opportunity or be able to give testimony when she has recovered.*

And, while Romeo never publicly judged his fellow *mafiosi* for killing children, he believed such acts against children were unforgivably wicked. Although a hardened criminal, Romeo realized he could never commit such acts of violence. Children are where Romeo drew the line. He was very thankful that his superiors hadn't yet ordered him to ensure the death of the captain's wife and child, as well.

Those would be despicable acts, thought Romeo, *and they are acts that have happened in the deepest and darkest corners of southern Italy and Sicily.*

His decision of how to perform his mission came to him like an epiphany: the captain would die in the parking lot outside his home, and his body would immediately be taken away to a deep body of water.

***

Aurelio Romeo had chosen the perfect spot in the parking lot. He felt surprisingly relaxed as he watched the Carabinieri captain drive his late-model gray Fiat sedan into the lot. Having observed the same maneuver a half-dozen times before, Romeo knew Captain Bondanella's preferred parking spot, as well as the backup one if the preferred spot was taken. As it turned out, the two spaces were within three spaces of each other in the fourth row of the parking lot away from the building.

On this evening, Romeo parked his white Volkswagen Passat station wagon in the fifth row away from the building. The Passat wagon's rear cargo space had been carefully lined with industrial-strength plastic sheeting. Two black body bags—to ensure sufficient strength for entombing the captain's body at the bottom of a lake, without the risk of tearing open—were in the cargo space. The Passat was not among the most popular cars in Italy, but it *was* popular among German and other European vacationers and owners of Italian property who ventured down to Italy from north of the Alps.

Seated on the passenger side was Romeo's hand-picked accomplice, a twenty-something mafia soldier who was striving to make a name for himself in the 'Ndrangheta. The young man called the mafia-beset town of Polistena, Calabria, his home. Renowned as a mafia hotbed by Italian governments but virtually forgotten and abandoned by the rest of Italy, it was located deep in southern Italy.

The kid had already killed two people. One was terminated in the Calabrian town of Cosenza, and the other in Rome, with the Rome victim thinking that a big, anonymous city like Rome was easier to seek refuge in than his Calabrian village of Sant'Ippolito. He could not have been more wrong. Both murder victims had gotten their wires crossed with the wrong people from the ruthless 'Ndrangheta, and, as a result, their pursuit by the 'Ndrangheta to the far corners of the earth was a foregone conclusion.

One of Romeo's mafia buddies recommended the *ragazzo* (kid). Romeo's friend said the young man was "calm, cold-blooded, and cocky, but completely loyal."

"He will do what is required," said Romeo's friend.

Romeo brought the kid along for two reasons: if Romeo failed to pull the trigger on his Beretta 92FS pistol (with silencer) or otherwise failed to get the job done, the young aspiring *mafioso* would serve as his backup. Romeo felt better having the extra insurance, knowing that if he failed this mission, it would come at a horrible cost to him and his family. Once the captain was dropped to the parking lot pavement, the kid would aid Romeo in quickly dragging the captain to the back of the Passat station wagon before the duo exited the lot.

Fortunately for the two assassins, throughout most of Italy, Italian urban designers and builders did not splurge on strong streetlights, and even less so for parking lots. The many shadows and dark spots in the parking lot, away from the meager light of the few streetlamps, aided in their plot.

They had removed their vehicles' interior dome lights and

disabled its alarms to mitigate the chances of unexpected surprises. As the Carabinieri captain began turning into his favorite parking spot, the two assassins were ready. Waiting with their car doors slightly ajar, they waited until Bondanella's car completed its slow turn into its usual parking space.

Just before the captain put his manual transmission into neutral and set the handbrake, the two killers exited their vehicle, their 9mm pistols drawn. They each moved up behind the two opposing vehicles that flanked the captain's car while being sure to stay low and out of any possible detection via the captain's side and rearview mirrors.

Captain Bondanella exited the vehicle, shut the vehicle's door, and pressed his key fob to lock it. Romeo, in a crouching position, eased out from behind the trunk and right rear tire well of the adjacent car. He aimed at the captain's upper back, slightly above the captain's left shoulder blade. Before Bondanella took his fourth step, Romeo fired two shots in quick succession. The captain fell forward on the pavement, his face grotesquely turned to one side.

Romeo's young accomplice, who had been hiding outside the captain's right front passenger door, immediately crossed in front of the captain's car, reached the collapsed captain, and fired an additional two shots into the captain's right temple. Romeo did not expect that. His eyes widened.

Romeo's criminal mind quickly calculated that with the kid firing the final two shots, Romeo might somehow escape full culpability if he was ever to be arrested and tried in court. In some ways, the two shots fired by the kid were an unspoken gift to Romeo, with the kid becoming more than an accessory to murder. He was the one who *ensured* that the Carabinieri captain was dead. Romeo appreciated the gesture.

As Romeo approached the body and the kid standing over it, Romeo's eyes met the kid's eyes. Romeo gave the kid a single affirmative nod and a slight smile. The kid knew his objective to please Romeo had been achieved.

Within seconds, the two men dragged the dead captain's corpse to the back of the Passat, loaded him in its spacious cargo area, and drove away. Before midnight, double body bags would enshroud the captain. A steel barrel, with its top sealed shut, would serve as the captain's coffin. A small, 14-foot fishing boat with a quiet outboard electric engine would serve as the captain's waterborne hearse. The bottom of Lake Bracciano, located 20 miles northwest of Rome and with a maximum depth of 541 feet, would be the captain's final resting place.

CHAPTER 26

No Need To Worry

CARLA BONDANELLA WAS NOT SOMEONE WHO PANICKED EASILY, let alone worried. Before she had met her husband, Captain Pietro Bondanella, she had seen and experienced more than her fair share of life's soul-jarring tragedies, as well as exquisite triumphs. As a nurse in a children's cancer ward for three years, life's highest highs and lowest lows presented themselves almost weekly.

God bless people who can do this for many years, she thought as she walked out on her last day of working at Rome's *Bambin' Gesu* Children's Hospital. *But as for me, after three years of treating those beautiful children, I need to take a different path.*

Her epiphany led Carla Bondanella to the field of hospital administration and management, one—except for the Catholic Church and other religious denominations—that had been dominated by men for centuries. In recent decades, however, it has been a field increasingly accepting of women.

She had met her husband, a young Carabinieri officer, when he had come to the hospital to interview a crime suspect who had been shot. After a four-year courtship, they married, and two years later, they welcomed a beautiful daughter whom they named Francesca. In her early thirties and a year older than Pietro, Carla understood the challenges of being married to a Carabinieri officer. Never in her worst dreams, however, did she think any of the worst challenges, threats, or news would arrive at her doorstep.

But this night felt different. A creeping, ominous feeling grew and lurked in her mind.

Pietro had been good about calling when he was going to be an hour or more late beyond his expected arrival time. That was typically between 6:45 and 7:00 p.m. Carla loved that Pietro had a more predictable schedule than when he worked for "that crazy general." Tonight, however, Pietro was more than an hour late, and Carla had heard nothing.

Is my phone in silent mode? She asked herself.

Rechecking it to be sure, she discovered it was on, and the volume was sufficiently loud to be able to hear a call from a phone that was right in front of her on the kitchen table.

At 8:33 p.m., she thought about calling Pietro but then decided to put it off for another thirty minutes.

No need to worry, she thought. *He'll be home soon.*

At 8:58 p.m., she called Pietro's phone. He did not answer, and the call went to voice mail. Carla left a message.

"Ciao, *Caro* (dear), I'm just calling to make sure everything is OK. Please call me when you get a chance."

Still, no reason to worry, she thought. *Perhaps he was going out for a drink or dinner tonight with a colleague but forgot to tell me about it? That would be rare for Pietro, so maybe he told me...and I was the one who forgot about it?*

She checked the calendar on her cell phone, the one she had been very disciplined in tracking both her and Pietro's appointments. It was devoid of any scheduled events for the evening.

At 9:17 p.m., little Francesca cried out from her crib. Unlike most 18-month-old children, she normally slept quite well for the first seven or so hours after falling asleep. Then, typically around 4 a.m., she cried out to her parents to come and rescue her from her crib. Tonight, however, was different, and as a mother, Carla felt anxious about Francesca's piercing cry—almost a scream—which grew into a sustained sob.

Carla brought the child into her bed after checking her diaper. It was dry. She put her experienced former nurse's hand on Francesca's forehead. Francesca's temperature was normal. Carla tried to comfort Francesca by lying next to her, and after twenty minutes of sobbing, sniffling, and feeling her mother's body heat, Francesca finally settled down in her mother's arms and fell asleep.

Carla silently thanked God for Francesca's steady breathing and peaceful state.

But where is Pietro? She pondered.

CHAPTER 27

Lake Bracciano

ROMEO FROZE AS HE GRIPPED THE TILLER OF THE ELECTRIC OUTBOARD MOTOR. He was guiding the 14-foot, flat-bottomed aluminum boat to the center of the volcanic lake and much deeper water. He had already gone about a mile from the shore of twenty-mile-circumference, 6.4-mile-diameter Lake Bracciano, reachable by car in twenty-five to thirty minutes from Rome's northern outskirts. In the darkness, with his own running lights off on a cloudy night with minimal ambient light, Romeo couldn't tell if the boat—he'd spotted its running lights roughly 200–300 yards off his right front stern—was directly approaching him or not. He cut the power to the quiet electric engine. The boat slowed and drifted forward. Romeo and his young sidekick listened. Off in the distance and over their starboard side bow, they could faintly hear the gas-powered outboard motor of the boat headed their way.

Obviously, it does not have an electric engine, said Romeo.

With the steel barrel at the front of the boat containing Bondanella's body, Romeo had concocted a pretty good story, one that his partner was well briefed and rehearsed on. The boat was full of just enough fishing gear, tackle, and a net to make it look like they were on a nighttime fishing expedition. The lake was known to contain huge pike, largemouth bass, and European perch (which provided an excellent food supply for the two larger species). Having fished with his older brother in Calabria, Romeo knew that the best fishing—legal or otherwise—was at night. This was something done throughout Italy.

To eliminate any air pockets from forming inside the barrel and thereby rendering it more buoyant, he punched several holes in its bottom and sides. The holes would allow water to enter quickly, thereby submerging the barrel as quickly as possible to the bottom of the 541-foot-deep lake.

Romeo and his mafia apprentice had already discussed their contingency plans if approached directly by another boat: 1. Dump the barrel over the front of the boat in plenty of time to make sure it sank below the water's surface before being approached by another boat. The barrel had to be dumped over the boat's squared-off bow, as dumping it off to the side might cause the boat to list and to take on water, a hazard that they needed to avoid at all costs. 2. If sufficient time was not available, and if asked what the barrel was for, tell any inquiring person that the barrel was being used as a "live well" to keep any caught fish alive until they could reach the shore and properly clean them for consumption. Given that two- and three-foot-long pikes were known to be pulled from Lake Bracciano, their story had some credibility, and Romeo knew that "some credibility" was all that was needed.

However, if someone wants to closely examine the barrel, it will be a problem when they see the holes, he thought.

Romeo believed that God had given gifts of talent to certain people, and his special talent was telling lies—even outrageous ones—and having people believe him like those lies were the Gospel truth. If by chance Romeo's story was not believed and law enforcement officers chose to inspect the barrel, "See the third option," Romeo told the kid. 3. If "through some terrible misfortune," according to Romeo, the approaching boat contained law enforcement officers who were intent on inspecting the boat, the two men still had their 9mm Beretta pistols and would "do what was necessary to be done."

Romeo calculated that there was not enough time—and too much risk—to dump the barrel now. Besides, the water they were in was only about 120 feet deep, and he wanted to motor out about another mile to get to much deeper water...*at least 400 feet deep*, he thought.

Romeo's young partner turned his head toward Romeo, who was barely visible in the darkness. The two men could barely make out each other's upper torso and head profiles. Romeo anticipated the young man's question.

"We will *not* dump the barrel here," whispered Romeo.

The two men sat silently as they observed the distant but steadily approaching boat. Within a very long two minutes, it had become clear: the boat was *not* heading directly toward them and most likely had not spotted them. It eventually passed off the starboard side of Romeo's unlighted boat. In broad daylight, at that distance, it might have been a problem. But the darkness, lack of moonlight, and gathering fog just off the lake's surface provided just the cover that they needed.

Once the small fishing boat traveled out of sight and into the light fog behind them, Romeo whispered to his younger mafia apprentice: "Poachers."

Romeo restarted the electric engine and guided the boat back on its course toward the center of the lake.

"About another mile or so, and we'll be in deep water," he said to his fellow criminal.

Romeo was thankful that his mission would soon be complete and that his family would, as a result, be removed from harm's way.

CHAPTER 28

The Car?

CARLA BONDANELLA OPENED HER EYES. Francesa was still sleeping peacefully beside her. She relished the moments snuggled close to her sleeping, steadily breathing daughter, *with her beautiful eyes closed to the darkness of the world,* she thought.

But what time is it?

Carla, unlike many people who depended on their ever-present cell phones to get the time, wore a luminescent watch that Pietro had bought for her on Florence's iconic *Ponte Vecchio*, the Old Bridge. She loved the watch, not only because she had picked it out herself but also because it was practical enough to be worn all the time, including at work or in the shower. While it exceeded their budget, Pietro offered to buy the sporty watch without hesitation.

Carla turned her wrist slightly so that the light leaking into the bedroom from the kitchen could catch the luminescent numbers and hands on the watch's face. It was 11:57 p.m.

My God, did I just fall asleep for almost three hours? she asked herself.

Moving gently and slowly as she got up from the bed, Carla softly repositioned Francesca in the center of the bed for added insurance that she would not roll off. Carla headed for the kitchen with a heavy heart.

Where, dear God, is Pietro?

She called Pietro's phone again. But this time, instead of her call going to voice mail, Carla heard the standard message one receives in most countries when service to a phone has been interrupted. She did not know that Pietro's cell phone, with the SIM (Subscriber Identity Module) card removed, was on the bottom of Lake Bracciano.

Before getting in the boat, Romeo flushed Pietro's SIM card down the toilet at a nearby public bathroom adjacent to a public parking area on the lake's shoreline. Pietro's car key fob was also crushed and then flushed down the same toilet. About a half-mile after Romeo and his accomplice departed the shore, Romeo crushed and tossed the useless, non-transmitting cell phone in dark, 110-foot-deep water.

The threat against Romeo's family had focused Romeo's mind. The threat provided Romeo with all the motivation he needed to be as careful, devious, and as precise as possible. He constantly reminded himself of the vow he had made on the Villa Borghese Park bench: "I cannot fail" this mission.

***

Carla stood in the kitchen, staring at her cell phone.

Who do I call next? A coworker? Perhaps a coworker might know something. My older sister? Perhaps she might have a thought. But it's too late to call her.

The Italian telephone number for emergencies, 112, came to her mind. But she fought the notion that the time had come to call that emergency number. That would be tantamount to giving in to despondency and hopelessness.

Or am I just being stubborn and stupid? she thought. *What would Pietro do?*

At that moment, she felt a cosmic tug—an urge—to go over to the kitchen window. Earlier in the evening, she had closed the window's wooden shutters. It was a habit, for security reasons, that Pietro had taught her, even though the apartment was on the fourth floor.

"Besides," he had said, "it's better to have the shutters completely shut during an evening storm. It creates less noise for the apartment, and it lessens the possibility that the shutters will get ripped off by strong winds."

Carla remembered learning that from her father when she was an eleven-year-old child, but she did not want to tell that to Pietro, thereby robbing him of his husbandly moment of wisdom.

Carla pulled the curtains to the side, then opened wood-framed windows inward and pushed the shutters outward away from the window frame.

There, in the parking lot below, at about sixty yards and not under the strongest parking lot lights in the world, she thought she could see Pietro's car. She lingered for a minute with a glimpse of hope and a prayer that he was in the car, safe. Still not completely sure at that distance that it was Pietro's car, she knew she had to find out.

Carla returned to the bedroom and gently cradled and picked up Francesca, carefully placing her in her crib. Carla grabbed her long wool overcoat and put it on over her pajamas. After slipping on her tennis shoes without socks, she diligently grabbed her apartment and stairwell front door keys, slipped them into her overcoat pocket, and headed down the apartment building's marble stairs, foregoing the elevator.

Perhaps Pietro fell asleep in the car? She thought hopefully as she quickly bounded down the stairwell.

CHAPTER 29

Testimony

ANATOLY ROMAN VOLKOV, AKA "THE WOLF," WAS FEELING RELAXED in his jail cell. While the lead Italian government prosecutor expected that some of the crimes committed by Volkov's Wolfpack were at the behest of the Russian oligarch Volkov, it was not clear how much influence Volkov had since the initial investigations showed that in almost every instance, the orders to conduct the crimes were given by his alleged deputy, Boris Stepanov. That is exactly the kind of obfuscation Volkov had hoped and planned for in the event he was arrested.

Boris Stepanov's fingerprints were on every single crime the Wolfpack had conducted. They included the thefts of the magnificent Caravaggio paintings, the hiring of a known torturer to join the Wolfpack, the merciless and gruesome torturing and murder of a Myanmar colonel, and the commercial procurement of just about everything the Wolfpack used to conduct its nefarious business, including two tactical nuclear weapons. One weapon had likely been detonated on European soil, and a second one was planned to be detonated on European soil. All criminal roads led to Boris Stepanov, with Volkov retaining significant plausible deniability for every crime and horror committed.

For his part, Stepanov knew his only choice was to take the fall for the Wolf, even if it included the remainder of Stepanov's life in a God-forsaken prison on some Italian island. Volkov, the second most wealthy and powerful oligarch after Russia's President Vasily Puchta, still had many powerful friends outside of the prison . . . and a few inside the prison. Were Stepanov to squeal to the Italian government legal authorities about Volkov's involvement, Volkov would have every single close relative—and even some friends—of Stepanov's killed. Those closest to Stepanov would meet the most gruesome, horrible deaths.

At the core of his soul, after years of doing the Wolf's criminal bidding for him, Stepanov somehow retained a surviving spark of decency. Stepanov knew his only choice was to resign himself to his fate in an Italian prison rather than have the few people he cared about have their lives ended in horrible deaths.

CHAPTER 30

It's Not Oil

CARLA BONDANELLA RECHECKED HER COAT POCKET before exiting the stairwell door and walking out to the parking lot. The stairwell key was there. As a typically fashion-minded Italian, she allowed herself a momentary, distracting, and humorous thought as the worry and fear about Pietro's fate continued to build.

I can't believe I'm walking out of this building wearing my pajamas, tennis shoes, and this old overcoat with my hair in an absolute mess, she thought.

With her first few steps out of the apartment building, she oriented herself on her husband's gray Fiat sedan. At about forty yards, she could barely make out its rooftop.

I pray that is indeed his car and that he has fallen peacefully asleep in there, she thought as she approached the vehicle.

As she got within ten feet of the vehicle, approaching it from the front, she could see the license plate number.

It's Pietro's car, she assured herself.

As she got close enough to touch the hood, she looked through the tinted windshield. She stopped and stared. The nearby parking lamp post provided just enough light so that she could make out the general form of the driver's seat. The seat was empty. Moving on to the driver's side door, she pulled on the handle. The door was locked. While peering as best she could through the tinted windows, she walked around the vehicle.

Is he sleeping in the back seat, maybe?

As her heart rate picked up, she knew she was grasping for any sign of hope.

Although the rear passenger doors were tinted a bit more heavily than the rest of the windows, something that Pietro had insisted upon to shield Francesca from Italy's strong sunshine, Carla did not find Pietro sleeping—nor see anything suspicious—in the back seat of the car.

She walked past the front of the car, stopped about six feet away, turned, and looked back at it.

Where is he? she asked herself. *Did he end up in another apartment?*

As Carla turned around and headed back to the apartment stairwell door, she felt guilty for thinking that Pietro might have ended up in another apartment, *perhaps with another woman?* She knew at this point, however, that she had to call the Italian emergency services number, 112, upon returning to the apartment. She also resolved to call her mother and then her sister.

Carla entered her apartment door, went to the kitchen table, and sat down on the black wooden kitchen table chair, intending to call 112. It was eighteen minutes past midnight. She couldn't believe it had come down to this. She realized she was so distraught that she had broken her iron-clad habit of removing her shoes as soon as she walked into her home. That habit helped keep the place cleaner, especially for Francesca, who often played on the small apartment's floors.

Folding her left leg up as she sat on the chair, she grabbed her tennis shoe to take it off. She immediately felt what she thought was a slimy liquid on the side of the shoe's sole. She looked down at it.

Is that dark red I am looking at?

She looked at her hand and then the shoe again. There *was* a small blotch of blood on her hand. It was also evident that something dark red—covering about the area of a euro coin—had seeped into the white sole of her tennis shoe.

Her breath almost left her as her heart pounded, and her mind led her thoughts to a gloomy place. It was a place that Sara did not want to go. The prospect that it might be Pietro's blood caused tears to begin to form. She immediately grabbed her keys again, bolted out the apartment door, and flew down the steps as fast as she could without falling and breaking her neck.

Once outside, she turned on her cell phone light as she began retracing her steps. Approaching Pietro's parked Fiat, she spotted—about six feet in front of the driver's side headlight—a dark spot on the gray concrete pavement. The stain was almost a foot in diameter.

Her mind racing, she desperately prayed for it to be an oil stain.

Or maybe hydraulic fluid? she hoped.

Carla sat down on the asphalt, putting most of her weight on her left side. She bent over and ran her right index finger through the thin layer of grimy film on the concrete surface. She sat upright and raised her right index finger to within about ten inches of her eyes. Carla shined her cell phone light on the tip of her right index finger. It looked to be dark red, a natural state after being exposed to the open air and absorbing dust, dirt, and grime from the pavement. She sniffed her finger, hoping to smell oil. It was not oil. Deep in her nurse's heart and soul, she knew what it was.

Carla threw her head back and looked through the weakly lit parking lights and up to the dark and gray-clouded Roman sky above her. She let out a scream, followed by shouts of "No! No! No!" Several people on the parking lot side of the building woke up, and soon, lights began leaking through their shut-

tered windows. A couple of the shutters opened.
Trying to breathe, Carla prayed fervently.
Please, dear God, don't let this be Pietro's blood!

CHAPTER 31

Can't Wait To See You

JAKE WAS EXCITED AS HE PRESSED the green phone receiver icon on his cell phone. During a break from the major NATO exercise, he'd called Sara once before. And now, at 9:45 p.m. on a Thursday, he had another opportunity to call her. Jake had just been informed that the NATO-US commanding general had officially declared "ENDEX" (end-ex, end of exercise) for the major NATO exercise.

The next morning would be filled with "after-action reviews" and "lessons learned" from the exercise. After twenty-one years of US Army service, Jake knew these "hot wash" sessions, as soldiers often called them, were—besides their actual follow-up—the most important aspects of any military exercise or training, be it at the 10-soldier army squad level or the 30,000-soldier corps level.

Jake was also looking forward to the next day's travels. They meant he was going *home*. By 4 p.m. the next day, Jake would get on the road and travel up Sicily's northeastern coast to the port of Messina, catch the half-hour ferry ride across the Straits of Messina to mainland Italy, and drive north to Rome. He figured he'd be home by midnight, and he and Sara would have the weekend together, just for themselves.

Jake smiled when he heard Sara's voice, which was clearly suppressing excitement.

After exchanging greetings, Sara, almost bursting, managed to say, "Sweetie, I have some good news, but I'd prefer to share it in person, so don't ask me another question,"

"OK, you have my head spinning right now, *Cara Mia*, but it wouldn't be the first time," Jake laughed.

"I can't wait to see you, *Caro*," responded Sara. "I know it's been less than a week, but I've missed you a lot."

"Not as much as I've missed you," Jake countered lovingly. "But I should be home by about midnight tomorrow night."

"Drive carefully," said Sara, "especially on that *autostrada* (highway) stretch between Naples and Rome. Over several years, my Carabinieri traffic colleagues have had to do entirely too much work on that road. Too many accidents to clean up and investigate. If a trucker is going to fall asleep on a road in Italy, odds are it will be on that one."

"I hear you, Sweetie," Jake reassured her. "I will be very careful and will see you late tomorrow night. Don't wait up for me."

"You know I'll be wide awake until after you walk through the front door," said Sara with a mixture of mischief and worry in her voice.

"Well, I don't expect that, but I do appreciate it, *Cara Mia*," replied Jake.

CHAPTER 32

A Perfect Match

LIEUTENANT COLONEL SARA SIMONETTI WAS SICK TO HER STOMACH. She thought it was too early in her pregnancy for the cause to be morning sickness. The entire Carabinieri Headquarters' mood had been somber all day long. It had been almost twenty hours since Captain Pietro Bondanella had left his workplace the evening prior. He had apparently driven home, parked his car in the parking lot outside of his apartment building...and disappeared. A Carabinieri colonel and friend of Sara's had just passed the news to her.

The evening prior, Bondanella's wife had discovered what appeared to be blood a few feet from her husband's car. She called 112, and two Carabinieri investigators were immediately dispatched to the scene, arriving by 1 a.m. Within thirty-five minutes, two additional Carabinieri investigators arrived. That morning, when the Carabinieri Headquarters building began to fill up for the day's duties, the rumors had spread rapidly. And now, in the late afternoon, came the latest devastating news.

With twenty-first-century technology, a focused sense of urgency, and the proper evidence, an accurate DNA test could be completed within two to three hours. As Carabinieri police officers whose daily lives were in constant peril, every Carabinieri Corps member provided a DNA sample, which was kept in an electronic file at the headquarters.

"I'm afraid the lab reported that it's a perfect DNA match to Pietro's blood," said the colonel, with deep sadness in his voice.

The colonel had known Pietro Bondanella almost as long as Sara had, first getting to know Bondanella at *L'Accademia Militare di Modena*. Italy's premier officer-producing military academy was founded in 1678, and today is the world's oldest military institution of its kind. While Sara Simonetti was serving on the academy's staff and faculty as a captain, she mentored Bondanella. He had known from early on that he wanted to become a Carabinieri officer. It was common for faculty and staff active-duty officers to mentor a handful of cadets from the academy.

Cadet and later Italian Carabinieri Lieutenant and then-Captain Bondanella had considered Simonetti as a kind of benevolent aunt, someone he could go to when he needed advice, career or otherwise. When Bondanella had heard his boss, the Italian Army brigadier general, having a conversation in the adjoining office with an American Army lieutenant colonel that sounded very wrong—if not downright criminal—in nature, Bondanella had wrestled with himself over what to do about it for three nights. Finally, he decided to go to Lieutenant Colonel Sara Simonetti for advice, and she advised him to report what he'd heard to the Carabinieri Corps' Deputy Commander. It was Bondanella's account of what he'd heard that launched a major investigation—as well as the electronic and human surveillance that followed—on the general.

The Italian Army brigadier general was later indicted for privately selling hundreds of AK-47s to an American lieutenant colonel, as well as for conspiracy. Without Captain Bondanella's brave intervention, the Italian general would most likely not have been caught. The brigadier general's trial was fast approaching, and one of the prosecutor's key witnesses had disappeared overnight.

Seated in front of the colonel's desk, Sara bowed her head and closed her eyes. She did not know what she should pray for first: God's forgiveness or the fact that Pietro Bondanella was still somehow alive. And then, visions of Carla Bondanella and little Francesca also entered her mind's eye.

"It's my fault," said Sara, with tears in her eyes. "Pietro would be here if I had not convinced him to take his information about General Cadorna to our Deputy Commander."

"You can't be sure of that," replied the colonel. "We don't yet know exactly what happened to Pietro. He might still be alive. Besides, Sara, you had no choice in the matter. Nor did Pietro. As a Carabinieri officer, he *had* to report what he'd heard. And you gave him exactly the right advice...that he should share it with our senior Carabinieri leadership."

Sara appreciated her friend's attempt to console her, but she couldn't get past the fact that she was the one who led Captain Bondanella to report the criminal-sounding information he had overheard. Sara again thought of Carla, Bondanella's wife, and Francesca, their cute-as-a-button daughter. Thinking of those two people, with their husband and father having gone missing, caused her even greater emotional pain. Sara had heard that women who are expecting a child can feel hyper-emotional at times, but this emotional pain was almost too much to bear.

CHAPTER 33

Distraught

SARA SIMONETTI WAS FULLY PREOCCUPIED AND STILL DISTRAUGHT. Earlier in the day, she'd heard from her Carabinieri colleague and friend that the blood found in Pietro Bondanella's apartment parking lot proved to be a match to his DNA. On this dismal and rainy Roman night, it was all Sara could do to get through *this cursed via Cassia traffic jam, get home, and await Jake's arrival,* she thought. *I have so much I want to share with him, face-to-face, with his arms around me.*

She visualized the scene when she would tell Jake that she was pregnant. She had run that joyous tape in her mind's eye several times. Sara knew Jake would be thrilled. But she also knew she needed to tell Jake about Pietro Bondanella's disappearance.

It will be bittersweet, thought Sara. *But that's how life is sometimes. And I know being with Jake will help my state of mind tremendously.*

***

As Sara started up the *via Cassia* in the heavy traffic heading north, the first mafia-driven vehicle, an Alfa Romeo Stelvio, passed her. The vehicle's driver, quickly passing on Sara's left, edged his vehicle to the right and stuck his car's nose in front of Sara's left front fender, indicating he wanted to squeeze into the car conga line that was jammed up on the *via Cassia*. His quick move had effectively cut Sara off. He did not use his turn signal. That would have been very un-Roman. Sara, used to this kind of Roman maneuver, especially in its more chaotic neighbor to the south, Naples, didn't think twice about letting the vehicle move in front of her. Her only other choice would have been to hit the car with hers.

A second 'Ndrangheta vehicle, a Jeep Compass containing two *mafiosi*, continued to trail Sara. Behind them was a third mafia vehicle, a designated backup. Its job was also to stop any impetuous driver who wanted to pass by and disrupt the operation that was about to go down.

Two mafia "ground soldiers," each on opposite sides of the *via Cassia*, stood curbside in their raincoats and black baseball caps. The bigger soldier's job was to assist the baby-carriage-pushing woman in stopping traffic in the oncoming lane if needed and help the "snatch and go" team in the Jeep. The second soldier's job was to hop in Sara's car and drive it away once the "snatch and go" team finished their mission.

The entourage's *Capo* had picked this night because of the high probability of rain. He had officially designated the operation a "Go" when it became evident that the rain would be incessant, thereby decreasing the evening's visibility as well as keeping most pedestrian Romans off the streets.

The two streetside men and one woman looked at their cell phones. The simple *"verde"* (green) text message told them everything they needed to know. Their mission was on.

They had rehearsed their well-planned missions several times.

One mafia soldier, the woman, waited for Sara's crawling vehicle, with its tires barely rotating forward, to approach.

As it did, the 'Ndrangheta woman began pushing an empty baby carriage out in front of Sara's car. Sara stopped immediately, thinking she would do at least one good deed on this otherwise dark and sad day.

Standing directly in the front center of Sara's car, the woman turned her head toward Sara and, without looking into her eyes, yelled a loud, "*Grazie!*"

Sara smiled at the woman's gesture. The woman continued with the baby carriage into the barely crawling oncoming single-lane traffic, which immediately stopped to let the woman continue crossing the street. 'Ndrangheta leaders and virtually all Romans understood that when a mother pushes a baby carriage into a slow-moving traffic jam in Rome, everybody—with the exception of the biggest *stronzi* (pieces of fecal matter) on the planet—would stop.

Sara immediately refocused her attention on the back of the vehicle in front of her. The vehicle, driven by a 'Ndrangheta *mafioso*, was stopped.

The two *mafiosi* trailing Sara in the gray Jeep Compass right behind her made their move, practically exploding out of the Jeep. One quickly took a one-inch-thick, eight-inch-long lead punch and thrust it into Sara's driver's side window. That maneuver was followed a half second later by the big mafia soldier in the raincoat, who did the same thing to the passenger door window, immediately sticking his hand through the glass's open space and pressing the button to unlock all four doors.

Sara's first instinct was to recoil from the shattered glass, but before she knew it, the second mafia soldier from the Jeep slid in the backseat behind her, threw a rope over her chest and arms, pulled back vigorously on the rope, and pinned Sara in the driver's seat. The passenger-side assailant quickly shot Sara in the neck with a dose of sleep-inducing propofol and then covered her head with a dark hood.

The woman who was pushing the baby carriage, now standing in the middle of the oncoming traffic lane, immediately turned and pointed her Beretta 9 mm pistol at the driver of the lead vehicle, which had stopped in the oncoming lane. The terrified driver immediately took her hands off the steering wheel and put her hands up.

Sara momentarily tried to struggle, but control of her body was leaving her, and within seconds, she was in another world. The big man in the front passenger seat grabbed Sara, pulled her out of the car, and, with the help of the *mafioso* who'd busted out the driver's side window, dragged Sara around to the Jeep's back storage compartment. As the big man hopped in the backup vehicle, and the other two jumped in and closed the doors on the Jeep, the second *mafioso* in a raincoat slid in and took the wheel of Sara's beat-up old car, with the keys in the ignition, and drove it up on the sidewalk to the right.

Their location for executing the kidnapping was perfect. The Jeep Compass team needed only to drive to the right of the vehicle in front of it, ride the sidewalk for about thirty yards, take a right, and drive onto the dark, rain-soaked road leading off the *via Cassia*. The driver in Sara's car drove right behind them, but his destination and mission would be different. The vehicle containing Sara would head to Italy's deep south to the rugged and steeply hilly—even mountainous—Calabrian area of Aspromonte, which for well over a century had been dotted with several 'Ndrangheta hideouts.

Sara's personal vehicle would be removed from the scene and, to keep Carabinieri investigators perplexed, hidden in a storage shed on the northeastern outskirts of Rome, less than 10 miles from where it was hijacked.

After 5 minutes of driving to pre-designated locations, the two cars' occupants put on new license plates and went on their separate ways into Rome's suburbs and well beyond.

CHAPTER 34

Nobody Home

IT WAS A FEW MINUTES AFTER MIDNIGHT. As Jake pulled up to the electronic gate, he pushed the remote-control button attached to his internal windshield visor. The ten-foot-high green metal gate, located just off northern Rome's *via Cassia*, opened with the creaky metallic sound that Jake had grown accustomed to. Beyond the gate was the *Centro Residenziale Condominio Avila*, a sixty-year-old collection of five apartment buildings, each containing eight to ten apartments. One of the apartments had once housed the former King of Afghanistan and his family in the 1970s, 80s, and 90s. In the 1990s, the Pheonix-born and Rome-raised American former racing driver Eddie Cheever, who raced for almost thirty years in Formula One, sports cars, CART, and the Indy Racing League, and who won the 1998 Indianapolis 500, also lived there.

As Jake descended the hill to his apartment building at the eastern end of the compound and farthest from the gate, Jake was feeling a bit nostalgic.

This will be our last week here, thought Jake. *And, in a few short days, I will be fully retired from the US Army. No matter what awaits, I know that Sara and I will be very happy in Rome...or perhaps in some small villa near Vicenza, or perhaps in the Dolomite mountains.*

As Jake wheeled his Fiat sedan around the back of the

apartment building and to its parking garage, his heart glowed with the thought that within minutes, he would be sharing the same bed with Sara. Would she be up? Jake was not sure.

Tomorrow is a Saturday, he thought. *So maybe she's awake. But I hope she is sleeping peacefully.*

After Jake parked the car, he headed through the underground parking garage's access door to the building's stairwell. Normally, he would walk up the five flights of stairs. But tonight, Jake was exhausted. He decided to take the elevator.

Not wanting to wake Sara, he gently inserted his skeleton key into the keyhole of the solid wooden and metal-framed door. Again, he gently turned it. Hearing the squeak of the hinges, he lamented that he hadn't applied some WD-40 to them earlier.

Jake removed his jacket and put it in the closet. He removed his street shoes and put on his house shoes. The movers would come in a few days to pack up and transport Jake and Sara's personal items like wall pictures, kitchenware, and so forth and move them across town. But Jake felt good that since he and Sara had agreed on Jake leaving the Army, they had been "purging"—giving some items away, throwing others out, and selling a couple of items of furniture before moving into their new two-bedroom apartment at the end of the upcoming week.

He went into the kitchen, grabbed a bottle of water from the fridge, and poured himself a glass. He drank it all in one go. Not hearing Sara nor seeing any light emanating from the master bedroom, he knew she had fallen asleep. He went to use the bathroom in the hallway and then quietly moved to the bedroom. The door was slightly ajar, and the room was dark. Jake entered the bedroom.

Quietly stepping toward the master bathroom, Jake found the door frame in the dark, stepped inside the bathroom, and shut the door. He was careful not to turn on the light until he had shut the door. Perhaps due to Jake's Army experience training and operating in blackout conditions, he knew by feel, proportion, and habit exactly how the room was laid out. He could just as well have been blindfolded, and he would have easily moved around the room without stubbing his toe or walking into a door.

Once inside the bathroom, Jake, being as quiet as possible, brushed his teeth and washed his face. He knew a shower might wake Sara, so Jake decided to wait until morning for that.

He turned off the light and exited the bathroom in darkness. His side of the bed was, fortunately, closest to the bathroom. Jake bent over and felt for the duvet cover and top sheet when his legs bumped into the bed. He peeled both covers back. Gingerly, he eased himself into the king-size bed, facing Sara's side, and slowly pulled the cover and sheet up to his chest. As his pupils slowly adjusted to the darkness, he expected to see the dark form of the love of his life lying next to him.

There was nothing. Sara was a quiet nighttime breather, so he didn't expect to hear anything coming from her side of the bed. But Jake could now see that Sara's head was not on her pillow, either.

Jake reached his hand across the length of the bed as far as he could. The bed was flat, and the duvet and sheets on Sara's side were undisturbed. Jake froze, heart hammering in his chest.

I know it's been a long trip, and I'm exhausted, but what is happening?

For a few twilight-zone-like seconds, Jake considered whether he was in the right room and apartment. He rolled back to the lamp on his nightstand and turned on the light. It was definitely his and Sara's bed.

And Sara was not there.

CHAPTER 35

The Fragrance

SARA OPENED HER EYES.

Where am I? she thought. *Am I coming out of a dream?*

Her mind searched for an answer. In a mental flash, a vision appeared of a glass explosion next to the left side of her face, followed immediately by a black-gloved hand reaching through her car window, searching for the door latch. Then, blackness.

The mild panic at the realization her mouth was taped shut was somewhat relieved by the air she felt flowing past her in the mostly dark space. A tiny shard of light, about 18 inches from Sara's face, gave her hope.

A paraphrased biblical verse from her Catholic catechism days entered her mind: *the light shall overcome the darkness.* Sara was thankful for the light. She was alive.

With each passing second, it increasingly made sense. She could feel the zip-ties cutting into her wrists, *fortunately in front of me instead of behind me*, she thought, knowing it was more comfortable to have her hands in front than torqued behind her back. Her ankles were also bound together.

But I'm alive, and I can breathe, she reminded herself.

She did not know she was in the most southern part of the Italian boot, but the presence of light and the zip-ties added pieces to Sara's mental puzzle. Sara quickly understood she was lying on her left side, and the slight hum of the vehicle's tires told her she was likely in the back of a vehicle, one big enough to allow her to lie in a semi-fetal position but not big enough to allow her to stretch out her long legs.

A thick cloth tarp loosely draped over her head and body. Her captors removed the black hood during the stop to change license plates, ensuring Sara could breathe under the tarp. The tarp's diesel smell reminded Sara of the old Italian Army tents she slept in when on training exercises with the Italian Military Academy.

The slight shard of light coming through finally made sense, too.

And then she heard some talk from inside the vehicle. One voice sounded like it was either coming from a female or an effeminate male. The other voice was clearly male. The chatty duo was talking about rolling down the car's windows "just a little bit." The trip had been "eight hours long," said the female occupant, "and we need some fresh air."

Sara heard the windows come down.

Not much, maybe two or three inches or so, she thought. But they were down enough to let the local fragrance into the car.

To Sara, whom the two people in the front of the car thought was still knocked out from a strong propofol dose that they were told would last "ten hours or so," it was an unmistakable fragrance. She had smelled it only twice before in her life, the first time as a nine-year-old girl on a trip with her mother to visit her deceased father's relatives in Sicily, and the second when she had taken a southerly five-hour excursion from the Nunziatella Military Academy in Naples, located farther to the north. Nunziatella was the competitive military preparatory academy for high school-aged students wishing to attend Italy's military service academies.

Sara had pleasantly surprised her Carabinieri grandfather when she told him that she wanted to attend the Nunziatella

Preparatory Academy. Sara's father, also a Carabinieri officer, had been killed by the mafia when Sara was four years old.

The citrus fragrance was delightful. It lifted Sara's spirits. Given the stops at stoplights the vehicle was making along the route, Sara knew they were not traveling on Italy's autostrada.

In fact, for the past five miles, the trio had entered a thin strip of coastline road running fifty miles from San Giovanni, on the Tyrrhenian Sea and on the western coast of Calabria, to where it became the Ionian Sea and Brancaleone on the eastern side. Along this climatically idyllic stretch of earth grew bergamot (*citrus bergamia*) groves. The grove's trees produced a citrus fruit that had been cross-pollinated from lemon trees and sour orange trees some three to four centuries prior. In the early 1700s, the Farina family distilled the bergamot fruit to be among the first, if not the first, *eau de cologne*—later, simply *cologne* in English—to cover up the unpleasant bodily odors of the then-rich and famous. The Farina family earned a fortune from their bergamot citrus enterprise.

Later, in the nineteenth century, the bergamot citrus was discovered to have extraordinary health, antiseptic, and antibacterial qualities. Slightly larger than a lemon and green in color, the discovery of the fruit's 368 separate chemical qualities made it a highly sought-after commodity in the mid-1800s, enriching many of the locals in this limited stretch of coastline and the western part of a Calabria region that was otherwise known as the poorest in Italy. Among the six well-known citrus growing areas (Lake Garda, Liguria, Florence, the Amalfi coast, Diamanté, and this strip north of Reggio Calabria) in mainland Italy, the bergamot fruit is today the most highly valued and is known in Italy and the world over as "Green Gold."

The duo of 'Ndrangheta members who had been guiding the vehicle from Rome had indeed been driving almost eight hours, and that was *after* they had switched the vehicle's license plates on a rainy sideroad in Rome. Now, they were driving on Italy's coastal road north of Reggio Calabria. The slight waft of sea air, intermixed with the occasional scents of citrus, further informed Sara of where she *might be*. She was surprised by the degree to which her senses of smell and sound had been enhanced with her mouth taped shut.

Then came further confirmation of her location.

At one stop light, she could hear local people crossing the crosswalk and talking loudly through the rolled-down window. What she heard was clearly a Calabrian accent.

Heading south, to their right—or to the west—were the Straits of Messina and the island of Sicily just beyond the straits. Their ultimate destination was to the east and south in Calabria's mountainous and perennially economically downtrodden sub-region of Aspromonte on the very southern tip of mainland Italy. It had long provided remote hideouts, ideal for hiding kidnapped political officials or whoever else would earn them a handsome profit of extortion money, and whatever else the 'Ndrangheta thought needed to be hidden there—including countless dead bodies buried by the local mafia over the intervening century and a half—from Italian law enforcement and uncorrupted government officials.

As her weight shifted to the right and back of the vehicle, Sara realized that the vehicle had made a left turn and that they were now headed to higher terrain. Her mouth was parched, and she needed to relieve herself in the worst way. Soon, given all the turns and switchbacks that the SUV was navigating, Sara realized she had to make a choice between peeing her pants or getting her captors to stop and allow her a moment to relieve herself. She thought the latter choice was a long shot, but it was worth trying.

If these guys had wanted me dead, they would already have taken care of business, thought Sara, trying to keep her mind as positive as possible. It was one of the many lessons she had learned as an *Accademia Militare* cadet and young Carabinieri police officer trainee, and one she would have to constantly keep at the forefront of her mind until she was—hopefully—released.

Trying to get her abductor's attention, Sara began to kick the back wall of the Jeep Compass's luggage compartment as best she could with the soles of her bound feet. It seemed to work, as the woman in the right front passenger seat said something to the driver, who said something back to the right seat passenger. And then the passenger shouted at Sara.

CHAPTER 36

Aspromonte

"IF YOU WANT TO STAY ALIVE, STOP KICKING, YOU IDIOT!" Screamed the woman at Sara Simonetti. "You do it again, and we will kill you and bury you twenty feet deep!"

Sara stopped.

She heard more conversation between her captors.

"Maybe she's thirsty," said the male driver. "Or maybe she needs to go to the bathroom. How long has it been, anyway?"

"It's been well over eight hours," said his female accomplice.

"That's a long time to go without water, and if she hadn't had a drink or gone to the bathroom a couple or three hours before we snatched her, that could make it almost ten or even twelve hours," said the driver.

"You know, Gio-..."

The eight-year-veteran female 'Ndrangheta member stopped herself short, not wanting to say her fellow 'Ndrangheta member's first name—Giovanni—in front of their abductee. Instead, looking at her partner, she began again.

"You know..." She paused again.

She was uncomfortable that her Carabinieri prisoner had heard their conversation and knew how long they had been traveling since she was abducted.

"You talk too much! You just need to shut up sometimes!" she continued.

"Me…I talk too much? What did *you* just say?"

The driver, a 'Ndrangheta member who hailed from the roughly 1000-person mountainous village of *Santa Cristina d'Aspromonte*, was chosen for this mission because he knew the area and the mountain hideout Sara was being taken to as well as anybody. And as part of an 'Ndrangheta-directed hit, he had already killed the "vice mayor" of the Calabrian village of Polistena, thereby proving his loyalty to the 'Ndrangheta "family."

The mayor deserved it for not allowing the 'Ndrangheta to reap its fair share of taxes from the town's businesses, thought the fully indoctrinated mafioso.

The murder was done in classic 'Ndrangheta style: while riding on the back of a slowly moving but agile motor scooter, driven by another 'Ndrangheta aspirant, and with both the motor scooter driver—and "Gio," the shooter—covered in darkly-visored motorcycle helmets, they had been waiting for the mayor to park his car curbside. Gio (pronounced Jee-o, short for Giovanni) had fired three well-aimed shots as the mayor exited his parked car. The then-18-year-old did not miss, earning his first real merit badge as an aspiring 'Ndrangheta *giovane d'onore* (honored youth).

"Well, if she craps or pees her pants back there, you're going to be the one to clean it up. And if she dies from dehydration, I'm going to kill you before we both get killed by the *capos*!"

That was not an overstatement by the man the woman had called "Gio." If they failed in their mission of keeping Sara alive and getting her to the remote hideout location, the 'Ndrangheta duo would pay the price of their failure with their lives, and along with Carabinieri Lieutenant Colonel Sara Simonetti, their bodies would be disposed of in any number of 'Ndrangheta ways, including in vats of acid, local sub-terranean vaults known and protected by only a handful of local

'Ndrangheta members, or buried deep in the nearby seas surrounding three sides of this southernmost part of the Italian peninsula.

After Gio's outburst, both *mafiosi* went silent for a minute.

The woman continued.

"OK, listen. Drive us to a safe spot well off the road somewhere, and I'll see what the hell she wants."

Gio knew they were very close to a remote area that only saw a passing car every hour or so at most. Within twenty to thirty minutes, they would be there. The only people who ventured into the area were occasional local hunters who knew the area well, completely lost tourists, or 'Ndrangheta members who were hiding their kidnapped victims.

Gio's mind flashed to his father, also a former 'Ndrangheta *mafioso*, who was involved in the Aspromonte kidnapping and extortion trade of the early 1970s through the mid-1990s. During that period, it's estimated that more than 200 abductions were carried out across Italy by criminals associated with the Calabrian Mafia. Perhaps most famous was the 1974 kidnapping of J. Paul Getty III, grandson of American oil tycoon J. Paul Getty. The ransom money was ultimately used to fund the 'Ndrangheta's meteoric rise in drug trafficking.

In November and December 1990, the Italian government sent a battalion of *Alpini* (Alpine Mountain) troops to the area to "show the government flag" to the Calabrian locals and better map the Aspromonte area. The local maps hadn't been updated since shortly after World War II.

***

Lia Ippoliti slowly raised the Jeep Compass's back hatch door, pulled the tarp off her human cargo, and, with Gio's help, dropped the tarp on the ground to the back of the Jeep.

The bright early morning sun caused Sara's pupils to dilate more than she expected. Lying on her left side, she turned her head slightly to the right to get a view of the woman leaning in from the back of the vehicle.

"Listen," said Lia, "I know that through all your bullshit military training, you were taught to play the stoic, heroic prisoner who would never give in to her captor's demands. I don't care if you're stoic; in fact, I'd very much prefer it if you kept your mouth shut. But in a minute, I'm going to rip that tape off your pretty face so my partner and I can find out what you're riled up about. Don't try to be a hero, because if we must, we will not hesitate to kill you and bury you in a very deep hole. And if you're really, really lucky, we might check to make sure you're dead before we bury you."

Lia let those words sink in. Sara was beginning to understand the mettle of this woman with the dark complexion, black hair, and green eyes. The 'Ndrangheta ensured a woman was one of Sara's captors to avoid potential recriminations about her treatment in captivity. That is, if the situation ever resolved favorably and the 'Ndrangheta gave her back to the Carabinieri.

"Now, I'm going to climb in the back of this thing and pull that tape off."

Lia got on all fours, crawled forward, and grabbed the tape covering Sara's mouth.

"Like Momma said when she pulled off a band-aid, it only hurts for a second."

Lia immediately ripped the tape off.

Sara winced slightly, but, truth be told, it hurt more than expected.

"Now see, you don't need to worry about sitting in front of a mirror all day pulling those vexing facial hairs out with a pair of tweezers. That was much more efficient, wasn't it?"

Lia laughed loudly.

Sara wasn't quite sure if Lia had a sick or truly funny sense of humor.

"So, what's your problem, little lady?" asked Lia.

"I gotta pee…and I could use some water," responded Sara.

Sara realized that, surprisingly, she didn't feel that dehydrated, but she also knew she had to drink for the unborn child that was growing daily inside of her.

"OK, this is what we're going to do," said Lia. "I'm going to free your legs up so that you can walk. Your wrists will remain tied. Once I get you out of here, I'm going to grab you by your right arm with my left hand, and in my right hand, I'm going to be carrying this," she said as she waved the 9mm Beretta pistol in Sara's face.

"Then I'm going to escort you behind that tree," she added, nodding to a big oak tree about forty feet away. "And I'm going to release you when we get there, and you're going to do your business there. Sorry that we don't have a powder room next to it…so don't take forever! Understand?"

"Understand," responded Sara.

"And if you try to get cute and run away, my partner has one of these, too," said Lia, again brandishing her pistol. "And he's a better shot than me."

Sara thought about asking the woman to cut the zip-ties off her wrist, but she felt quite sure what the answer would be, so she decided not to push her luck at this early stage of being captive.

Around the back of the tree, it was no small feat for Sara, with her wrists bound together and her hands only movable as a pair, but fortunately, with her fingers still able to function, she got her pants and panties down so she could squat and relieve herself. Lia watched Sara struggle with her jeans and waited, almost offering to help. However, when Sara struggled to pull her pants all the way up to her waist, Lia grabbed Sara's blue jean belt loops from behind and pulled up to better position the jeans on Sara's waist. Sara was surprised at the assistance.

Walking back to the vehicle, Gio was standing there with an opened, small plastic bottle of water and handed it to Sara.

She took the San Pelligrino bottle of water as gracefully as possible, lifted it to her lips…and drank the whole thing.

"Damn, woman, are you sure you want to drink that much? We might be on the road another six hours without stopping again!" Gio laughed, tormenting Sara.

Lia frowned at Gio with that "Really, Asshole?" look she occasionally gave him.

Sara remained expressionless. Inside, although she was not quite sure about Lia and even less so about Gio, Sara was thankful that her captors seemed to retain some sense of humanity. And the "six hours" part that Gio had just mentioned?

That's bullshit. This feels and smells like southern Italy, thought Sara, recalling the scents of citrus, sea air, and the higher temperature than Rome, *and any direction we drive from here—except for due north, where we just came from—a coastline is no more than two, maybe three hours away.*

After putting a fresh strip of tape on Sara's mouth, getting Sara back in the vehicle, rebinding her ankles with plastic zipties, re-covering Sara with the tarp, and shutting the hatch, the two 'Ndrangheta killers got back in the Jeep. They continued their sun-splashed journey along the gravely, dusty, twisting, mostly forest-lined, and sparsely populated Aspromonte hills of southern Calabria.

CHAPTER 37

The Darkest Day

IT WAS A SATURDAY EVENING in the Italian Carabinieri headquarters. While there was a constantly manned, 24–7 operations cell active in the building, most Saturdays and Sundays were quieter days for the headquarters staff. Sure, some of the department leaders who held the rank of general and several hard-charging underling colonels and lieutenant colonels were habitually there on Saturday mornings. But by the afternoons, the building got as empty as it would be all week long. On this Saturday, at 6 p.m., the Carabinieri's senior leadership had convened a special meeting.

"This is the darkest day our Carabinieri ranks have experienced since Nasariya," began the Italian three-star general, addressing nine fellow Carabinieri officers and two civilians, one a public relations officer and the other a liaison to the Italian Parliament. Half of those seated around the large mahogany table had heard about the Italian senior officer's recent disappearance, but the other half had only heard rumors or nothing at all. That is until they sat down at the table and spoke to their colleagues just before the meeting began.

The general's reference to Nasariya hearkened to the Iraq War, where on November 12, 2003, eighteen Italians and eight Iraqis were killed by a suicide truck bomber in the southern Iraqi city. It was the worst single-day military loss for Italy since World War II. Twelve of the dead were Carabinieri police officers, while four were Italian Army soldiers, and one was a civilian working at the base. It was the first major attack on Western troops in southern Iraq during the Iraq War.

"Three nights ago, one of our most promising young officers, Captain Pietro Bondanella, disappeared. The only trace he left behind was a pool of his blood. It was discovered by his wife, Carla, in a parking lot northwest of the city, near their apartment building. Early last night, Lieutenant Colonel Sara Simonetti left this headquarters but never made it home to her apartment, just off the *via Cassia*, north of the city. We suspect she might have been involved in an orchestrated accident that occurred on the *via Cassia* and that she was perhaps kidnapped. Her personal vehicle is nowhere to be found, nor is she. We got a call just after midnight last night from her American husband, who I believe at least some of you know."

Three officers at the table solemnly nodded their heads.

"I know what some of you might be thinking," said the general. "We all know that close relatives or neighbors can perpetrate these kinds of crimes."

The general paused.

One of the officers who had nodded now shook his head and whispered to himself, "No way." *There is no way Jake Fortina is involved in this*, he thought. *Jake truly loves Sara.*

The general continued.

"Of course, we will vigorously pursue all evidence and leads. We have followed up with Lieutenant Colonel Jake Fortina this morning, and he is not a suspect, at least not for now."

The officer who doubted Fortina's involvement slowly nodded his head.

"Since last Sunday, Fortina was involved in a NATO exercise at the Sigonella Air Base, which I'm sure you all know is in southeastern Sicily. He did not return from that exercise until about midnight last night."

"So, where does that leave us?" the general inquired of his

staff. "You should all remember the attacks on Sara and Lieutenant Colonel Fortina, which occurred a few months back. The first was in the Vatican, and the second, immediately following the first, was on the streets adjacent to the Vatican, near the *Castel Sant'Angelo*. We unfortunately lost a dear colleague during the *Castel Sant'Angelo* attack." He took a moment of silence for his fallen officer. "Somebody wanted Sara and Jake Fortina dead, and most likely still do. Let us pray that our sister-in-arms, Sara Simonetti-Fortina, is still with us and is found safe and that nothing befalls our American colleague, Jake Fortina. But beyond praying, we must act with a sense of urgency." His voice rising, he continued, "And we—and all of our Carabinieri officers in the streets of Rome, and from the southern tip of our Italian peninsula to the Dolomite mountains—must do everything we can to resolve what happened to Sara and bring her safely home, as well as Pietro Bondanella."

Several heads around the table nodded in agreement.

One of the two colonels in the room, who was a recent friend to both Sara and Jake—though was unaware of their previous roles in countering national security threats—asked a question.

"Sir, I know the safe recovery of our fellow Carabinieri officers Bondanella and Simonetti-Fortina is clearly the priority here. But what about Jake Fortina? Since he is on Italian soil, don't we have some responsibility for his well-being?"

"Yes, I suppose we do," the Italian general replied. "But first, we must commit all hands to find out what has happened to Pietro and Sara and how to get them safely back from wherever they might be."

The three-star general, while he was certainly concerned by the question, was also frustrated by it. He knew that he had to tread carefully in terms of how to answer the question. Only three officers in the room knew about US Army Lieutenant Colonel Jake Fortina's participation in the operation to raid the Russian oligarch's "Farm" east of Rome several months prior. It was a raid that successfully recovered a suitcase nuclear weapon being held by the Russian, and that was intended to be used against US Naval Forces, with serious potential collateral damage to Italian civilians.

Only one of those three—a Carabinieri intelligence officer—seated at the table knew of Jake and Sara's involvement some four years prior in preventing an Iranian agent and his accomplices from carrying out the spreading of a lethal virus against Jews and Americans around the world.

The sharing of this knowledge had been limited to as few people as possible for obvious reasons, not the least of which was the health and well-being of the Italian and American officers. Now, the question was, who could be further trusted to know this information?

CHAPTER 38

Rumors

THE 'NDRANGHETA MAFIA WAS PUTTING the recently hired Cyberkid to good use. Typical of the 'Ndrangheta's methods of operation, the mafia organization did whatever it took to obfuscate, confuse, and dissuade Italian law enforcement—especially the Carabinieri—from following evidence to discover the true nature and source of 'Ndrangheta crimes.

Vincenzo Mangione, a *Vangelista* (evangelist) in the 'Ndrangheta's "major society" upper leadership ranks, was responsible for the mafia organization's social media campaigns. He was very pleased—even cautiously optimistic—after his introduction to Alexei, a.k.a. "the Cyberkid," now in his thirties. The Russian whiz kid's cyber talents, background, and experience reached back to the US presidential election of 2016 when Alexei was part of a covert Russian cyber organization whose sole mission was to flood US and international social media platforms with pro-Republican and anti-Democrat messages leading up to the 2016 US presidential election.

In February 2018, a US Federal Grand Jury indicted thirteen Russians for "federal crimes while seeking to interfere in the United States political system, including the 2016 presidential election." Alexei, because he had not been part of the Russian cyber group's leadership ranks, evaded indictment. Later, in December 2023, "a binder containing highly classified information related to Russian election interference" was reported by US and international media outlets to have gone missing. And now, the Kid's cyber efforts in support of the 'Ndrangheta were working beautifully, and Vincenzo Mangione was ecstatic.

Soon after the Kid's hiring, Mangione had given the Kid guidance for the kind of narrative the 'Ndrangheta leaders wanted out in the media. *So far*, thought the veteran *mafioso*, *the political mice—and duped Italian citizens—are having a feeding frenzy on the smelly cheese the Kid has been putting out there.*

"The rumors you have been planting are working their magic!" said Mangione to his Russian underling.

It was a rare moment of praise by Mangione, who was more used to employing fear and even terror—sprinkled with the occasional reward—as the main motivator for those young mafia members he had brought up through the 'Ndrangheta's ranks.

"Thank you, *signore*," replied the Kid. "It's not that hard. People eat this stuff up—even the most egregious lies—as if it were the Gospel truth."

"Well, keep spreading the good word!" responded Mangione.

The main narrative, approved all the way up to the 'Ndrangheta Godfather level and that Mangione and the Kid were focused on, was that there were other Italian Army general officers and senior government involved in the conspiracy to sell AK 47s to an extremist, white supremacist US militia group based out of the United States. Only half of that narrative was true. Italian Army Brigadier General Constantino Cadorna was the sole Italian Army officer—let alone general officer—who had acted in the conspiracy.

But the 'Ndrangheta knew there were at least a half-dozen Italian politicians involved in the conspiracy. Why? Because they, the most fascist-leaning of the far-right Italian government politicians, wanted a return to a Mussolini-style authoritarian government, one that would "make Italy great again," and rid the country of the "scum" who were increasingly filling Italy's cities and villages from places like North Africa and the Middle East. The 'Ndrangheta also knew these politicians were on the 'Ndrangheta payroll, and if push came to shove, the 'Ndrangheta would expose the politicians as the corrupt Italian government officials that they were.

"We want to diffuse the Italian government's focus on General Cadorna and get the government focused on their own internal problems," said Mangione. "We want Cadorna to either receive a significantly reduced sentence for selling the AK 47s to the Americans or have any potential jail time for Cadorna completely done away with!"

"I understand, signore," replied Alexei. "I will do everything I can to make that goal happen."

Mangione nodded affirmatively.

"*Buono* (good)," he responded.

Mangione knew it was critical that the Kid succeeded. Otherwise, through Cadorna's prosecution and court proceedings, the 'Ndrangheta's massive illicit weapons trafficking operation reaching all the way to places like Afghanistan, Pakistan, Russia, and Venezuela might be exposed.

CHAPTER 39

The Hideout

GIO AND LIA APPROACHED THE FINAL TURN TOWARD THE HIDEOUT. Gio had performed a reconnaissance of this route before. He hated to go anywhere without first having done a trial run, even in his home region of Calabria. The terrain was just too easy to get lost in, even for old-timers like him. As they began to turn right and leave the relatively passable gravel road, where they would get onto a dirt—and sometimes muddy—two-track road, Lia was surprised to see a herd of sheep heading their way. Their shepherd, *who*, she thought, *was probably around twenty and stunningly handsome, if a bit weather-worn*, was traveling in the opposite direction from their destination.

Gio was not surprised by the bleating and pooping entourage and their human leader. Both mafia members knew the almost mystical Aspromonte region fairly well, but it was so remote, and its terrain so varying and thickly wooded, that one would never know what to find out here.

Gio looked at Lia.

"They've been here for centuries. I went to school with two kids whose father was a shepherd. The kids left school at the age of sixteen and were never seen again. Tough way to make a living."

"Or not," said Lia. "Imagine all the modern-day bullshit these kids—and later adults—never have to worry about."

Gio nodded.

When the sheep had passed them by, Gio and Lia focused their attention down the road. After about a half-mile of slowly creeping through the thickly wooded, old-growth forest on the rocky, bumpy road that was barely wide enough for one vehicle, they knew they were getting close to the sunlit clearing. Once they could see the light on the other end of the heavily shaded tunnel getting brighter, they knew the old cement and stuccoed building that stood at the clearing would soon be visible.

Other than it being a 'Ndrangheta hideout, the provenance of the two-story building was not known to either of them. But there had been plenty of speculation. In their preparation for this trip, they had driven to the hideout just once.

"Whoever and whyever they built this place here," said Lia, "it creeps me the hell out."

Gio nodded in agreement, goosebumps prickling his skin.

"But I suspect I know what it's been used for. If it could tell stories, even I, a badass mafia girl, would not want to hear them," she added, laughing to keep the nerves at bay.

Both Gio and Lia knew of the 'Ndrangheta's decades-long practice of kidnapping victims and holding them for ransom in Aspromonte, the thickly wooded, ravine-filled, often-steep, and remote province of Calabria. Unbeknownst to Gio and Lia, some former occupants of the hideout survived while others died in captivity. Some, who died in captivity, had their bodies dumped in the middle of the night in a local village square—sending a clear message to locals. In other cases, the bodies were hidden deep in cavernous caves, with loved ones forever left to ponder their fates.

The duo had never heard of a single instance where Italian law enforcement successfully ventured into this area, let alone was successful in recovering a single kidnapped victim. The word *Aspromonte* had almost a mysterious fatality to it, not only to southern mainland Italy locals but to the highest government and law enforcement officials of the land as well.

The area was so thickly wooded that, as the story went, a British Army and German Wehrmacht unit had practically stumbled upon each other after a British Army soldier left his foxhole one morning to relieve himself, only to find out he was within throwing distance of the German lines. A young Wehrmacht soldier, perhaps because he was just coming out of his early morning slumber, did not immediately react, allowing the Brit to quickly return behind friendly lines.

For a moment, Lia thought about how she had come to this place in her life. Her grandfather had been a Carabinieri *maresciallo* (equivalent to a US warrant officer). But when he had been abandoned—or so the story went—by the Italian government in his later years of service, Lia's grandfather decided to take bribes from the 'Ndrangheta. After that, he looked the other way from 'Ndrangheta-committed crimes, eventually even helping to commit them.

Lia's father noticed how the family's economic fortunes improved after his father joined the mafia, and he, too, decided to commit his loyalty to the 'Ndrangheta. The tangible result was a comfortable—albeit not grandiose—country home where Lia grew up. Her family never suffered the poverty common to many families in this "forgotten" part of Italy. Lia deeply loved her attentive father and, wanting to please him, didn't hesitate to express her desire to join the mafia after the 'Ndrangheta opened the door for "a few women." Her father was initially concerned about it and objected to his only daughter joining the criminal organization, but he later relented.

Once the Godfather-at-the-time had announced his concise manifesto to the *Crimine*, some six years prior, it was a done deal for Lia to make her move.

"In this day and age," said *il Capo*, "we'd be stupid to think that women—just a few, not many—won't help us in sustaining over a century of respectable 'Ndrangheta tradition. The Italian government goons and thieves, whose only purpose is to steal from the people of our beautiful Calabrian homeland, will be too stupid and slow to realize that women have joined our magnificent ranks and traditions, and we will use this Italian government stupidity to our advantage."

On the first floor of the off-white hideout that was seriously in need of a paint job, there was a large, cement-floored, and thickly walled room. There was a cot with a single wool blanket on a wall across from a sink that sat under the single window on that floor. The sink served as both a drinking and bathing facility for the room's occupant.

Three feet to the left of the sink was a "squatter" toilet. Consisting of two porcelain pads where one placed their feet, there was a six-inch diameter hole in the center and just behind the foot pads. Good aim and strong thighs were important for using the squatter effectively.

Two sides of the room were the exterior, twenty-four-inch-thick cement and stucco walls. An interior stucco support wall constituted the cell's third wall, and interior iron bars constituted the cell room's fourth side. In the summer, the thickness of the two exterior cement walls would provide some respite from the oppressive Calabrian summer heat, as would the building's 2100 feet of elevation and the surrounding mixed deciduous-coniferous, old-growth forest.

The top of one exterior wall—opposite the bed on the wall with the sink and toilet—was an open-air window with three vertically running iron bars. Calling it a "window" was a stretch. Twelve inches high and sixteen inches wide, the window was positioned nine feet off the floor. While rare were the occupants who could reach the windowsill *and* had the strength to pull themselves up to see out of the window, it did allow natural light in. And for most occupants caged in the cell room, that was the one thing they looked forward to each morning: the light. For those who could not manage to jump up, get a good finger hold on the window's sill, *and* pull themselves up, the depth of the windowsill and the wall's thickness allowed only for a quick glimpse of distant treetops, located just across the seventy-yard-diameter clearing. Yet, somehow, the rectangular aperture provided most occupants a beacon of hope.

On the cement walls were ageless engravings, some giving hope, some not so much.

On the wall above the bed was a single, fourteen-inch-high dark brown wooden cross, fashioned decades prior from a one-inch-thick beech tree branch found just outside the building's front door by a bored but faithful guard of the 'Ndrangheta.

The room was not for the faint of heart.

CHAPTER 40

Silence

THE SILENCE WAS DEAFENING. Jake knew he would only spend three more nights in the now silent apartment before moving into the smaller place he and Sara had purchased closer to Rome's city center. As Jake entered the dark bedroom he and Sara had shared, he felt Sara's absence in the depths of his soul. Jake had lost his first wife and two children in a horrific car accident several years prior, and the familiar ache of losing those dearest to the heart surged again in his soul.

Is she still alive? he asked himself as he slipped on his pajama bottoms. *Is she hurt? Dear God, please let her be in good health and spirits.*

At that prayer, he smiled bracingly. Jake knew just how resilient and resourceful his beautiful Italian bride was. As a former Italian Military Academy cadet and current Carabinieri officer, Sara had received extensive training to stay alive and vigilant, including survival techniques, how to resist interrogation, and hand-to-hand combat. The thought bolstered Jake's hope, keeping the dark thoughts that were trying to worm their way into his mind at bay. Jake had learned that Sara had that extra gear, that "extra something" that had set her apart from many other people—let alone women—that he had encountered in his life of military service. Sara's quick thinking had saved Jake's life some four years prior when they chased Iranian terrorists.

He carried those thoughts with him as he knelt at the edge of his bed to pray. Jake rarely closed his eyes for the night before consciously reaching out to the Almighty. Indeed, his faith was with him all day. In the mornings, after readying himself for the day and making a double espresso, he always grabbed his well-worn copies of *Jesus Calling* and the *Holy Bible* and spent several minutes in quiet reading and reflection.

While prayer was a habit he had developed over the years, getting on his knees for prayer was not something he frequently did. Truth be told, though, it was something he did for life's weightier concerns, the ones that literally brought Jake to his knees.

He knelt now, the heaviness of his thoughts and emotions bringing him to his knees at the side of the large bed. His elbows rested on the mattress. Facing the wall opposite the glass balcony door, he tracked the familiar shadows cast by the diluted evening light and the balcony's side curtains. Jake bowed his head in deference and sent a fervent prayer to Almighty God. It was a prayer that lasted almost two minutes.

After he finished his prayer, Jake slowly raised his head... and saw what he thought was a change in the shadows cast on the wall. Jake refocused his eyes, thinking perhaps he had seen the shadow of a moving tree branch just beyond the balcony behind him. He quickly realized how ridiculous that thought was, as the closest tree was forty feet away and not in front of the balcony at all. Jake's Spidey sense began to tingle. He saw the shadow again, only this time it was larger. He quickly turned his head and saw a hand reaching for the balcony glass door. Simultaneously, the person whose hand was reaching for the glass balcony door handle saw Jake's sudden movement and Jake's face, and the man reaching for the door realized his element of surprise was gone.

As soon as Jake got to his feet, he saw the darkly clothed

figure go over the balcony. By the time he opened the door, got to the edge of the balcony, and looked down, he could see the person bounding from the balcony below to the next one below that. Then, somehow, the man slid down the apartment building's robust drainpipe for the last twelve feet to the ground. Jake bolted toward the apartment's front door, slipped into his shoes, pulled the door keys out that were in the lock on the interior side of the heavy metal door, and raced down the apartment building's stairwell to the ground floor in his pajama bottoms, T-shirt, and street shoes.

The person was nowhere to be found.

CHAPTER 41

Skeptical

AZAR ZADEHA WAS DISAPPOINTED AND SKEPTICAL. Her handlers back in Tehran had promised her that Kamran Masoumi was the right operator for the job. He had been ruthless in torturing men, women, and even children of parents who had protested in the streets and on social media against the Iranian regime.

However, Zadeha had discovered from a couple of her intelligence contacts in Iran that while Masoumi was efficient at doing the Iranian government's deranged dirty work of torturing confessions out of Iranian protestors and that he might have successfully performed one (confirmed) or two (unconfirmed) assassinations of domestic enemies of the Iranian regime, he was "not that competent as an assassin nor gatherer of high stakes intelligence." One of Zadeha's contacts even went so far as to say that some in the Iranian regime wanted Masoumi out of the country because he was too much of a liability to certain members of the Iranian regime.

That is probably why, speculated Zadeha, *the government sent Masoumi here. They thought Masoumi could do the job, and if he didn't, he would be expendable.*

Zadeha wanted to hear directly from the supposed "professional hit man" as to why he failed to assassinate the American Army officer, Jake Fortina.

"Tell me again," she began, "about what happened on the

Change of Mission 143

night you were supposed to kill the American."

"I had observed his residential area, with its electronic entry gate, for two weeks," began Masoumi. "I was able to quickly gain access to the compound. While the immediate gate area was video-surveilled, no part of the rest of the fenced-in compound was. So, I scaled the outer fence each night until I could determine what apartment building the American and Italian couple were staying in. Eventually, by determining when their vehicle came into the compound and when certain apartment lights came on and off, I was able to determine what apartment was theirs. For a few days, the American no longer returned to the apartment. Then, when he did, his wife did not return. I was not sure why."

"Not sure why? Of what?" asked Zadeha. "Why the American eventually returned, and why his wife didn't?

"Precisely," replied Masoumi. "He came back to the apartment, and she didn't. So, unsure of what would happen next, I realized I needed to act quickly."

"Go on," replied Zadeha.

"At that point, I decided that after only three nights of observing him in his apartment, I needed to make my move," said the assassin. "So, on the third night, I scaled up to his third-floor apartment balcony."

"How did you do that?" asked Zadeha.

Thinking *she will be impressed by what I have to say next*, Masoumi continued.

"Partially by climbing up the drainpipe and partially, for the last floor, with a rope and grappling hook, to get to his bedroom balcony."

"And...what happened next?" asked the Iranian intelligence agent.

"I stayed on his balcony and waited for him to turn on the light and enter his bedroom. But I never saw him come in," said Masoumi. "So, I decided to open the balcony door and enter his bedroom to find out where he was in the apartment because I knew he was in there."

"So, you got impatient," replied Zadeha.

Taken aback at Zadeha's comment—somewhere between an outright accusation and negative implication—Masoumi quickly defended himself.

"No, not really," he responded. "I was thinking more that I needed to take action rather than just wait."

"Action? When you had no idea where in that fucking apartment he was?"

Zadeha was growing increasingly impatient and frustrated.

"Well, yes," responded the Iranian assassin.

"What were you armed with?" asked Zadeha.

"I was armed with a stiletto knife and pistol, with a silencer. My plan was to find him in that apartment and kill him," said Masoumi, repeating himself.

"Well, what the hell happened?" asked Zadeha, her tone increasingly aggravated.

"As I reached for the balcony door handle, the nearby streetlights that were shining through the door glass reflected on the American's face. He must have been kneeling at the side of the bed; his face seemed to come out of nowhere."

"So, now you're saying the American is some kind of ghost?" said Zadeha wryly, decreasingly able to believe her supposed hitman's story.

"No, I'm not. But I must confess, it did surprise me..."

Zadeha interrupted with another question.

"So, what did you do when you saw the ghost?" now ridiculing Masoumi.

"I quickly lowered myself off the balcony to the next balcony below, and then shimmied down the drainpipe and got the hell off that compound."

Zadeha looked down at the paper in front of her. She sighed a long sigh and nodded her head in silence.

"Do you think he saw your face?" she asked.

"He couldn't," responded Masoumi.

"How sure are you about that?" asked Zadeha.

"I'm quite sure. I had a black skull cap and a black ski mask on. Everything I was wearing was black."

"So, how do you intend to do to fix this?" asked Zadeha. "Our leaders at the highest levels of our government want this American dead."

"I will find him and kill him, I promise," replied the Iranian.

CHAPTER 42

A New Home

SARA HEARD THE VEHICLE'S BRAKES SQUEAK as the vehicle came to a stop. In less than thirty seconds, while Gio got out and walked toward the building, Lia Ippoliti exited the vehicle, walked around to the back, and opened the back hatch. Ippoliti quickly pulled the tarp away from Sara, cut through the zip-ties holding her ankles together, and, with Sara's wrists still zip-tied, firmly told Sara to "get out of the vehicle."

Sara quickly complied, wriggling her way out the back of the Jeep Compass and standing.

"We are going to your new home," said Lia to Sara as she grabbed Sara by the arm and began walking Sara to the hideout. "It's not air-conditioned, but the walls are pretty thick. So, when it starts heating up around here you won't be cooked."

Sara instantly focused on the second "thick walls" part of that comment. The comment gave her an inkling of hope that the walls might protect her against the oppressive Calabrian heat, which would surely come as spring, soon to begin, would turn to summer. Sara, trying to keep her thoughts positive, also thought that Lia might be showing concern, however slight, for Sara's well-being. Sara's awareness sharpened. Every sense now acutely attuned to the sights, sounds, and sensations of her surroundings, including the intensity of the sunlight, the blue sky, the slight breeze, and the smells of the surrounding forest.

Change of Mission   147

As Lia led Sara to the hideout's only entrance—secured by a thick, scarred wooden door hung not long after World War II—Sara mentally photographed and sensed everything that she could about the area surrounding her soon-to-be prison. She filed it all away in case the opportunity to escape presented itself.

As Lia pushed her toward the entrance, Sara's careful optimism faltered. She felt like she was entering some kind of tomb. With Gio in front of her and Lia behind her, Sara was led through a stucco-covered hallway, barely wide enough for two people, with a stone floor and a low, arched ceiling. It was no more than seven to eight feet high. The hallway extended for a few feet before a narrow stairwell opened up on the right side. Opposite the stairwell was a solid wooden door. A small wooden sign marked "STORAGE" was tacked to it. Inside the "storage" room was a toilet for the captors. She followed Gio another eight feet or so beyond the stairwell before the low hallway ceiling exited into a room with a ten-foot-high ceiling and a prison cell to her left. The cell had floor-to-ceiling bars on the side facing Sara and cement walls on the other three sides. The part of the room she stood in as she stared in trepidation at the cell was bare. No windows. No furniture.

With Sara and Lia now standing in front of the bars, Gio inserted a skeleton key into the cell door's lock. As Gio turned the key, the old lock's tumblers made audible click and clunk sounds. Then Gio pulled the door open. Lia nudged Sara into the space. Once inside, Lia grabbed Sara by the arms and slowly turned her around so they faced each other. Lia again grabbed her Leatherman-style tool and cut the zip-ties from Sara's wrists.

"Enjoy your stay," said Lia unceremoniously.

Lia stepped out of the cell, and Gio shut and locked the door. Both 'Ndrangheta members turned and walked toward the hallway. They disappeared around the corner, and Sara could make out the groans and squeaks of the wood as they climbed to the second floor.

Sara turned around and examined the rest of the room. Above her, hanging from a simple, thick, black wire that extended a foot below the ceiling, was a single bare lightbulb. The bulb was three feet above Sara's extended reach. What Sara did not yet realize was that she had no control over the light switch, as it was on the wall about four feet outside of her cell.

Sara looked at the cot. It had a simple, gray wool blanket folded on it. It encouraged her. It could provide warmth on cold nights, but, folded up, it would make an excellent pillow when the nights began to warm.

Above the cot, Sara looked at the simple wooden cross on the wall. She smiled. The cross gave her hope. She resolved to always remember she was never alone and remember those who she loved and who loved her.

Etched crudely into the wall between the cross and the cot, apparently done at different times and by different hands, judging by the letters, were *"non morire"* (don't die) and *"non ho paura"* (I'm not afraid) and *"ti amo"* (I love you).

Sara turned around and looked at the sink and the squatter toilet. She was very thankful that there was a hand towel hanging from a hook near the sink as well as a solid white bar of soap on the sink. Those simple items would allow Sara to keep *a minimum level of hygiene*, she thought.

They also mean that they want to keep me alive, at least for a while, she half-thought and half-prayed.

Sara did not know it yet, but the sink's faucet only had one temperature setting: cold.

The toilet, which, *thankfully*, thought Sara, had a roll of toilet paper next to it, was squatter-style, common throughout the southern parts of Italy.

She recalled using a squatter toilet when she was an adolescent, telling her mother how "disgusting" it was. But she also knew that for much of the country, these toilets were common through much of the twentieth century. The resolute soldier inside of Sara dismissed it as *just a slight inconvenience.*

As Sara sighed, resigned to the situation, she was encouraged by the small sounds she could hear through the floor upstairs—the movement of a wooden chair on the cement floor and occasional *bumps* and *clunks*, the water coming through the pipes in the walls. While she could hear no voices, as time went on—*I pray to God time* will *go on,* she thought—Sara knew those sounds would help her overall situational awareness of what was happening above and around her.

Looking at the small window above her, Sara smiled. The window allowed some natural light in. And natural light meant life.

Her mind quickly flashed to more hopeful thoughts that included decent treatment and a sojourn of weeks, not months... and certainly not years. While Sara had never worked kidnapping cases as a Carabinieri officer, Sara understood that it could take a year or longer to resolve them if they were able to be resolved. She knew some victims were never found. She fought off those thoughts with the sustaining hope that her case would be different.

***

Upstairs, Gio switched on the burner of the forty-year-old but still workable electric stove. He removed a vintage Bialetti steel espresso coffee pot from the single wooden shelf above the sink and filled the pot's base with water. He stuffed some Kimbo espresso grounds into the top part of the pot and set the pot on the burner.

He looked at Lia and the man sitting at the wooden table,

which was barely big enough for four.

"As long as we have espresso, life will not suck here," said Gio. He laughed.

The man seated at one side of the table and opposite Lia responded.

"I don't see how you can drink that swill."

"Swill? What do *you* drink, Ivan? Vodka? Morning, noon, and night?" responded Gio.

Ivan was not the man's real name. But the 'Ndrangheta had given the man, a former Wolfpack member, refuge from Italian government law enforcement, so Ivan became his cover name.

The man at the table shot Gio a menacing glance. What the man did not know was that many people underestimated Gio. He was much more attuned to the greater world and more well-read than the average *mafioso*. In World War II, Gio's great-grandfather left Calabria to fight with Italy's *Alpini* (mountain troops), eventually ending up in Russia. As most of the alpine troops came from the northern alpine and Dolomite mountains of Italy, with some also coming from the Apennine Mountain range, the spine of mountains running north and south along much of the Italian boot, Gio's southern-raised grandfather had to practically fight to enlist with the *Alpini*. But the dense mountains and hills of Calabria had made the young man accustomed to trudging up and down difficult terrain, and it made him physically tough. And to the *Alpini's* recruiters, he *looked* tough and athletic, too. Italian Army World War II recruiters finally accepted Gio's grandfather into the ranks of the Italian mountain troops.

Over four decades later, when Gio turned sixteen, Gio's father gifted Gio a book and said, "Read this. This is what your grandfather did. He was a *real* man."

Gio read the book, and it sparked his interest in history and politics.

The book, originally published in 1963 to wide Italian acclaim, was authored by Giulio Bedeschi. Bedeschi was an Italian Army second lieutenant assigned to the Italian Army Medical Corps and, ultimately, to the *Alpini*. The book was titled *Centomila Gavette di Ghiaccio* (*One Hundred Thousand Frozen Mess Kits*). Bedeschi's book described the harrowing and deadly consequences of underequipped and poorly supplied Italian mountain soldiers who, much like Napoleon's *Grande Armée* and Hitler's *Wehrmacht*, had to face not only incessant Soviet artillery barrages and horrifying combat but also the brutal and heartless 1942–1943 Russian winter.

On the evening of January 17, 1943, on the Axis Eastern Front, believing his corps no longer combat-effective, the Italian Alpine Army Corps commander ordered a full retreat. A 40,000-strong mass of stragglers—*Alpini*, Italian soldiers from other commands, Germans, and Hungarians—formed two columns that followed the *Alpini Tridentina* Division westward to the German lines. Bedeschi's own *Julia* Division suffered heavy losses: less than a tenth of the Division's 18,000 troops survived. The combined Italian losses on the Eastern Front in the late fall and winter of 1942–1943 amounted to over 100,000 dead. Gio's grandfather miraculously came home to Calabria.

The Russian seated at the table was not quite sure how to respond to Gio's comment.

"Real men drink vodka," offered the Russian.

"How lame," responded Gio. "How many real Russian men live beyond the age of fifty?"

Gio knew the devastating effects of alcohol on the Russian population, especially the "real men" Ivan was referring to.

"Now, boys, let's settle down," implored Lia. "We have a job to do. And it's not going to be any easier with you two bickering like a couple of schoolyard punks."

CHAPTER 43

Just A Matter Of Time

"HENNADIY, I'M NOT SURE IF YOU HAVE HEARD," said Jake Fortina, speaking into his new burner phone.

"Heard what? That you will officially retire tomorrow, with no ceremony for your friends to attend and cheer you on?" asked Ukraine's Defense Attaché to Italy.

"No, not that," replied Fortina. "After tomorrow, nobody in the US government or army will give a rat's ass about me. Do you have some time in the next day or two when you and I can meet?"

"Next day or two? Hell, Jake, I can meet you in the next hour or two. You tell me when and where, and I'll be there."

Jake deeply appreciated that his relationship with Colonel Hennadiy Kovalenko was not just professional. Kovalenko was the foreign military attaché in Rome that Jake trusted the most, and truth be told, he and Colonel Kovalenko would entrust their lives to each other if it came to it. And in some sense, they already had, exchanging intelligence about Vasily Puchta, Russia's president, as well as a runaway oligarch living in Italy.

"You know our humble place...the one with the brown paper?"

Fortina knew the chances of someone listening in on his cheap burner phone, which he had used only a couple of times, were next to zero. But if somebody was listening in on Kovalenko's phone, it was extremely unlikely that in a city of over 13,000 restaurants and several thousand bars and gelaterias, that listeners wouldn't have an inkling about what the brown paper reference meant, let alone that Fortina was referring to a restaurant.

Kovalenko went silent for a minute. Although Fortina couldn't see it, Kovalenko eventually smiled broadly when his mental light bulb came on. A vision of fried cod wrapped in brown paper revealed the very place Fortina was referring to.

"Yes, I do, my friend. *Dimmi quando* (tell me when)," said Kovalenko, switching to Italian.

"*In tre ore, va bene?*" (In three hours, OK?)

Kovalenko checked his watch and marked the time.

"*Perfetto*," replied Kovalenko.

***

Jake Fortina walked into the *Filetti di Baccala*, a small Roman bar and restaurant located at *Largo dei Librari* 88. It was an unassuming place. Its specialty was fried cod filets. As Jake walked by the dark and shiny wooden bar and into the back dining room, with off-white paper serving as tablecloths, Fortina spied Kovalenko sitting in the back corner. Both military attachés had learned early on to always pick the restaurant table—or train or subway seat or standing place—with the best view of the entire space, including the space's primary and secondary exits.

Jake was raised by his parents to give the restaurant seat with the best view to his date or partner. But Fortina and Kovalenko knew that in the gray international world of overt information gathering and security cooperation—as well as the covert world of espionage—the best seat for situational and security awareness should always be claimed by the professional.

As Fortina took his time walking to a back corner of the restaurant, he was aware—and happy—that the languages he heard at three tables along the way were American English, the King's English, and German. Fortina approached Kovalenko's table and gave the Ukrainian colonel a big smile. Kovalenko stood up, reciprocated, and gave his old friend a hug. As Fortina pulled his chair out, he could see that Kovalenko had already ordered a liter of uncarbonated water.

But what Fortina was not expecting were two shot glasses on the table, each with clear liquid inside them. The shots were normally reserved for *after* a meal.

"Looks like we are getting off to a good start, my dear friend," said Fortina. "Is this grappa?"

"Hell no," replied Kovalenko. "It's Ukrainian vodka, the best vodka on the planet."

What Kovalenko did not tell Fortina was that when Kovalenko walked into the restaurant, he gifted a sealed bottle of Ukrainian vodka to the female bartender, with the only caveat that Kovalenko and his dinner partner would each get a shot to start their dinners with. The bartender confirmed that the bottle's seal was intact, and she thought that *if this guy and his partner don't croak after drinking their shots, I'll do a little taste test myself.*

When Fortina and Kovalenko spoke on the phone some three hours earlier, Kovalenko could feel the tension and negative energy in Fortina's voice, and this was Kovalenko's way of showing that he cared. But he also wanted to celebrate Fortina's almost twenty-one years of dedicated and honorable US Army service.

The two clinked their shot glasses, looked each other in the eyes, and said, "*Salute*" (pronounced sa-LU-tay, the Italian toast for "to your health.")

Toasting Fortina's service, Kovalenko said, "To one hell of

a run, my friend. And God bless you, the US Army, your government, and the millions of Americans who support Ukraine. Without you and them, our kids would be speaking Russian in a few years."

The two men put down their glasses, and Fortina responded.

"Thank you, my dear friend."

Kovalenko continued.

"Tell me, Jake, what is on your mind. What has happened?"

"Tomorrow, Hennadiy, what I am about to tell you will be all over the news, depending on how the Carabinieri decide to approach it," said Fortina. "They've been sitting on this announcement for a few days now. I guess they wanted to throw the bad guys off a bit. Now, it seems, they are ready—hopefully—to conduct a massive investigation."

Kovalenko raised his eyebrows, and his face portrayed concern. He nodded but still had no clue about what Fortina was about to tell him, so he interjected, "An investigation of what?"

"Sara has disappeared," said Fortina.

Kovalenko inhaled deeply and let out a discernible sigh.

"*What*? I'm so sorry to hear that," responded Kovalenko.

"When I got back from Sigonella last Friday, after midnight, she wasn't in our apartment. I had just spoken with her the previous evening. Her—our—old junker car is also nowhere to be found. The Carabinieri said she had left work around 6:30 p.m. that same evening in a driving rainstorm, and within about thirty minutes of her leaving the building, a couple of witnesses driving on the *via Cassia* reported that they had witnessed what they thought was some kind of carjacking. However, that old beater car we had wasn't worth more than 2000 euros (about $2100-$2200), so there is no way the assailants or thieves were focused on hijacking the car."

Questions were beginning to form in Kovalenko's mind. But he thought it best to simply nod to Fortina.

"And last night, somebody was on my balcony, trying to open the balcony door. By the time I responded, the person, with the height and build of a man, lowered himself off the balcony and disappeared by the time I got downstairs and outside."

The overall picture was now becoming clearer in Kovalenko's head, and Fortina soon confirmed that picture.

"I'm pissed that somebody managed to surveil my place and confirm where Sara and I lived, but I also know that somebody wants both Sara and me dead. Unfortunately, there is more than one candidate out there who would like to see Sara and me six feet under. I'm going to need your help, my friend."

Kovalenko had anticipated Fortina's comment and was ready for it.

"If you need a place to stay, you are welcome to stay at my place. We have an extra room, and Mila and I would love to have you."

"I feel like that's asking too much, Hennadiy. And it might also put you and Mila in danger."

"No more danger than we're already in," responded Kovalenko, chuckling. "Between the Russians, their good friends, the Syrians, the Turks, and even some Hungarians, I'm not sure who would draw the short straw—or seek the prize more—to have me done away with."

Kovalenko smiled.

"I'm serious, Jake," continued Kovalenko. "We'd love to have you for as long as you need to stay. Not just days…weeks, months, whatever. Heck, we could even alternate pulling guard duty, haha, just like when we were young bucks."

Fortina paused to consider Kovalenko's offer.

"OK, I'm deeply grateful for your generosity, Hennadiy.

But I don't intend to stay for more than one, two weeks max. I just need to get my bearings and figure out what the hell is going on."

"And you need to stay off the X," replied Kovalenko, referring to the most vulnerable spot where people are targeted, either lethally or, as in the case of Sara, non-lethally.

"Your old apartment that you just left was obviously targeted," continued Kovalenko, "and wherever you intended to move next in this city—no matter how big you think it is—is most likely targeted as well. All your enemies need to do is slip some corrupt Roman official a few hundred euros, and they'll find out what lease or real estate contract has been publicly registered in your or Sara's name. It's only a matter of time before the bad guys get another shot at you, and you know as well as I do that with each successive try, their odds of killing or kidnapping you will only get better."

Jake nodded his head in agreement.

CHAPTER 44

Much Speculation

THE CAREFULLY PREPARED CARABINIERI PRESS RELEASE stirred much speculation among journalists, pundits, and the greater Italian population: what happened to Carabinieri Lieutenant Colonel Sara Simonetti-Fortina? Her beautiful face was splashed across social media and the few remaining newspaper kiosks—once prolific across Italy—that still existed on some Italian city street corners. Old men who had known each other for decades sat in cafés and speculated about what happened to the senior—and "attractive"—Carabinieri officer. Old ladies lit candles for her in the Roman Catholic churches across the country. In Carabinieri police stations in Italy's cities, towns, and villages, Sara Simonetti-Fortina's disappearance was the subject of much talk and speculation.

The press release was simple and straightforward, noting that she was likely the victim of a carjacking and kidnapping that took place on Rome's *via Cassia* on a rainy Friday night. It included a description of her old beat-up car and approximately where the incident took place. Unfortunately, nobody had yet reported seeing her face where the incident occurred, nor since. Nor had her car been spotted.

Once the media received the official press release, even more talk, questions, and speculation began at dinner tables, in bars, in lunchrooms, and gathering places small and large across Italy.

"Did you know she was married to an American?"

"Do you think he was CIA?"

"You know, it's the nearest relatives who are usually involved in this kind of thing."

"The American probably was involved. Where is he, anyway? Has anybody spoken to him?"

The Cyberkid, working for the 'Ndrangheta, was having a field day on social media.

CHAPTER 45

This Is For You

SARA AWOKE TO THE SOUNDS of shuffling feet and what sounded like chairs scraping on the cement floor above her. The cell room's light had been left on by her captors for the entire evening. To avoid the light from the single light bulb in the center of the cell, she had slept facing the wall. Sara slept with her clothes on—a light green long-sleeve shirt and blue jeans—that she was wearing when she had left the Carabinieri Headquarters some thirty-six hours prior, leaving her uniform in her locker.

She had folded up her rain jacket, from which her captors had removed her cell phone, and used it as a pillow. She placed her light brown leather loafers under the cot. Sara was thankful that the old gray blanket that she had found on the cot provided more than enough heat during her first cool night in the cell.

Once Sara had laid down on the cot, she prayed to God that she be allowed to live and be able to return to Jake and other family members and friends whom she held dearest. She prayed that God grant her the daily gift of hope. And she prayed that she would always find the strength to live each day with dignity. She imagined pushing these and all her concerns at the feet of Jesus, and she prayed that He would take care of all of them.

The clop, clop, clop on the wooden stairs alerted Sara to a

visitor. A man came out of the hallway and turned the corner. Sara instantly realized she did not recognize this third person.

He must have been upstairs when I arrived early yesterday morning, she thought.

Sara did not know that Gio, who was ultimately responsible for following the Capo Crimine's orders on how to handle the female Carabinieri officer, was standing in the hallway. Gio was there to watch the man's first encounter with the captive.

The man, about five feet, eight inches tall with a wiry build and short, dark hair, had cold blue and lifeless eyes. Sara knew that Italy's invaders, like the Vandals, who had invaded Italy and sacked Rome in AD 455, and the Normans, who invaded Sicily and southern mainland Italy some 450 years later, had brought much of their blue-eyed DNA to Sicily and mainland southern Italy. But for some reason, Sara did not think the man to be of Italian origin.

"*Buongiorno, Cara*," said the man, holding a cheap, semi-clear plastic drinking cup with both hands as if about to present a special gift.

"*Buongiorno*," replied Sara, ignoring the "dear" part of the man's greeting. Sara did, however, detect a foreign accent.

"This is for you," said the man.

The man bent over, reached through the cell's bars with the cup in his right hand, and set the cup on the barren cement floor.

The man stood upright and continued to look blankly at Sara.

Sara went down on one knee and picked up the cup. She thought about whether she should say thank you. She decided not to say anything and simply nodded.

With a smirk on his face, the man continued to stare at Sara. Then he broke eye contact and looked at Sara—ogled, actually—from head to toe and then back up to her eyes. The second stare lasted for thirty seconds. Sara, still holding the cup, unflinchingly stared back and then mimicked the man, looking at the man from head to toe and back in his eyes again.

The man nodded slightly and then left the room.

Let the psychological games begin, thought Sara.

CHAPTER 46

One Person

THREE DAYS HAD PASSED SINCE JAKE FORTINA was officially retired and off the active army's radar. He had turned in his active military ID card and received a card of the "retired" variety in exchange. Overnight, his access to the US Embassy became limited. With a US passport and a retired military ID card, if someone inside the embassy wanted to see Jake, made an appointment for him, and informed the Marine guards ahead of time, Jake could likely be allowed access. But only for the expressed purpose of an appointment with the official inside. But for Jake, knowing that the US Embassy, located on Rome's storied *via Veneto*, was likely being surveilled by whoever his intended assassin or assassins were—or perhaps even the Italian press—visiting the embassy was no longer an option. He needed to keep a very low profile, both for his sake and Sara's.

There was one person inside the US Embassy, however, with whom Jake wanted to see and stay in touch. That person was US Army Sergeant First Class Manuel "Manny" Alvarez. Alvarez, a Special Forces medic at the time in the rank of "buck" sergeant E-5, and then-Captain Fortina had served together some ten years earlier in the crucible of combat in Afghanistan's hellish Korengal Valley. Later, when Alvarez was serving in Vicenza, Italy, Alvarez volunteered for US Embassy duty. When hearing of Alvarez's interest in embassy duty,

Lieutenant Colonel Fortina immediately notified US Army Human Resources personnel that he wanted to draft Alvarez as his noncommissioned officer assistant for duty in Rome. Alvarez, who not only spoke Spanish but, by then, excellent Italian, was a perfect fit for the job.

"Done deal," said the army.

Now, Jake wanted to meet Manny Alvarez on his terms and not according to some embassy regulations or any other strictures. Using his burner phone was relatively safe, but Jake couldn't guarantee the safety of anybody he reached out to. For this conversation, Jake had decided he needed to meet Alvarez in person.

***

The Roman taxi let Jake out exactly where Jake told the driver: on *via Eugenio Vajna* in northeastern Rome, in the *Parioli* district; the street ran through a mixed middle-class, mainly upper-middle-class neighborhood. No army sergeant nor the vast majority of army officers could afford to live in this part of Rome. However, the US Embassy leased a couple of relatively small three-bedroom apartments in this safe neighborhood for someone of Alvarez's rank and family size. The third-floor, 1400-square-foot apartment also came with a relatively secure underground parking option, an additional security feature that appealed to the US Embassy's regional security officer. For Manny Alvarez, his Italian bride from Vicenza, and their two-year-old daughter, the apartment was a great fit.

After stepping out of the taxi, Jake walked down the tree-lined side of *via Eugenio Vajna*, found a park bench, and sat down. In his hand, he had a copy of *The Soul of a Nation* by one of Jake's favorite historians and writers, Jon Meacham.

Jake knew the neighborhood. He and Sara had visited the Alvarez family for some prosecco and *panettone* (a type of Italian sweet bread typical for the Christmas holidays). They later returned to the neighborhood to do some "house dreaming," as Sara called it, but even they thought it to be rather expensive.

This part of *via Eugenio Vajna* was one-way, so Fortina knew there was only one way Manny Alvarez could travel to reach the gate, which opened to a short downhill drive before reaching the security-code-required gate to the underground parking garage.

After more than thirty minutes on the park bench, Jake could see Alvarez's six-year-old silver Volvo sedan climbing the slightly inclined *via Eugenio Vajna*. As Alvarez's vehicle approached the gate, Jake stepped away from the park bench and got to the opposite side of the street, where Alvarez's apartment was and where Alvarez could easily spot Jake before turning in toward the gate.

When Alvarez spotted Jake, who slightly raised his right arm in a casual wave to Alvarez, Alvarez's face lit up like a Christmas tree.

Jake approached the car as Alvarez rolled down his passenger-side window. Jake bent over so the two could clearly see each other through the window.

Alvarez began before Jake could get the first word out.

"Holy crap, sir! It's great to see you! How are you?"

"I'm great, Manny. How are you and your beautiful family?"

"Everybody is fine, thank you."

Before Jake could say, "I'd like to talk to you," Alvarez interrupted him.

"Sir, how about you get in the car? I have a couple of cold ones in the fridge waiting for both of us."

"Yes, sir. That sounds like a plan!" replied Jake.

Jake got in the passenger seat, and Alvarez drove the car through the gate.

CHAPTER 47

Nobody Home?

KAMRAN MASOUMI STARED AT THE APARTMENT BUILDING from his hidden position among the shrubbery and trees just inside the compound's fence line. The Iranian had chosen the perfect spot for conducting surveillance. He could see the apartment compound's gate, easily observing which vehicles came in and went out. He could observe the road from inside the gate, leading to the three five-story apartment buildings on his side of the compound. The road allowed Masoumi plenty of time to positively identify Jake Fortina's vehicle before Fortina drove around the back of his apartment building and entered the underground parking garage. Masoumi also had a clear view of the third building at the end of the road, and more importantly, using opera binoculars, he could clearly see Fortina's apartment. The apartment was dark, and it had been that way for eight straight nights.

Where the hell is this guy? thought Masoumi.

He again questioned the timing of his surveillance.

Did I get here early enough? It was right after it became dark. Of course, I got here early enough.

Masoumi felt the handle of his 9 mm pistol, safely secured by a leather shoulder harness under his dark blue jacket. He continued to peer at Fortina's apartment while listening for the sound of the compound's front gate to open. A couple of cars drove in, but they went to the opposite side of the compound, on the other side of the Olympic-sized pool situated in the middle of the six apartment buildings.

Where has Fortina gone? Does he still even live in that apartment?

Masoumi knew his handler was growing impatient with him. He needed to get results, and the only result she and the Iranian government officials back in Tehran were interested in—*demanded*, actually—was a dead US Army Lieutenant Colonel, Jake Fortina. For a select few Iranian government officials, his death would be a double win: killing the man who disrupted Iran's strategic goal of developing a deadly virus intended to kill hundreds of thousands, if not millions, of Americans and Jews and earning a sweet and easy $10 million in the process.

Masoumi's realization was one he did not want to face. The last time he tried to enter the American officer's apartment, the American spotted him, and Masoumi fled. He was within seconds of being physically caught. But he knew it was his only choice: he needed to get into that apartment to not only see if the American might be in there but also to confirm if he even lived there anymore.

CHAPTER 48

Where Is Jake Fortina?

KAMRAN MASOUMI SMILED. The glass balcony door had not been changed since the building was constructed in the 1960s. His manual glass-cutting tool—Swiss-made and the newest of its type—was advertised to cut tempered glass up to 20 mm thick. The double-pane glass Masoumi aimed to cut, first developed commercially in the 1950s, did not exceed 8 mm for each pane, with a 6 mm air pocket between the panes.

In the shadows of Jake Fortina's balcony, Masoumi worked his cutting tool perfectly. All he needed to do was to cut out a hole large enough to reach his hand through. Then, he could put his hand in and flip the small metal locking mechanism on the inside of the balcony door. He attached a small but strong suction cup that was fastened to the end of a stick to the section of glass he was cutting. After twenty minutes of careful attention and producing more sweat than he expected, he used the suction cup to remove first the outer and then the inner pieces of glass without them falling to the hardwood floor or the cement balcony outside. Within seconds, he found the locking switch and gently eased the sliding door open.

As he stepped into the bedroom, he froze. The bed that was there before—and from which Jake Fortina seemed to come from out of nowhere—was gone.

Am I in the right place? he asked himself.

Masoumi doubted himself, thinking that perhaps he had

made a careless mistake by not counting the number of floors correctly and that he was in the wrong apartment. He stepped back out onto the balcony to make sure he was exactly where he needed to be.

This must be the right place, he thought.

He counted the balconies below him.

I KNOW I'm in the right place.

He stepped back inside the bedroom. He stealthily picked up his feet with each step and moved forward, deciding to leave his small torchlight off. The outside streetlights, as weak as they were, provided minimally sufficient light spillage so that he could make out the apartment's walls and doors.

He stepped into the master bathroom, shut the door behind him, and switched on his torchlight. The bathroom was completely bare, devoid of everything, even a roll of toilet paper. He turned off the torchlight, reopened the bathroom door, and stepped back into the bedroom.

He hesitated for a minute, allowing his pupils to readjust to the semi-darkness.

Is Jake Fortina still living in the apartment but decided to stay out of the bedroom because of the nearby streetlight? Masoumi asked himself out of an abundance of caution...and fear.

Masoumi needed to be sure. He stepped out of the bedroom into the marble-floored hallway and then slowly moved into the larger marble-floored living room. He could see a large dark object near one wall of the living room. It looked like a couch. He slowly approached it, concerned that Jake Fortina might be watching his every move.

With his pistol at the ready in his right hand, he eased his left hand onto the cloth couch, just to be sure there was nobody sleeping on it. There was nobody there.

What Masoumi did not know was that US Embassy workers had left the couch in the US Embassy-leased apartment but had moved other temporary furniture to another embassy-leased apartment, making it ready for a recently arrived State Department family's temporary use.

It was quickly becoming clear that there was nobody home and that the apartment was uninhabited.

He moved on to the next bedroom. It was completely bare. He then continued to the kitchen. Empty.

Where is Jake Fortina? The Iranian assassin was mystified.

CHAPTER 49

The Message

THE ITALIAN CARABINIERI *MARESCIALLO* entered the headquarters building through its main entrance. He was right on time for his 10 p.m. night shift in the 24-hour Operations Center. Once inside the building, the warrant officer immediately saw—and almost stepped on—a manila envelope on the marble floor. Someone had typed *"Per il Comandante Generale"* (for the Commanding General) on the face of the envelope. He stepped back and examined the envelope from a distance. It was thin, suggesting that it likely did not contain explosive material.

However, it might contain anthrax powder or fentanyl traces, he thought.

The *maresciallo* recalled the spate of anthrax powder mail some 20 years prior when he first joined the Carabinieri. Its intended victims varied, but often they were high-ranking political officials. Although he could not discern any powder on the outside of the envelope, the Carabinieri officer knew not to touch it. In today's world, deadly fentanyl was more prevalent and less obvious—if detectable at all—to the human eye than anthrax powder.

As he pondered his next move, he could see a Carabinieri sergeant approaching the building's glass and steel doors from the outside.

The young sergeant walked in, looked down at the envelope, and looked at the officer. The officer responded.

"Look, I need your help, sergeant. Could you go up to the Operations Center and tell them I am looking at an envelope that was likely pushed underneath our entrance doors and that I want to have it checked for anthrax or other hazards? It does not look like it's big enough to contain any explosives, but that's still a remote concern. We need the right team to be called out to inspect this thing. If you are late for your shift, I will let your supervisor know it was my fault."

"Will do," replied the sergeant.

**

The four-star general looked at the letter. Over the previous eight hours, it had been cleared by a Carabinieri special screening team to make sure it was not explosive and was not covered in anthrax powder, fentanyl, or any other dangerous substance. As an added measure of precaution and per their standard operating procedures, the Carabinieri screening team placed the document in a clear, plastic document protector and sealed it.

When the Carabinieri checked the building's video surveillance cameras, they found an hour prior to the envelope's discovery, at 9:57 p.m., a black-hooded figure wearing a ski mask was recorded sliding the envelope under the door before briskly walking away. Within less than fifteen seconds, he was out of view of any of the building's video cameras.

When the general came into his office at 7:30 a.m., he found the plastic-covered document on his desk, exactly where his aide-de-camp had placed it an hour earlier.

To make sure handwriting analysis would be a non-starter for handwriting experts, the message's letters were produced by a common printer. The message was clear and direct.

WE HAVE SARA SIMONETTI. SHE IS SAFE. WE WILL GIVE HER TO YOU IN EXCHANGE FOR GENERAL CADORNA, WITH ALL CHARGES BEING DROPPED AGAINST HIM. YOU HAVE 72 HOURS TO RESPOND. AFTER THAT, WITH EACH PASSING HOUR, SIMONETTI'S SAFETY WILL BE IN SERIOUS DOUBT. ANY ATTEMPT TO RESCUE HER WILL RESULT IN HER IMMEDIATE DEATH.

Within thirty minutes, the Carabinieri commander assembled his three closest advisers.

His first question to them was, "How the hell do we contact whoever typed this letter?"

CHAPTER 50

News

THE BUZZER WENT OFF ON JAKE FORTINA'S BURNER PHONE. It was one of three burner phones he had bought while living in or visiting three countries: France, Germany, and Italy. He marked them with white tape and black letters on the back, with "FR," "GE," and "IT." He gave his French phone number, beginning with France's international code "33," to Manny Alvarez and Hennadiy Kovalenko. They were the only people who had his number. He knew going forward that misdirection, building doubt in his adversaries, and staying off well-established phone lines were critical for his survival. His life had been threatened, and so had Sara's.

As an added layer of caution, all three soldiers not only had their own burner phones, but they had established duress signals—a specific word or words—to be used to convey that they were in trouble or under immediate threat without actually saying that they were in trouble. The "I'm under duress" word (e.g., somebody has a gun to my head, my life is in danger, etc.) was simple: *cazzo*. The Italian f-word was ubiquitous among Italian and other soldiers, could take many forms, and could be inserted in almost any conversation at any time. The three were Italian speakers, and they agreed they would switch to Italian if under duress. For example, "*che cazzo*" (what the *cazzo*), "*chi cazzo*" (who the *cazzo*), or "*porque cazzo*" (why the *cazzo*—though this was less common), would all work to indicate a threat.

Jake answered the phone with the Italian greeting, "*Pronto!*" (Directly translated, it means "ready," but on the phone in Italy, it also means "hello.") Jake knew Manny Alvarez was on the other end.

Alvarez spoke in Italian, and Jake followed his lead.

"Sir, I have news for you. I got a call this morning. See you soonest."

"Soonest" was their standard code for "one hour" and "I'll meet you at our regular coffee shop." The shop was about a half-mile from Hennadiy Kovalenko's apartment, where Jake was now taking up residence. After two trips to the neighborhood coffee shop, he and Alvarez would select another neutral location for meeting.

"Many thanks," replied Jake. "See you soon."

***

Manny Alvarez, wearing casual clothes bought locally, including a snazzy Massimo Dutti (A Spanish company with a "Made in Italy" line) jacket, walked into the café. Given his Hispanic background, much like Fortina's Italian Lebanese background, Alvarez blended in well in Rome. He was trained to know that blending in was important for personal security. His dress and look certainly did not scream, "I'm an American." Over the past decade, thousands of Latin Americans had emigrated from places like Argentina, Chile, and Columbia to Italy, seeking better economic conditions, and Romans—and foreign spies—did not give Alvarez a second look.

"Hey, Manny. How about a cappuccino?" asked Jake as Alvarez pulled out his chair to sit down at the round, small table for two.

"Done deal, sir."

That's the last time Alvarez would use "sir" to address the recently retired US Army lieutenant colonel. There was no doubt that Alvarez respected Jake, and his respect for Alvarez was mutual for Jake. But too much formality between them, and anybody within earshot would soon suspect these two were not a couple of regular Joes. They both, however, despite having been thrown together in dealing with serious national security matters, thought of themselves as just that: regular Joes. And that's how they wanted others to perceive them as well.

When Alvarez saw the waitress heading toward their table with two cappuccinos, he immediately mentioned the local Rome major league (*Seria A*) soccer team, Roma. It had been well over a year since Roma had departed ways with its colorful Portuguese manager, Jose Mourinho. And they had just taken a 3–0 drubbing by Juventus the evening prior.

"Roma sucked last night," said Alvarez. "I wonder if they wish they had Jose Mourinho back."

"He's arguably one of the best soccer coaches around. That thought must plague Roma's owners and fans right now," Jake laughed.

They continued their sports banter for a couple of more minutes, then got down to business. Jake was very interested in hearing what Alvarez had to say.

Alvarez cut to the heart of the matter.

"A Carabinieri colonel called our attaché office this morning wanting to speak to you. I took the call since your replacement is not expected to roll in for another two months. I guess the Carabinieri colonel didn't know you were retired. He sounded frustrated when I told him that you weren't there and that you weren't coming back. I told him I could get in touch with you if he wanted me to pass a message to you. He hesitated for a long time on the phone and then finally told me that it was urgent that you contact him."

Jake nodded, and Alvarez continued.

"I then asked him, 'Is it good news or bad news?' Again, hesitation. Then he told me to keep this confidential, but...the Carabinieri Headquarters received a letter which claimed to be from Sara's captors, which in their opinion, gives hope that she's alive. That's all that he told me."

Jake's heart leaped in his chest. He looked away for a moment. He fought off a tear. He knew this was far from the best news that he could have received but it at least provided a ray of hope. It was a glimmer of hope that Jake had been praying for. Not knowing anything about Sara—whether she was dead or alive—was the worst.

Alvarez showed his cell phone to Jake.

"The colonel, last name Ricci, said to call him at this number."

Jake copied the number into his cell phone contacts under "Richie." Three times, he checked that he'd copied the number correctly.

"*Mille grazie*, Manny," said Jake.

"Listen, Jake," replied Alvarez, "I'm here for you. That's not just some nice-to-hear bullshit. I'm *seriously* here for you, no matter what it is you need. We've been through a lot together. I may not have survived that firefight in the Korengal Valley were it not for your leadership, and I certainly would not be here in Rome had you not reached out to the Pentagon to bring me and my family here."

Jake felt the same way about Alvarez, who, as a Green Beret medic, had performed miracles under constantly life-threatening conditions in Afghanistan.

"The feeling is mutual," replied Jake.

CHAPTER 51

Hungry

SARA'S STOMACH GROWLED. It had been almost 40 hours since she'd had anything to eat.

Thankfully, though, thought Sara, *there is plenty of water for me and my child.*

She had kept her mind on positive thoughts, dreams, and memories. A hiker, she imagined herself hiking along the magnificent Dolomite Mountain trails and peaks, seeing glorious vistas in her mind's eye. They settled her soul and gave her yet another reason to never, never quit mentally or spiritually. She pictured herself driving along beautiful roads and going to the beach with Jake. She mentally visited magnificent landmarks, like the Uffizi Gallery in Florence or the Sistine Chapel in the Vatican.

Sara planned out daily physical routines, including light abdominal exercises on the cot and simple exercises like calf-raises and wall sits, that could be done almost anywhere. Sara knew that her physical condition would affect her mental well-being, and vice versa.

Sara heard the clop, clop, clop of someone coming down the wooden stairs. However, these sounds were a bit different from the ones she'd heard earlier that morning. She vowed to herself that she would attune her hearing to each person's pace and sound on the steps so that she would know who was about to appear around the corner.

Sure enough, it was a different person. It was Lia. She was holding a simple white plastic plate in her hand. It had two pieces of sour-dough bread, each covered in olive oil. Lia looked at Sara. While it was not a sympathetic look, it was far from the look the Slavic-accented man had given her earlier in the morning. Sara looked at the plate and then looked at Lia. Sara felt more comfortable saying *grazie* to Lia than the man who had been there with the plastic cup some five hours earlier.

Lia slid the plate under the bars, and Sara said, "*Grazie.*" It was businesslike, but a thank you nonetheless. Lia, in her quirky way, came back with a businesslike *prego* and shoulder shrug.

The two ladies looked at each other for a few seconds. Sara, thinking it might be against her better judgment as a captive, gave Lia an ever-so-slight smile. Lia nodded in return, expressionless. Then she turned toward the hallway and departed.

For Sara, it was the best bread and olive oil she'd ever tasted.

CHAPTER 52

We Will Stay The Course

AS THE 'NDRANGHETA'S SUPREME COUNCIL, the *Crimine* meeting had an air of high tension. The weight of the decisions to be made at this meeting was too great for it to be otherwise. It had been five days since Sara Simonetti had been taken hostage and driven to a remote hideout in the remote Aspromonte Hills of Calabria, mainland Italy's southernmost region. If Italy is shaped like a boot, then Calabria is the big toe.

Handled unwisely, the decisions could re-inflame God-fearing and law-abiding Italian citizens against the 'Ndrangheta even more than they had been in the past. The *Capo Crimine* and his "board of directors"—including the *Mastro di Giornata* (master of the day), the *Capo's* right-hand man, and the *Mastro General* (general master), the *Capo Societa* (head of the society), and *Contable* (accountant)—knew that over the decades and centuries, the Italian population's attitudes about the mafia had varied. At one extreme, attitudes included outright local support to quasi accommodation ("It's a police matter," citizens were heard to have said). In the middle was distant apathy. At the other extreme were, arguably, the most effective weapons of Italian citizenry, the absolute outrage and protests of angry mothers and wives. When infuriated Italian mothers and wives raised hell in the streets, the local and national governments took notice.

On the one side of the *Crimine* was a majority of seven board members who thought the Carabinieri officer being held in the Aspromonte hills should be used only for leverage to get Brigadier General Cadorna released from incarceration and that it would be a fair trade to release the female Carabinieri officer unharmed in exchange for Cadorna's release. On the other side were those five *Crimine* members who thought her captivity should be used to extract as much information as possible from her, including who the Carabinieri were that had infiltrated the 'Ndrangheta's ranks, as well as where and how the Carabinieri Corps was targeting their efforts to stop the 'Ndrangheta's massive, organized crime operations, and whatever other revealing information they could—forcibly or otherwise—extract from her.

"If she talks, great," said one of the more cold-blooded of the five. "If she doesn't, we convince her to."

With a little shrug of his shoulders and shake of his head, it was clear that he meant—or at least strongly implied—the use of torture.

"And if she still doesn't talk, what do we do then?" replied one of the seven majority.

"Well, you know, we take care of business like we normally do. We find her a lovely final resting place where nobody will find her."

"Look, *signore*," came back the reply, "We need her for a trade. She is not some fucking slimeball who has cheated us out of our hard-earned money. We all know law enforcement officers are the enemy. But she is not any old traffic-ticket-punching police officer. She is a Carabinieri officer! How do you think people will respond if they ever find out we were behind her disappearance?"

The mafia man speaking knew that the Carabinieri were held in high regard in cities and towns across Italy. Their national publicity and social media campaigns over the recent years had featured Carabinieri officers, normally a pair of them, with beautiful views of iconic Italian landmarks as backdrops. Each day, the Carabinieri would select a new village, town, or city from which to feature their officers—and the towns they protected—on social media. The message was always the same: "How can we help you?"

The speaker at the table continued.

"For Christ's sake, there is even a popular television series about the Carabinieri. Right now, the Carabinieri are more popular—only slightly more, however—than us."

He chuckled. Several *Crimine* members laughed. He continued.

"Hell, they are even more respected than our priests!"

The amped-up *Crimine* member, who had a magnificent villa in the Calabrian seaside town of Tropea, continued.

"The *merda* will seriously roll downhill if her disappearance or death are linked to us."

The *Capo Crimine*—the Godfather—spoke.

"Both of you pipe down for a minute. I appreciate both sides of your arguments. Yes, we must know more about what the Carabinieri are doing to try to disrupt our operations. That is *always* true. But we started down this path to get General Cadorna out of prison. If we are successful, he might someday be seated at this honorable table as one of us. I believe that is worth trying for. We will stay the course. If conditions change, then maybe we will change our plans. But for now, exchanging the woman for Cadorna is our goal. Any questions?"

The *Crimine* member whose people were responsible for overseeing Lieutenant Colonel Sara Simonetti-Fortino's captivity raised his hand off the table with his index finger extended, indicating he had a question.

"Yes, Antonio?" asked the *Capo Crimine* from the end of the massive wooden table.

"How do we treat Simonetti? Like a princess, living in a

5-star accommodation?"

Several *Crimine* members laughed while others smirked.

"Or can we, you know, rough her up a bit to try and get some information from her while we have her, how do I say it…attention?"

The *Capo Crimine* sighed and smiled. He liked Antonio. Their fathers had been good mafia friends. And he knew that Antonio had enough experience, intelligence, and street wits to be sitting right where he—the *Capo Crimine*—was sitting. The *Capo Crimine* also knew that he had to walk a fine line between doing what was best for the 'Ndrangheta and its global "business" operations and avoiding a palace mutiny, which, most assuredly, would result in his premature removal as *Capo*, and possibly, death.

He understood he had to speak to the wider audience in the meeting.

"Roughing her up is fine. But you *must understand* what the limits are. If this deal goes through, we have to give her back as the one beautiful…God, how in the hell is it possible that such ugly Carabinieri officers can birth such beautiful offspring?"

The *Crimine* erupted with laughter.

The *Capo* remembered Simonetti's father, a Sicilian, was a Carabinieri officer who was killed in neighboring Sicily when little Sara was four years old.

"As I was about to say, we must give her back in one piece, not like some crazy person who is babbling to herself. You may interrogate her, but you may leave no marks on her. And she can never, ever be touched in the wrong places. If you need help understanding what I mean by that, ask a woman."

Again, most of the *Crimine* members—all men—laughed out loud.

Antonio smiled and nodded, signaling his understanding.

"I'll say it one more time, so listen the hell up: aggressive interrogation is OK, but no marks are to be left on the Carabinieri officer, and she is not to be touched in the wrong places. *Got it?*"

CHAPTER 53

All We Know

CARABINIERI COLONEL GIORGO RICCI looked at his ringing desk phone. He hesitated. The country code showed 33 instead of Italy's 39. And then he remembered what the American Army sergeant had told him.

Jake Fortina will be calling you from a French phone number.

The colonel picked up the desktop phone's receiver.

Instead of the *"pronto"* typically used, he said, "*Si?*" This was also a way—if much less common—to answer the phone in Italy.

"It's me...Jake Fortina," answered the caller. "I understand you might have some information for me."

"*Signore*....Jake...are you on a secure line?" asked Colonel Ricci.

"It's as secure as it can be without being militarily secure, if you know what I mean," responded Jake.

The colonel again hesitated. He knew what Jake was saying. Their conversations were not encrypted and could *possibly* be intercepted. Should he risk his and Jake's conversation being potentially monitored, even as remote as that possibility was? He decided he had to. Time was of the essence. The colonel knew his line was secure and took the former US Army lieutenant colonel's word that his "was as secure as it can be."

"Jake, listen. This is not the last time I expect to have to talk to you, so please keep this line available. I'm sure we will be speaking again. But let me get down to it: we received word about Sara—if the letter we received last night can be believed—that indicates she is alive. That is all we know right now. We are going to try to contact her captors. Right now, we have no idea—well, we have ideas, but nothing firm—who her captors are. As soon as we know more, we will let you know. You know as well as I do that the next steps—hopefully—might include proof of life. For that, we might need your assistance."

"I deeply appreciate this information," replied Jake, feeling relief. "I will make sure this line remains available and look forward to our next conversation."

In a bedroom in Colonel Hennadiy Kovalenko's apartment, Jake Fortina put down the cell phone, got on his knees, and thanked God for the news, praying that the outcome would be positive.

***

The 'Ndrangheta member of the *Crimine* who was responsible for communications with the Carabinieri directed his mafia underling to make the call. The man complied, dialing the number to the commanding general's office in Rome.

"Pronto," replied the Carabinieri colonel, who answered the phone.

"Is this the commanding general's office?" came the response.

"It is," replied Colonel Ricci. "How may I help you?"

"Your general or his deputy should have read our friendly greeting this morning. Write this number down. It's the only number we will answer."

The 'Ndrangheta Mafia member spelled out the number, and the colonel duly jotted it down, repeating it back for confirmation.

"You know our demands. When you are ready to make an exchange, call us. You have 72 hours."

The *mafioso* hung up the phone.

Colonel Ricci took the phone number and went to his supervisor, the two-star general who was in the adjoining office and, in effect, responsible for managing the Carabinieri commanding general's office. Their next stop would be a meeting with the boss.

CHAPTER 54

You Need To Find Him

AZAR ZADEHA TRIED TO LISTEN PATIENTLY, but her patience was running out. Zadeha was told by her handlers back in Tehran that Kamran Masoumi "was one of the best." But instead, he was full of excuses. He'd had an opportunity to kill the American Jake Fortina, and he'd blown it. Instead, he had to flee for his life. Now, Masoumi had no idea where the American was.

Zadeha's Iranian handlers—once they could provide proof of Jake Fortina's death—had been promised $10 million by the 'Ndrangheta leadership. The "Ndrangheta had already made a $2 million down payment for the assassination, depositing the payment in Bank Pictet, a Geneva, Switzerland-based bank that grew to have offices around the world, including places like Hong Kong, Liechtenstein, Luxembourg, and Singapore.

Zadeha didn't like Masoumi from the moment she met him. He'd come to Italy with the reputation of being a devout supporter of the Islamic regime, willing—with depraved perversion—to torture confessions out of innocent civilians and even children.

That kind of activity proves his loyalty to Iran, thought Zadeha. *But that is not the same thing as being a competent assassin. As a hunter and killer, he sucks.*

Zadeha again questioned Masoumi.

"Tell me again how the hell you lost him," she asked. "Is it because he's a ghost like you told me last time?"

"I didn't call him a ghost," replied Masoumi, "you did."

"You said his face came out of nowhere."

"It did."

"Well, where the hell is he now?" said Zadeha, practically shouting.

"I don't know. He's dropped off the radar. He's not even showing up at the US Embassy anymore. I've been watching that place each day for the past week—and Fortina's apartment at night, which, as I told you, is now completely empty—and he's nowhere to be found."

"You need to find him and finish the job you were sent here to do," said Zadeha. "I don't know how our leaders will react if you don't. But I can promise you this: it will not be pretty."

CHAPTER 55

Contact

IT WAS THREE HOURS BEFORE the 72-hour deadline for responding to the 'Ndrangheta's initial phone call. It had been received at the Carabinieri commanding general's office of the Italian National Carabinieri Headquarters. The Carabinieri leadership was set to make the call in compliance with the caller's 72-hour deadline.

Colonel Ricci had been briefed by his boss, the two-star Carabinieri Major General Sebastiano Comitini, about what to say on the phone and how to say it. Given the national gravity and interest in the case of a missing Carabinieri female lieutenant colonel, who was now apparently being held hostage, this crisis was being directed and operationally managed from the very top of the Carabinieri chain of command.

Colonel Ricci looked at his desktop phone, focused his senses, and took a deep breath.

Present in the room were Major General Comitini and Colonel Giorgio Martini, the Commander of Italy's crack Special Intervention Group (GIS). Employed primarily for counter-terrorism operations, the elite 100-person GIS also specialized in hostage rescue, intervening against hijackings, as well as against nuclear, chemical, biological, and radiological threats.

Also in the room were the GIS's operations officer, a lieutenant colonel; and a slightly built, middle-aged civilian wearing a blue sport coat, white dress shirt, black pants, and black lace-up shoes. Professor Doctor (Europeans often combine titles like this) Maximo Cecchi was a PhD-holding professor from the University of Siena. He was Italy's foremost expert on Italian language dialects and accents. There were over thirty dialects and many more accents in the country.

With the desktop phone's speaker on, Colonel Ricci placed the phone call to the number he had been given.

The phone rang five times before it was answered.

"*Si,*" replied the experienced, mid-level 'Ndrangheta Mafia member. His boss and two other senior 'Ndrangheta members stood beside him, listening in.

The 'Ndrangheta member, too, had been thoroughly briefed by the 'Ndrangheta high-level leader who was overall in charge of the Sara Simonetti kidnapping and captivity and, ultimately, the goal: negotiating Italian Army Brigadier General Cadorna's release in exchange for Sara Simonetti. Cadorna was languishing in pre-trial confinement for conspiracy to sell AK-47 assault rifles to a US militia group, and he was a close associate of the 'Ndrangheta's highest leadership.

"I am calling about Sara Simonetti," replied the Carabinieri colonel.

"What about her?" replied the 'Ndrangheta member.

"We have communicated your demands to national authorities. The decision to exchange General Cadorna for Lieutenant Colonel Simonetti is not ours to make. That decision will likely have to be made at the level of the Prime Minister..."

"Bullshit," interrupted the 'Ndrangheta *mafioso*. "We know you have something to say about that. And you better say the right thing."

"OK, OK," replied Colonel Ricci. "I expect we will. But we need positive proof of life before moving ahead. When you are ready to provide that, we will talk again."

Colonel Ricci knew "positive proof" was redundant, but that is exactly what General Comitini told him to say. The Carabinieri wanted to be doubly sure Sara was alive and in good health before committing to further steps. But this assurance would also buy the Carabinieri more time to figure things out.

The 'Ndrangheta caller at the other end looked at his boss. His boss nodded slowly; he half-expected that would be the next step requested by the Carabinieri. The mafia boss knew that the Carabinieri possessed almost no leverage in making demands, but requesting "proof of life," the mafia boss thought, *was a reasonable request since we are asking for a prisoner swap.*

The 'Ndrangheta caller responded.

"*Va bene.* (OK.) *We will get back to you.*"

He ended the call.

Colonel Ricci put his phone's receiver down. He felt relief that the call went about as well as could be expected.

The four Carabinieri officers and the Italian professor looked at each other.

Major General Comitini spoke first.

"So, *dottore*, what do you think?"

"There is no doubt it was definitely a *meridionali estremi* accent," responded Cecchi, referring to the 'Ndrangheta member's accent from extreme southern Italy.

The GIS lieutenant colonel smiled and nodded. He was from Palermo, which had its own accent, but he'd heard the Calabrian accent before.

"Well, that's a good start," replied General Comitini. "The southern Italian accent is practically the 'Ndrangheta's national language." He chuckled. "But that does not necessarily mean Simonetti is being held in Calabria. She could be five miles from here. But this at least gives us a start in figuring out who might be holding her."

CHAPTER 56

Nobody Ever Wins

SARA WAS THANKFUL. After two weeks of captivity, she had been given sufficient food to be kept alive and physically functioning. Some bread and light pasta—occasionally with some pretty good red sauce made by Lia—kept her sufficiently fed that she did not feel famished. Still, she felt like she'd lost maybe three pounds or so. Under normal circumstances, this would be no problem. But carrying a child, it began to weigh upon her that the human being growing inside of her might not be getting sufficient nutrition.

Sara heard someone coming down the wooden stairs. The steps sounded like Ivan's. He only visited her cell once every two or three days. It was normally—and *always with that creepy look of his*, thought Sara—to push some bread to her from under the bars. More often, it was Gio or Lia who performed that task.

And then, oddly, she heard more sounds of steps coming from the staircase. The steps sounded like two people were now coming down rather than one.

The first person to turn the corner out of the hallway was indeed the man with the Russian accent. He brought a brown, back-slatted wooden chair taken from the kitchen table upstairs. Setting the chair down near the cell room's door, he unlocked the door. He pulled the chair into the middle of the cell room—with the chair's back to the cell's single wall of iron bars—and pulled the cell door shut behind him. It automatically locked. The keys remained in the lock outside.

The man with the Russian accent spoke.

"Sit down," Ivan said.

Sara complied.

"Put your arms through the slats in the back of the chair and the small of your back."

Sara again complied.

Quietly, Gio and Lia emerged from the hallway. They stood outside the cell room and anxiously looked in, with Lia standing with her arms crossed and Gio with his hands in his pockets. They were there not only to listen to Sara's responses to the interrogator's questions but also to make sure the Russian did not cross the redlines established by the *Capo Crimine*. Namely, the Russian was to "leave no marks" and to "not touch her in the wrong places."

Ivan moved around the back of the chair. He pulled a set of handcuffs out of his back pocket and placed them around Sara's wrists.

Still standing behind Sara, he paused. His breathing became deep, easily audible to Sara. Sara stared straight ahead.

Ivan leaned over Sara from behind, with his upper chest and head now straight above Sara's head. She could feel the slight pressure from his lower chest on the back of her head. He inhaled deeply again.

"You have a wonderful scent about you," he said.

"It's soap," shot back Sara. "You might want to try it sometime."

Ivan was surprised at Sara's bold and quick response. He could usually smell fear in his interrogation victims well before any torture began. But so far, he noted no fear in Sara. He moved around to Sara's front and looked straight into Sara's eyes. Sara looked straight ahead, avoiding eye contact.

"I'm going to ask you some simple questions," he began.

"If you answer them, you can have an enormous bowl of pasta smothered in Lia's delicious red sauce."

"And if I don't?" replied Sara.

"We'll have to see," replied Ivan.

"Actually, as good as Lia's pasta is, I'd prefer to call for takeout," responded Sara.

She might be mouthing off now, but she is not going to win, thought Ivan. *Nobody wins when I am in control.*

CHAPTER 57

Ready For Contingencies

DAVIDE BOVO PULLED BACK THE TARP. Jake liked what he saw. He walked around the red and black motorcycle. It had been many years since he'd ridden one. At some of the earlier army bases where he'd served, riding a motorcycle was not outright banned, but it was frowned upon by the chain of command. Over the preceding decades, the army had lost too many 18–20-year-old soldiers—mostly men—who, their first time away from home, got a bit too careless with their new-found freedoms. The result was sometimes tragic.

But Jake knew the Ducati would give him great agility on the roads. Add in the knobby tires he'd asked Davide to add to the bike, and he knew that if he needed to, he could maneuver in between jammed traffic, guide the bike up onto a sidewalk as he'd seen Italians do, or off-road safely at high speeds. The Ducati was a great transportation option and contingency. At least until he got Sara back and they bought something more practical for the two of them. And hopefully, one day, for their child, too. He and Sara had been trying for more than a year, but so far, no luck.

Perhaps it is not in God's plan, Jake increasingly worried.

Turning to his longtime friend Davide, from Peschiera-del-Garda, on Lake Garda's southern shore, he sealed the deal.

"How about cash?"

"Old school, eh?" replied Bovo with a wink.

Jake smiled in return as he pulled out a white envelope

containing 11,000 euros (about $12,000).

"Anything special I need to know about it?" asked Jake, referring to the 2021 Ducati Competition Hypermotard RVE motorcycle.

"Yes, there are a few things you need to know if you don't already. This thing is a crotch rocket. It will rip your stones off if you are not careful. And if you are ever in a hailstorm, get off the road immediately," said Bovo, remembering a cousin who had died when a hailstorm came out of nowhere while he was riding at 70 miles per hour on a state road in Austria.

"Maybe more importantly," laughed Bovo, "last year's 2023 version was named the "*Moto più Bella*" (the most beautiful motorbike) in the world at the big motorcycle expo in Milan. So, she produced good offspring. Take good care of her. She will not only maneuver like a missile, she—and you—will look good doing it, too."

"And why is *that* important? Hell, Davide, I'm not looking for a runway model. I'm looking for a quick and agile athlete!"

Jake smiled at his old friend.

"Well, this bike is all that. But remember, you are in Italy. So, whatever you are doing, you *must look good* doing it!" Bovo teased Jake.

Both men laughed riotously.

Davide reached into his old garage refrigerator. He pulled out a frosted bottle of homemade grappa and two frosted shot glasses from the top freezer compartment. He filled the two shot glasses with the clear, chilled liquid. He handed Jake a glass and poured a shot for himself.

"I'm old-fashioned, too," said Davide. "A good deal is not consummated until we celebrate it properly. *Salute!*"

The two men clinked their glasses, looked each other in the eye, and consumed the fiery grappa in one go.

"Damn," said Jake. "Speaking of rockets...this stuff is *rocket fuel!*"

Davide smiled and nodded.

"My grandfather's recipe. Good for what ails you, too."

***

Jake felt good with the Ducati roaring beneath him. On his trip back to Rome, he had chosen to travel mostly off Italy's *autostrada* (principal highway, with tolls). He'd wanted to test the Ducati's handling on the secondary, two-lane state roads and some of the back, more-dirt-than-road tracks. It did extremely well. He was impressed with the bike's snap-your-head-back acceleration, too.

Davide was right, thought Jake. *This Ducati is an athlete*.

The bright spring day in Italy, with the fields full of colorful red, yellow, and purple flowers, made Jake feel more alive than he'd felt since Sara had disappeared some two weeks earlier. But the bright ball of sunshine and blue sky did not take away the ever-present ache in his gut and heart about Sara's absence. He was not ready yet, but he knew the day was coming soon when he would go look for her—and *God-willing*—find her.

Like the good US Army Special Forces soldier he once was, he knew he had to be ready for all contingencies. Now that he had the transportation problem part mostly solved, and he'd solved the communications problem with his three international cell phones, he needed another kit to be ready for all contingencies: a first aid kit, Leatherman tool, water bottle with filtration tablets, and some light rain gear; and night vision goggles and a pistol, *maybe*...if he could procure them in Italy.

Jake knew the latter two items would be a challenge to get in Italy. Night vision goggles—at least the military ones—were highly controlled items, not only by US military forces stationed in Italy, but by Italian military forces as well. Except for those used by hunters, pistols and ammunition for private citizens were also difficult—but not impossible—to get in Italy.

CHAPTER 58

She's Tough

IVAN STEPPED BACK FROM SARA. She was stoically seated in the wooden chair with her hands cuffed behind her and the chair. Ivan knew his interrogation limits: "Leave no marks and do not touch her in the 'wrong' places." He now understood that extracting information from the Carabinieri officer would be far more difficult than back in Syria when he was a part of Russian military forces. In Syria, he had full license to physically torture his victims. He often began with the humiliating and obscene. In an "interrogation" center in some nondescript warehouse, he was able to force confessions as well as critical military intelligence from unfortunate souls, many of whom were innocent civilians and who simply wanted the Richter scale, soul-jarring pain to stop.

This one thinks she's tough, thought the Russian. *But I will get what I want. I always do.*

"Aren't those handcuffs a bit uncomfortable?" asked Ivan, doing his best to sound empathetic.

"Not at all," replied Sara. "They fit like a glove. I kinda like 'em. I prefer the diamond-encrusted ones, though, not these cheap ones."

Again, that was not the answer Ivan was expecting. This early in the game, he figured there was about a fifty percent chance that Sara would either not answer at all or say something like, "They only hurt a little." But Sara gave a full-throated reply, *almost like she enjoys this*, thought Ivan.

"So, let me ask you a simple and easy question," asked Ivan. "About how many Carabinieri officers do you have dedicated to combating mafia operations in Calabria?"

"Hmm, let me think about that," answered Sara. She pretended to consider the question. "Actually, I have no idea. And if I did, you'd never find out from me."

Ivan thought that if he could get his prisoner to answer easy, softball questions, she might eventually feel more comfortable in answering increasingly confidential questions. At least, that's how traditional interrogation measures sometimes—but not always—worked. The one variable was always the captive. Some—albeit rarely—resisted strongly enough to take their secrets with them to their painful and often slow deaths. But the vast majority had a breaking point. Ivan just had to find Sara's. But how could he, with his limited boundaries of what was permissible within the bounds of rough handling of Sara?

With his pain-inducing options limited, Ivan knew he had to apply those measures that would "leave no marks." Given his prisoner's defiance, Ivan also knew he had to step it up, and soon.

Gio and Lia, standing against the bars outside the cell, observed him closely as he moved behind Sara.

For about a full minute, Ivan stood behind Sara. He breathed audibly and deeply. He realized Sara was one of the most beautiful and athletic women he had ever seen. His sick mind flashed to Syria when he had, during his interrogations, sexually assaulted men *and* women, normally using physical objects to do his evil, humiliating, and perverted work. Occasionally, when there were only one or two witnesses in the room who *also* had committed such disgusting and horrifying acts, he personally assaulted them. He smirked at the thought.

As he put his hands on Sara's shoulders, his heart rate

picked up. With his fingertips, he felt around for Sara's shoulder socket and tendons on the front and inner side of Sara's shoulders. In Syria, he had cut or punctured people on those very spots, causing excruciating, mind-altering pain. Most victims were divided among those who were willing to tell Ivan whatever he wanted to hear and those who eventually either begged to die or were resigned to their tortuous end.

But that is not allowed here, he had to remind himself.

With the middle fingers of each hand, he located the tender spots on Sara's shoulders. He was aware that the middle finger was the strongest of his five digits.

"You seem kind of tight," said Ivan. "I think you need a massage."

Ivan pressed his pelvis through the open space in the chair's back and against Sara's spine. He could feel Sara's handcuffed hands between his inner thighs, just above his knees.

"And you need to go fuck yourself," snapped Sara.

She prayed that she would be ready for whatever came next and that she would be able to resist at all costs.

Seeing Ivan's hands resting on Sara, Gio pressed himself hard against the cell's bars. His hands grasped two of the bars. It was Gio's duty to make sure Ivan did not exceed his limits.

And Gio worried Ivan would exceed those limits. Gio did not like or trust Ivan. From the very first moment, Gio knew there was *something very crude and dark* about Ivan. Gio wasn't sure if it was some darkness in the Russian's soul or because of his grandfather, who had recounted the horrors he experienced in World War II. The Russian soldiers were brutish and pitiless on the Eastern Front. Whatever it was, it did not sit well with Gio.

Lia also stepped closer to the bars. Truth be told, she didn't like the Russian either. Her Spidey sense was up all day long around Ivan. Lia was thankful she had her own separate room upstairs. She didn't envy Gio having to share the adjacent room—their single beds only six feet apart—with Ivan.

For the past couple of days, Lia also had curiosity, bordering on a concern. Lia thought she'd discerned a slight, unexpected roundness in Sara's tummy. It was easy to miss, but Sara had yet to ask for any feminine items, which Lia thought was odd, *although the timing could be such that she doesn't need them yet.*

Maybe it's just my woman's intuition, thought Lia. *But is Simonetti pregnant?*

Ivan began to slowly massage Sara's shoulders, arousing himself with the perverted satisfaction of the woman being bound and helpless in front of him.

He then tried what he thought was another easy question.

"So, where is the Carabinieri Headquarters in Rome, exactly?"

Ivan knew it was a ridiculously easy question, one which he already knew the answer to. Anybody with access to Google Maps could answer the question in a heartbeat. There was absolutely nothing confidential about the answer.

"I didn't know the headquarters was located in Rome," responded Sara. "How interesting. Are you sure? Are you sure the headquarters is not in Palermo? Or Moscow?"

Sara had finally figured out where the man's accent was from. And it wasn't from Italy.

Ivan was growing hair-on-fire angry.

This spaghetti-eating bitch needs to be put in her place, he thought.

Ivan sighed deeply. With all the force he could muster, he focused his full strength on the ends of his two middle fingers, digging them into the highly sensitive junctures of Sara's shoulder joints, tendons, and nerves. He pressed as hard as he could.

Sara's mind flashed with pain. She fought back tears.

What happened next surprised even Sara. She leaned as

far away from Ivan as she could, ostensibly to get away from him. But really, it was so she could tip forward onto the chair's front two legs and stabilize it with her front legs. She heard him chuckle under his breath. Then, Sara simultaneously pushed up on her feet and thrust her hands about six inches upward into Ivan's crotch. It was a very difficult and slightly painful maneuver for Sara's shoulders, but her hands, still locked in the handcuffs, had reached their target. Seizing as much flesh as possible, she squeezed as hard as she could.

Ivan let out a scream and immediately removed his hands from Sara's shoulders. He slammed his arms and hands downward, breaking Sara's grip on his testicles, almost breaking her forearms.

Ivan then stepped off to his right and slapped Sara as hard as he could with the inside and lower, fleshier part of his lower hand. She did not see the strike coming. The blow landed on Sara's right eye and temple. The force of the strike caused Sara, still handcuffed to her chair, to tumble to the left, with Sara's left side and the chair underneath her as she hit the floor. Somehow anticipating the fall, Sara tried to keep her head from slamming on the cement floor. While she couldn't prevent it, Sara's efforts saved her from receiving the full blow of the concrete on the left side of her head.

Gio reached for the cell door and immediately turned the skeleton key to open it. Lia was right behind him.

"Did you see what that bitch did?" shouted Ivan, still bent over in pain, as Gio and Lia entered the cell.

Neither Gio nor Lia answered him. Lia glanced at him with complete disdain.

Gio and Lia immediately approached Sara, still locked in her chair and lying on her side.

"Give me your handcuff key," barked Lia at Ivan.

The Russian hesitated.

"Give it to me, goddammit!" shouted Lia.

The Russian reached into his pocket, pulled out the key, and handed it to Lia, who handed it to Gio.

Lia was angry. Gio was upset. Gio's job was to make sure the Russian did not go too far in extracting information from the Italian Carabinieri officer. And looking at the unconscious Sara lying still on her side as he unlocked her handcuffs, he was not yet sure if he had failed in his oversight mission.

Ivan stood by, his hands on his hips, feigning mild interest in the scene before him. *What the hell are Gio and Lia doing*, he thought. As far as Ivan was concerned, *Gio and Lia should just leave the bitch there, locked to her chair and lying on her side on the cold cement floor. That'll teach her to talk back to me.*

Gio and Lia gently slid the chair away from Sara. With her left arm still underneath Sara and folded behind her back, Gio gently lifted Sara off the floor a few inches while Lia moved her arm back to the forward position.

"We need to get her on the cot," said Lia. "You grab her shoulders, Gio. I will grab underneath her waist, and you grab her by the ankles," said Lia, looking at Ivan. "Do you think you can do that without jacking it up?"

"Why do that?" asked the Russian. "Why don't we just leave her on the floor?"

"Shut the hell up and do what she tells you," Gio barked.

Ivan nodded and grabbed Sara by the ankles.

The threesome lifted Sara and moved her onto the cot.

"Leave the chair here and go upstairs," said Gio.

Ivan left the cell in a huff, disappeared into the hallway, and noisily climbed the wooden staircase to the small apartment above. The pain between his legs made it difficult to climb the stairs.

Lia felt the roundness she thought she had discerned in Sara's tummy before. Her previous curiosity bloomed into certainty. Sara was with child.

"You or I need to be here when she wakes up. The right side of her face and eye are already turning purple and black," said Gio.

He looked at Sara, lying on the cot and on her left side.

"And we won't know how the left side of her face will look until she wakes up. Which she hopefully will."

Lia took Sara's wrist and felt for a pulse.

"She will, Gio. She will," said Lia. "I will take the first shift. Two hours at a time?"

"That's perfect. And we have to make sure that Russian jackass is never allowed down here alone if he's allowed down here at all. Antonio Di Salva is going to be super pissed with me if Simonetti ends up with evident bruises on both sides of her face," replied Gio. "And I have no idea how the *Capo* will react."

"He'll get over it," said Lia, not sure there was any truth to what she said.

CHAPTER 59

Get Rid Of Him

AZAR ZADEHA STARED AT THE MESSAGE. It was unequivocal.

"Get rid of him," said the message.

Once Zadeha contacted the Iranian authorities about Masoumi's "incompetence and imbecilic behavior," it did not take long for Iran's Deputy Prime Minister to make the decision. Iran's intelligence minister was embarrassed that he had recommended Kamran Masoumi for the job and now realized he was more a liability than an asset. Masoumi knew too much about the horrors the Iranian state had perpetrated on Iranian citizens who dared to voice—and demonstrate—their opinions against the suppressive Iranian regime. But what was worse was that Masoumi had the American in his sights and then totally botched the hit when he fled from the balcony of the American officer's apartment.

The $10 million contract on the American, brokered by the 'Ndrangheta, for a Russian oligarch now in prison, still stood. If the Iranians could prove they were the ones who killed the American, they could reap the $10 million.

Azar read the rest of the message.

"Once M is completely gone, the mission to take out the target will be on you, Azar Zadeha."

Zadeha realized her life of running several Iranian intelligence agents in Italy had just taken a new and completely unwelcome twist. Not only did she have to kill Masoumi and hide his remains, but she had to kill the American, too.

CHAPTER 60

I Come In Peace

LIA HEARD SARA MOAN. She saw Sara touch her right cheek before slowly putting her feet on the floor and trying to sit upright on the cot. Lia approached the cot. Sara turned her head to the right as Lia approached. Lia put her hands out as if to say, "I come in peace."

"How are you feeling?" asked Lia. "Can I have a closer look?"

"Sure," replied Sara, "but please tell me what the hell happened. All I seem to remember is that asshole digging his fingers into my shoulder joints."

"Well, we couldn't see too well because he had his back to us, so I'm not exactly sure what happened. All we heard was your chair move, then he screamed, and then we saw him make some kind of downward motion with his arms before coming around to your right side and landing a roundhouse punch to your right temple."

Lia got closer to Sara. Lia was not afraid to do so, nor did she think there was any risk in doing so.

It's not like Sara is some wild animal or criminal, she thought, *and she has nothing to hurt me with, which would, in any case, be very stupid to try on her part.*

Lia bent over and looked at Sara's right cheek. Sara had a black eye, and her eyeball was bloodshot. The bruise from her eye ran down to her cheekbone. Her other eye was not as bad, but there was also a bruise on the left side of her cheek.

"You look like you've been in a fistfight," said Lia.

At the word "fist," Sara was triggered out of her mental haze to remember what had happened.

"Well, I guess I did grab him by his *coglioni*," said Sara.

Lia nodded her head, smirking.

That makes sense, thought Lia, *especially the way Ivan's knees buckled right before he broke off Sara's vice grip with that quick downward motion.*

"Well, you must have got him right where it hurts because he was no more Mr. Nice Guy after that!" exclaimed Lia, barely holding back her laughter.

"Do you hurt anywhere else besides your face?" asked Lia.

"Other than my shoulders throbbing a bit, I'm fine," replied Sara, incredulous that she and Lia were having a very friendly—and almost intimate—conversation.

Lia wanted to ask Sara if she was pregnant, but she decided to ask later. She thought about getting Sara some aspirin, but she couldn't remember if aspirin was OK to take when a woman is pregnant.

CHAPTER 61

What The Hell?

"WHAT THE HELL ARE YOU SAYING?" asked Antonio Di Salva, the senior 'Ndrangheta *mafioso* who was responsible for the disposition of one of the 'Ndrangheta's highest profile hostages in decades, Carabinieri Lieutenant Colonel Sara Simonetti.

"Are you saying that you allowed that Russian goon just to beat the hell out of Simonetti? Weren't the *Capo's*—and *my* orders—clear enough?"

"*Signore*, it was not quite that way," replied Gio. "The Russian's method to force Simonetti to talk did not work out so well for him. He caused her some discomfort—OK, pain—to..."

"Where?" interrupted Di Salva.

"To her shoulders..." said Gio.

"He better not have left any marks!" interrupted Di Salva.

"He didn't, at least not to her shoulders."

What Gio did not realize was that bruises the size of a quarter, or roughly a two-euro piece, had formed on the front of each shoulder. However, Gio guessed nobody would ever see those, but he now had much bigger problems that he had to confess.

But the bruises to her face are another matter, thought Gio.

He hesitated and then grabbed the courage to spit it out.

"But...she has bruises to her face," blurted out Gio.

"Goddammit!" shouted Di Salva over the phone. "How the hell did that happen? How are we supposed to provide proof of life if our prized hostage has marks all over her face? If this ever leaks out, the entire country will be enraged, and the women will be in the streets again. The *Capo Crimine* is gonna kill me, but not before I kill you and that Russian!"

Di Salva knew that because the *Capo's* and Di Salva's fathers were partners in crime together, the *Capo Crimine* would do no such thing.

Not over this jacked-up affair, anyway, he thought.

Still, Di Salva was professionally embarrassed. He tried to imagine how bad Simonetti's bruises were.

Did this Russian scoundrel jackass break the skin? He asked himself.

Di Salva had earned his mafia spurs as someone who had not only killed but had ordered the deaths of two locals who had seriously crossed the 'Ndrangheta. Both had ended up taking "their last bath" in a vat of acid. But in this case, orders were orders, and if the *Capo Crimine* said "no marks" were to be left on the Italian woman and that she should not be touched in the "wrong" places, so be it. Di Salva's utter loyalty to the *Capo Crimine* and the 'Ndrangheta meant that "when the most senior *Capo* issues an order, that's the Gospel!"

For his part, Gio prayed that his lack of effective supervision of the Russian would not cost him serious punishment. Deep inside, he believed that his transgression was not bad enough to result in death as punishment. But the orders had come from the very top of the 'Ndrangheta, and he had failed to make sure the "vodka-swilling Russian son-of-a-bitch" did not exceed his boundaries. So, he was worried.

CHAPTER 62

Special Meeting

IT WAS A SPECIAL MEETING. Called by the *Capo Crimine*, the meeting was in response to a phone call with the Carabinieri Headquarters in which the Carabinieri said they wanted "proof of life" of Sara Simonetti. Not wanting the Carabinieri to somehow think they were in the driver's seat, the *Capo Crimine* did not intend to respond quickly to the Carabinieri's first demand. He wanted the 'Ndrangheta to take its "sweet time" in responding. In his calculus, the call did not require the convening of all twelve members of the *Crimine*. Only the *Capo Crimine's* three closest advisers, which included Di Salva, were present.

Di Salva was anxious. He had not yet told the *Capo Crimine* about the phone call from Gio—from the day prior—in which Gio had admitted to Sara Simonetti receiving bruises to her face. When he received the call, Slava already knew the "proof of life" issue would be the subject of this meeting convened by the *Capo*.

"Well, it's been a while since we had our little chat with the Carabinieri," said the *Capo Crimine*. "And as we expected, they wanted proof of life for Simonetti before engaging with us further on the exchange of her for General Cadorna. The question is, how do we show proof of life without compromising where and how we are keeping her? We all know there are all kinds of ways that electronic traces can occur these days."

The *Capo* looked at Bruno. Bruno was his senior expert

on operational and personal security and how the 'Ndrangheta kept its fingerprints—electronic or otherwise—from being discovered by not only Italian, EUROPOL, and other law enforcement agencies, but by the 'Ndrangheta's other mafia competitors like the Naples-based Camorra, the Sicilian Cosa Nostra, or the recently emerging—and as brutal as they come—*Foggia* mafia.

Further afield, the 'Ndrangheta had to worry about other transnational organized crime competitors, like the Brothers' Circle from Russia, the Yamaguchi-gumi (Yakuza) from Japan, and Los Zetas from Mexico. Sometimes, the 'Ndrangheta *wanted* their fingerprints left on their activities and crimes, if only to send a message to whomever they thought needed to hear it. However, most of the time, full confidentiality and security were the best approaches.

Bruno responded.

"*Signore*, I suggest we do a simple but very short videotape. We can put in a false background, like they do with Zoom, to not compromise anything about her location or conditions."

"What is Zoom?" asked the 77-year-old *Capo Crimine*.

"It's a video teleconferencing system. We can send one of our experts to the hideout and have the video recorded there. All she has to say is, 'I am Sara Simonetti, and I am safe.'"

Antonio squirmed in his seat. He had yet to tell the *Capo Crimine* about Simonetti's facial condition.

"Sir, and Bruno, there is something I need to tell you. I received a call yesterday from the hideout from Gio. He said the Russian interrogator we positioned there went crazy in his recent questioning of Simonetti. Apparently, Simonetti has a black eye and a pretty bad bruise on the right side of her face. She has another bruise on her left cheek from hitting the floor. If the Carabinieri find out about this, they will use this information to their advantage, and the people will revolt against us."

The *Capo Crimine* looked at Antonio sternly. He was extremely angry and disappointed in his old friend.

"Weren't my orders about how to handle her clear?" he asked.

"*Si*, they were very clear, *signore*. And so were mine to Gio, who is in charge of the hideout. They were made clear to the Russian we hired, too. I believe the Russian just downright ignored them."

"Well, it sure sounds to me like he did," replied the *Capo*, shaking his head with visible disgust on his face. "That was very disrespectful of him."

As Antonio expected, the *Capo* did not come down hard on Antonio. They had been trusted friends for far too long. In the brutal business of organized crime, deeply trusted friends were extremely rare. A very anxious Antonio was also very thankful for the trust that existed between him and the *Capo*. But Antonio also had no idea about the angry thoughts flashing through the *Capo*'s mind, many of them directed at Antonio.

Turning back to Bruno, the *Capo* asked, "Now what? What do we do?"

"We can try an audio tape or a live phone call, with Sara speaking on either one," replied Bruno. "There is more risk in the live call because she could try to blurt out something, like her location. With an audio recording, we have more control. However, in today's world of artificial intelligence, they may not believe a recording."

"OK, that's it, then," said the *Capo Crimine*. "We do the audio recording first. If that does not work, we do the live call."

CHAPTER 63

He's A Clown

AZAR ZADEHA FELT CONFIDENT as she quietly climbed the steps in the apartment building stairwell. She knew it was a better choice than the elevator, which made an audible "thump" when it reached the fifth floor.

Zadeha had the key to Masoumi's apartment. She had also placed hidden cameras—about half the size of a pea—throughout the apartment as well. After all, she had furnished the simple Roman one-bedroom apartment with the bare bones basics before her supposed "top assassin" arrived in Rome to fulfill his contract on the American military attaché, Jake Fortina.

He's a clown, she had thought a week earlier. *He might have been good at torturing confessions out of people, but he sucks at surveillance and murder. Tehran has made it clear. My mission is to get rid of him.*

Zadeha had checked her laptop just thirty minutes prior, and Masoumi had gone to bed and fallen asleep some thirty minutes before that.

She slowly and gently eased the skeleton key into the apartment's door, getting it to release the deadbolt. She knew that Masoumi had a bad habit of forgetting to lock the second, separate, sliding inside deadbolt.

The door hinges creaked ever so slightly. She froze in place and listened for thirty seconds, making sure there were no sounds coming from Masoumi's room.

Silence.

She gently eased the door shut, not making a sound.

Zadeha stood like a statue, slowly breathing through her nose while letting her pupils adjust to the blackness. She could see some very faint light spilling from the street into Masoumi's bedroom. She had anticipated that.

Zadeha slowly and deliberately stepped through the blackness toward the open bedroom door. She pulled the silencer-muzzled pistol from her large leather purse, strapped diagonally across her chest and resting on her right hip.

She slowly turned into the bedroom, hesitating briefly at the foot of Masoumi's bed before proceeding along the right side of the bed toward the headboard. The open bedroom door was folded back toward the wall on her right. She slowly approached the pillow. She could see what she thought was Masoumi's head protruding from the sheets and resting on the bottom half of the pillow. But it was not Masoumi's head. It was his two black house shoes, placed together and made to look like Masoumi's head in the darkness.

Zadeha extended her arm, intending to pull the trigger.

Masoumi pounced, reaching around Zadeha from the back and grabbing her face with his left hand, jerking her head back, and nearly simultaneously pulling hard on the butcher knife with his right hand. It sliced hard into the soft tissue under her jaw before Masoumi slid the knife across Zadeha's throat, making sure to cut her carotid artery, located off to the side of her neck. Partially decapitated, Zadeha's knees buckled as blood spurted from her neck.

Masoumi let her drop. Zadeha was dead within seconds of her knees and torso hitting the floor.

CHAPTER 64

Unbelievable

NOT ALL OF THE SPECIALLY convened five Carabinieri officers in the room were convinced beyond a shadow of a doubt that it was their colleague, Lieutenant Colonel Sara Simonetti, on the audio recording. The voice was clearly that of a female. And for a couple of the officers in the room, the recording sounded like Sara's voice. However, three of the officers were not convinced enough to be 100 percent sure that it was Sara's voice.

"It kind of sounded like her, but why no video?" asked one officer.

"The recording could have been produced with artificial intelligence," said another. "They could easily have copied Sara's voice from the internet. She's done more than one public affairs interview for the Carabinieri Corps."

"I don't think we can unequivocally say we have proof that Sara is alive, at least not with this recording. And if we say it, we must be able to say it strongly and with full confidence that she is alive," said Major General Comitini, the senior officer in the group that heard the recording. "We must go back to her captors and demand a video recording of her."

Major General Comitini still had no confirmation of who Sara's captors were, but the 'Ndrangheta Mafia organization was on his short list. The Italian language accents were clearly from deep southern mainland Italy.

***

"*Signore*, it's the Carbs on the line again," said the senior 'Ndrangheta member on the phone.

"What the hell do they want?" Antonio Di Salva asked, exasperated. He was one step below the *Capo Crimine*, who stood at the apex of the massive—and massively wealthy—transnational crime organization.

"They are rejecting the audio recording of Sara's voice," responded the mafia member.

"Why they hell for?" responded Di Salva.

"They can't confirm it's her voice."

Ten seconds of silence passed as Di Salva looked down at the table.

"What do they want?" asked Di Salva.

"They want a video," came the response.

"They can kiss my ass with their video. We are not going to do that."

"Do you want me to tell them that?"

"Yes. But right after you tell them that, let's give them another option: a live phone call right into the comandante's office. It does need to be the commanding general on the line, but I want the call to go right into the same office we are speaking with now. Tell them this will be their only chance to get proof of life. Let them know if they don't like it, our hostage may never be seen or heard from again. Take it or leave it. And we want an answer now. The clock is ticking."

The senior mafia member conveyed Di Salva's entire message to the Carabinieri caller.

There were two minutes of silence on the line as the Carabinieri discussed the proposal and Major General Comitini made the decision. The Carabinieri caller came back on the line.

"OK, it's a done deal," replied the Carabinieri caller. "With one condition: you call us at least 6 hours before the call to schedule the call."

The Carabinieri did not want the key members of their special hostage crisis group to have to be tied to their desks—or the headquarters building—while this proof of life issue was being (hopefully) concluded. So, if they needed to recall key Carabinieri players to the building, they would have plenty of time to travel there.

The *mafioso* member relayed the message to Di Salva.

Di Salva did not like demands, and this one just did not smell right.

"Bullshit," replied Di Salva. "We'll give them a two-hour warning, and that's it. That is our final offer."

The *mafioso* relayed the new condition for the call.

"They said '*va bene*'(OK) to the two hours," he replied after waiting a minute for the Carabinieri officer to respond.

CHAPTER 65

Live Phone Call

JAKE'S BURNER PHONE VIBRATED, practically bouncing across the table. The call was from "Richie." That was the only part of the caller's name Jake had entered into his phone's contact list. But it was also one of the few and most important names on the list. The last time "Richie" called, Carabinieri Colonel Giorgio Ricci informed Jake that the Carabinieri Headquarters had received word from Sara's anonymous captors. The captors had indicated that they were holding Sara and wanted to trade her for the release of Italian Brigadier General Cadorna, who was in an Italian jail awaiting trial.

With the sight of Ricci's cover name, a thought—more like a prayer—flashed through Jake's mind.

Dear God, let this be good news about Sara.

Jake reached for the cell phone.

"*Ciao*, Giorgio," Jake said.

"*Ciao*, Jake," responded the colonel. "We contacted Sara's captors again."

Jake held his breath.

"And?" he responded.

"And they want to set up a proof of life call with us."

"When?" asked Jake.

"That's just it...we don't *know* when," said the colonel. "They said they would call this office and give us a two-hour warning before the phone call. That's it. We had to take the deal."

Jake was hopeful.

Actually, a two-hour warning is a good deal, thought Jake.

"Thanks for this, Giorgio," responded Jake.

"But there's more," said Colonel Ricci. "Right after we get the two-hour warning, we want you to get to this office for the call. We will feel more prepared for it if you are here when it happens. The general thinks you'll provide some added insurance to help us confirm that it's Sara. They have agreed to a live phone call but no video. We will, of course, record the conversation, but we may only get one good shot at this."

Jake's heart soared. He knew he was a long way from having Sara in his arms again, but Jake's hope meter had just swung strongly to the positive side.

"So, Jake, we need you on standby, and with the ability to get here within ninety minutes of our warning call to you. I have no idea what time of day the call will come in, but at night this number will be answered in the Operations Center, so somebody will be ready to answer the phone around-the-clock...at all times."

"I can respond to a ninety-minute leash," answered Jake. "I live thirty-five minutes from you on a good day and maybe ninety minutes to two hours during the worst traffic periods of the day. But I'll make it there in time, rest assured."

"I have no doubt," replied the colonel.

Colonel Ricci hung up the phone.

I have no idea how hard it must be to be in his shoes, thought Ricci.

Jake, for his part, was very grateful and optimistic.

CHAPTER 66

I Thought So

AS LIA HEADED DOWN THE OLD WOODEN STAIRS, she felt like this day would be different. It was one of those feelings she always got when a new day would turn out to be a good day. Like many Italian Mafia members, Lia was faithful in an Italian Mafia kind of way. She believed there was a God. But for some reason, her God *seemed to give the rich people—especially the government people, 'who stole from the poor'—all the breaks*, but she still believed. She knew she was not perfect, and even though she had done some terrible things in her day, she also knew the door was always there for her to move away and become somebody "normal," with a husband, maybe, and some kids. At 33, she had known only the mafia as a way of life.

It had been several days since Sara had gotten beaten up. Tomorrow was the day Gio had been told—and Gio had duly informed Lia—that three 'Ndrangheta members would pay a visit to the hideout. Gio was told not to announce the reason for the visit to Sara, but she suspected she knew the reason.

But tonight, it was Lia's turn to bring the pasta down for Sara's dinner. She'd added a little extra sauce to it simply because she thought it the right thing to do. Lia would soon find out if her intuition was right.

Instead of pushing the dinner underneath the bars, which was customary for her and Gio—but "no longer allowed for that jackass Russian guy, until the bosses figure out what to do with him," Gio had said—tonight Lia decided to carry the pasta into the cell room.

Sara looked quizzically at Lia as she unlocked the cell door, shut the door behind her, and brought the pasta in.

"*Buona sera* (good evening)," began Lia.

Sara's jaw almost dropped. Never before had Sara offered a civil greeting like that. In fact, there had been exactly zero such salutations during her captivity. "Please" and "thank you" had been spoken a few times, mostly from Sara: never to the Russian, sometimes to Gio, and more often to Lia. Usually, Sara only got a head nod from Lia in response, but recently, Lia had once slipped up and said, "You're welcome."

Sara wasn't quite sure how to respond to Lia's surprising salutation. But then Sara decided to do what came naturally.

"*Buona sera*," she responded.

Lia walked up to Sara, who was still seated on the cot. Lia stopped a couple of paces away from Sara, with both hands holding the white bowl of steaming pasta.

"Please stand up," said Lia.

Sara complied.

Standing, Sara could see the abundant amount of food in the bowl, and she could easily smell the wonderful aroma of the sauce. Both were a first. While Lia had, upon occasion, added some basic red sauce to the basic penne or spaghetti pasta, this bowl smelled flavorful.

Sara knew not to take the bowl until Lia got closer and clearly offered it.

"Look me in the eye," ordered Lia.

A negative thought flashed through Sara's mind and soul. Lia's borderline bizarre behavior was beginning to concern Sara. Sara was puzzled.

Is this when she tells me this is my last supper? Pondered Sara, her heart rate began to elevate.

Sara raised her eyes from the delicious-looking bowl of food to meet Lia's eyes.

"Now, tell me the truth," said Lia. "Are you pregnant?"

Sara hesitated. Her eyes blinked as she fought back a tear, not knowing what her answer would mean for her or, more importantly, her unborn child.

Sara's hesitation was all that Lia needed to make up her mind.

"I thought so," continued Lia. "For how long?"

"Eleven weeks, maybe twelve," replied Sara.

"Well, with your trim and sporty frame, you are starting to show earlier than most. But neither one of those two goombahs upstairs—especially that Russian prick—would have a clue. But me? I could tell," said Lia, proudly.

"Here, *mangia* (eat)!" said Lia, presenting the bowl to Sara.

"*Grazie*," replied Sara.

What just happened? thought Sara as Lia walked out of the cell room.

The wonderful taste of the pasta, *the best food I've had here*, thought Sara, carried her mind to more positive realms. She could almost feel herself cracking a smile.

CHAPTER 67

It's On

JAKE SAT ON A LAWN CHAIR on the bedroom balcony of Colonel Hennadiy Kovalenko's spacious Roman apartment. A few minutes before 8 a.m., after he'd already completed a 40-minute workout in his bedroom, Jake was enjoying the warmth of the rising Roman sun. Trying to keep his life as normal as possible, he had just read his daily dose of *Jesus Calling* and the *Holy Bible*. It fortified his soul to understand that just as things had been turned upside down in his life, it could all be made right in an instant. Not by his timeline, but that of the Almighty. He just had to believe that.

Jake's burner phone buzzed. It was Colonel Ricci calling.

"Good morning, *mon colonel*," answered Jake, throwing in a little French.

"Good morning, *Giacomo*," responded Ricci, adding his own twist to his greeting.

"How can I help you, sir?" responded Jake.

"Jake, get here as soon as you can. It's *on*...in one hour and forty-five minutes from now."

"Roger that," responded Jake in military speak.

Ricci hung up and told the Carabinieri warrant officer in the adjoining office to notify the guards at the headquarters entrance gate that Lieutenant Colonel Jake Fortina, a retired US Army officer, would be rolling into the headquarters within the next two hours.

"Make sure he gets prompt access to the parking area and gets escorted into the headquarters building," added the Italian colonel.

Jake grabbed a 90-second shower, toweled himself off, threw on some casual clothes with a light jacket, grabbed his motorcycle keys, helmet, wallet with ID, sunglasses, and burner phone, and quickly got down the stairs and into the basement garage, where he had parked the Ducati.

The motorbike's engine roared to life inside the cement structure. Its growl reverberated off the low ceilings, walls, and every piece of metal and glass. Jake guided the bike up the parking garage's inclined exit, drove out the apartment complex's gates...and soon found himself in heavy morning Roman traffic.

Within five minutes on a one-way road, the line of cars ahead of him was completely stopped.

He took the bike up on the sidewalk and, within 10 seconds, almost hit a middle-aged Italian couple as they exited a café.

The man waggled his finger at Jake, every cuss word he knew flying from his mouth as Jake passed by on the motorcycle. The woman beside him followed suit.

Jake caught a glimpse of the couple in his rearview mirror and knew it had been a close call. He guided the motorcycle back into the now-slowly creeping traffic. He thought about trying his luck on the sidewalk again but changed his mind. Thankfully, like the good soldier he was, he had already performed a reconnaissance of the roads leading to the Carabinieri Headquarters. So, he knew what was ahead. But he also knew this was absolutely the worst time to be traveling toward the heart of the city.

While continuing to ease the Ducati forward, he grabbed his cell phone from his pocket and called Colonel Ricci.

Ricci picked up on the first ring.

"Jake?" answered Ricci.

"Giorgio," began Jake, "I'm stuck in really bad traffic. I will do my best to get there on time, but…"

"Where are you?" interrupted Ricci.

Jake described his location to Ricci, including that it was about 300 meters off the *Viale Goffredo Lombardo*.

Ricci had served three tours in Rome, and he knew the *Viale Goffredo Lombardo* area well. It was full of modern apartment complexes. He also knew that there was a Carabinieri station not far from *Viale Goffredo Lombardo*. Ricci snapped his fingers at the nearby *maresciallo*, who was standing by, ready to support in any way he could.

Jake could hear Ricci muffling the phone's speaker, but in the background, he could still hear some fast-paced Italian being spoken between Ricci and the warrant officer.

The warrant officer consulted Google Maps and knew that on a perfect day, Jake was thirty-five minutes from the headquarters. On a bad day, it could be an hour and a half or longer. This was a bad day.

Ricci and the junior officer had been at it almost three minutes before Ricci came back on the line.

"Listen, Jake, I need you to get to this intersection as soon as you can."

Ricci described the intersection's location.

"If traffic is crawling, you'll be there in ten minutes," added the colonel. "What kind of car are you driving? What is your license plate number?"

"I'm not in a car. I'm on a red and black Ducati," responded Jake.

"Did you say *Ducati*?" responded Ricci.

"Yep," replied Jake.

"Typical ballsy American," laughed the Italian warrant officer, who was listening in on the conversation.

The colonel chuckled with him.

"What was that?" asked Jake, trying to hear above the noisy traffic, with the sound of impatient drivers blaring their horns every thirty seconds or so.

"Nothing," replied Ricci. "Just get to that intersection. There will be a Carabinieri vehicle waiting there for you. It will escort you to our headquarters building. We'll tell the welcoming crew to look for a red and black Ducati."

"Got it!" responded Jake.

CHAPTER 68

Upstairs

SARA WAS DOING SOME STRETCHING and isometric exercises when she heard the thump, thump, and thump of three car doors closing outside the building. Not having heard the sound before, especially through the small window above her, she wasn't quite sure what she had heard. From down the hallway, she soon heard four hard knocks on the old wooden front door. Someone from upstairs scurried down the steps and opened the door.

Sara heard "*Buongiorno*" exchanged. *Perhaps two, maybe more people*, she thought as she heard the group trudge upstairs.

What might this mean? Sara wondered.

She resolved to stay positive as she considered the implications. Sara's mind flashed back to the previous day's conversation with Lia, the *kindest contact I've had with a human being since I left the Carabinieri headquarters that rainy night*, she thought as her mind took her back to the fuzzy blur that was her kidnapping.

Would Lia have been so kind to me if they were going to kill me and bury me today? The analytical law enforcement part of her mind asked, now coming to the fore.

Sara heard the kitchen chairs moving on the floor above her but could barely hear the muffled voices in the room.

***

Less than an hour later, Sara could hear two people coming down the steps. Lia and Gio emerged from the hallway. Lia walked up to the cell's door, unlocked it, and entered the cell. She was carrying what looked to be a bandanna and handcuffs. Gio remained at the cell room's slightly open door.

Sara saw both items. She fought the urge to become anxious. She resolved to be strong.

"I have to take you upstairs now," said Lia firmly. "And I need to put the handcuffs and blindfold on you before I do. Stand up."

The firmness in her voice was as much to impress Gio—who was observing Lia from outside the cell—as it was to be clear to Sara about what was expected and about to happen. Lia did not want Gio to know the familiarity that was beginning to bloom between her and Sara.

In as low a voice as she could, Lia said to Sara, "Don't worry."

Gio heard the whisper.

"What was *that*?" asked Gio.

"I told her she was not going to be slapped upside the head this time. Is *that OK*?" said Lia with a belligerent tone.

Finding himself somewhere between not caring and suspicious, Gio did not respond.

Lia took Sara by Sara's right arm, led her out of the cell room, and took her up the steps to the open kitchen and living area.

Lia led Sara to the wooden chair in the middle of the open space. It was the same chair Sara was shackled to before. Once more, she felt the handcuffs close around her wrists after Lia had guided them through the back of the chair. The room's window was open, and Sara was seated about six feet away from it. She relished the fresh morning air that flowed in from the nearby field and forest. These were spring smells she hadn't yet experienced in Calabria.

With the blindfold on, Sara could feel the presence of more than Lia, Gio, and the Russian in the room. Sara didn't know it, but one of the most senior members of the 'Ndrangheta Mafia clan, Antonio Di Salva, was sitting at the kitchen table about ten feet from Sara. Two of his henchmen were standing near the chair. One of them had a burner cell phone in his hand. The two had recommended that Sara be brought out of the cell room, with its thick walls and tiny window, to the upstairs area with less thick walls than the first floor and with a larger window. Their concern, as confirmed by Gio shortly after their arrival, was that the cell coverage was terrible on the first floor, and while not great on the second floor, it was better than the first.

The *mafioso* with the cell phone had already tested connections from the room with another mafia colleague about seventy miles away. He told Di Salva it "worked OK but not perfectly" on the second floor. Antonio Di Salva agreed with the duo's recommendation to make the call from the second floor.

The man holding the cell phone was in charge of what was about to happen.

He addressed Sara, stoically seated, blindfolded, and handcuffed to the chair.

"Listen, we are going to make a phone call in about ten minutes," he began. "It's for the Carabinieri on the other end to know that you are alive. I'm going to tell you what to say. I will be holding the phone next to your mouth and will have it on speaker. If you say anything but exactly what I tell you to say, I'm going to terminate the call. And after that, I have no idea what will happen to you, but it most likely won't be good."

The man looked at Di Salva, who nodded his head affirmatively.

CHAPTER 69

Carabinieri Escort

THE TWO CARABINIERI SEATED IN THE PATROL CAR spotted Jake approaching the intersection on his red and black Ducati motorcycle at about the same time Jake spotted the Carabinieri patrol car. The patrol car immediately turned on its blue flashing rooftop light and its siren. The patrol car entered the intersection, with the Carabinieri officer seated on the passenger side waving aggressively from his rolled-down window, signaling to Jake to follow closely behind. Fortunately for Jake, he had observed a few police escorts not only by the Carabinieri but also by the Gendarmes of France. Jake understood that his job was to follow the patrol car as closely as possible without ending up in its trunk.

As Jake traveled behind the patrol car, he was delighted to see the stalled traffic, making every effort to provide a passable lane for the blaring patrol car. Jake figured some of the drivers assumed he was taking advantage, but he didn't care. Jake was not going to let some wise-ass Roman driver knock him from his spot, so he stayed right on the patrol car's bumper.

Initially, the progress of the Carabinieri car and the motorcycle went on in fits and starts. Just like for an American football running back, sometimes it was three yards of progress and a cloud of dust; other times, it was a thirty or forty-yard gain.

Jake smiled an impromptu smile, which was rare for him

since Sara had disappeared.

This is fun, he thought. *And it sure as hell is much faster than if I had tried to get there by myself.*

Within thirty-three minutes of Jake getting behind the patrol car, they pulled up to the Carabinieri Headquarters. The electric gate was already open. He stopped at the guard shack just inside it.

As the gate closed, the young Carabinieri guard approached Jake and asked for his identification card. He needed to verify Jake was the right guy. For the first time, Jake pulled out his new US Department of Defense/Uniformed Services Veteran's ID card.

The young officer examined the card and asked Jake to raise his motorcycle helmet's visor. Jake felt like a bit of a jackass for not having raised his visor as soon as he pulled up to the gate, but in the excitement of the journey, he had simply forgotten.

The man looked into Jake's eyes and looked again at Jake's ID card. He handed the card back to Jake and waved Jake into the parking lot.

Another pre-positioned officer in the parking lot pointed to the parking space reserved for Jake. As soon as Jake parked the bike and removed his helmet, a third officer, who spoke pretty good English, told Jake, "Please follow me, sir."

As Jake followed, he struck up a conversation in Italian. The young man was quite surprised by how well Jake spoke Italian. He even detected the slight Veneto accent Jake acquired during his first army assignment when he'd spent three and half years in Vicenza. The local Veneto accent had stuck.

Within ten minutes of Jake having entered the gate, he was surprised to find himself standing in the Carabinieri commanding general's outer office.

CHAPTER 70

Garlic, Olive Oil, And Red Peppers

AT A FEW MINUTES PAST 10 A.M., the phone in the Carabinieri's commanding general's outer office rang. The five Carabinieri special task force members were present to listen to the call, as was Jake Fortina. Colonel Ricci picked up the phone on the third ring.

"*Pronto*," replied Ricci.

"Is this the comandante's office?" asked the caller.

"It is," replied Colonel Ricci, now used to hearing the voice on the other end of the line.

"Stand by for Sara Simonetti," said the caller.

The phone connection was not great, but the voices could be heard on either end clearly enough, or so they thought.

In the hideout, the 'Ndrangheta member who had instructed Sara on what to say, followed by a veiled threat in the event she said anything else, held the phone six inches from Sara's mouth.

"Speak," he said to Sara.

"This is Sara Simonetti," said Sara. "I am safe. I am in good health, and my treatment has been good."

The 'Ndrangheta member pulled back the phone and put the receiver next to his mouth.

"Get what you want?" he asked.

"Give us a minute," came the response from Rome.

Everyone assembled looked at Jake Fortina.

He shook his head.

"I'm not sure that was her," he replied.

"What do you mean?" asked Major General Comitini.

"I mean exactly what I said, sir," answered Jake. "I'm not 100 percent that's her. I need something more concrete to be assured that it's her. That was too short, and it was not very clear."

"I get it," said another member of the special task force. "The connection is not great. I know Sara personally, but I'm not sure, either."

"How do we confirm it's her, then?" asked Ricci, his hand over the speaker.

Di Salva, sitting in the Calabrian hideout, was getting anxious over the delay.

"What's the problem?" he asked.

"What's the problem?" relayed the 'Ndrangheta member speaking from the hideout to his Carabinieri contact.

"We need some way to verify her *bona fides*," replied Ricci.

"Her *what*?" shot back the 'Ndrangheta speaker.

"Her true identity," said Ricci. "Nobody here thinks it's her, especially her husband."

Ricci looked at the general and Jake as if to say, "I'm sorry that slipped out."

Jake immediately nodded affirmatively to Ricci, and with two thumbs up, conveying, "That's perfectly OK. No harm done."

With the knowledge that Jake could hear her voice, Sara's heart leaped in her chest.

Back in Rome, "I know what we can do," said Lieutenant Colonel Martini, Commander of Italy's GIS, almost out of the blue.

He looked at Jake.

"What is something Sara would know about Lieutenant Colonel Jake Fortina" he pointed emphatically, "...about you,

Jake...that *only she* would know?" He clapped once as he thought of the perfect thing. "Like, what is your favorite meal? What is one of your most favorite wines?"

Major General Comitini nodded affirmatively.

"Ok, let's try that," he declared. "Let's ask that."

Colonel Ricci took his hand off the receiver and asked the 'Ndrangheta caller, "What does Lieutenant Colonel Simonetti say is her husband's favorite meal? And...what is *one* of his favorite wines? If she answers correctly, we will acknowledge Sara Simonetti is there, and we will acknowledge proof of life."

The group at the hideout stared incredulously at the phone.

"What the fuuucck?" said the 'Ndrangheta member with the burner phone in his hand, now covering the receiver tightly so the Carabinieri could hear nothing.

He looked at Antonio Di Salva and asked, "What do we do, boss?"

The longer the telephone conversation went on, the more nervous Di Salva was getting. But he did not want to have to do this again.

"OK," said Di Salva. "Let Simonetti answer the question."

The 'Ndrangheta man, still with his hand over the receiver, looked at Sara, who, of course, could not see him.

"You better talk about nothing but food and wine. If you do mention anything else, I will terminate the call, and you will be in serious trouble. Understand?"

"Yes, I understand," responded Sara.

"Speak," said the 'Ndrangheta member firmly to Sara.

"Well, his favorite wine is Bordeaux. Sadly, I was not able to convince him that Italian wine is better than French wine."

Several of the people on both ends of the line smirked; a couple of people even chuckled, and some raised their eyebrows. Everybody in the commander's office looked at Jake, a couple feigning daggers in their eyes.

Jake nodded affirmatively and put his hands up as if to

say, "What can I say? It's true. I do prefer a Bordeaux."

"But his favorite meal is *aglio, olio*, and the strongest Italian *peperoncino* (garlic, olive oil, and *Calabrian* chili peppers), and bergamot pie."

Everybody on both ends of the phone connection loved *aglio, olio,* and *peperoncino*. The Carabinieri officer's faith in Jake was restored. Most within earshot of the statement in both Calabria and Rome knew the Italian spaghetti dish had gone global, too, with most reputable Italian restaurants around the world serving it. Italian purists consumed the simple pasta dish without any cheese, while many people around the world, including many Italians, like it with grated parmesan cheese sprinkled on the top.

Jake half nodded his head at Sara's favorite food answer.

Colonel Ricci looked at Jake for confirmation.

Jake was sure it was Sara. He *loved* garlic, olive oil, and the *Calabrian* pepper chili, the strongest of Italian chili peppers. But while he didn't remember ever eating bergamot pie, he now knew it was Sara on the other end.

"It's her," replied Jake. It's Sara."

"OK, we agree, it's her, Sara Simonetti," replied Colonel Ricci on the phone. "We acknowledge proof of life. And let me be very clear. If you lay a finger on her, you'll have hell to pay."

"Fuck you," came the response. "You are in no position to dictate terms or to negotiate until you are able to assure us that Brigadier General Cadorna will be handed over in a trade."

The line went dead.

CHAPTER 71

Grateful And Hopeful

JAKE FORTINA WAS GRATEFUL. He was grateful to have heard Sara's voice and to know that Sara was alive. He was grateful for the way the Carabinieri responded and the way they let him into their inner circle.

The five-person team in the room had just concluded an intense 45-minute discussion on Sara's status. Three of the officers were fairly optimistic, and two were not. Hostage crises and negotiations were a very tough business. Once a hostage or hostages were located—a massive challenge in itself—one could never fully tell how the captors would respond when confronted.

"*Mille grazie,*" Jake said to all of them gathered in the room. "I know we don't have her back home yet, but I thank you for making this tremendous effort thus far."

They all nodded their heads in agreement and appreciation for Jake's comments. They each had their thoughts on the region of Italy where Sara might be, and most of them thought it was somewhere south of Rome. But a couple of them knew that was a long, long way from actionable intelligence. For an American, it would be like saying, "She is somewhere in Southern California." Jake understood that Italy, being about two-thirds the size of California, geographically America's third largest state, is deceptively large and diverse, with highly variable terrain. Jake knew the challenges ahead, and he prayed for the Carabinieri to get enough of a break to give them an opportunity to rescue Sara.

"But I cannot wait for them," vowed Jake. "I have to do everything I can do to bring her safely home. This is now my sole mission in life."

As he rode to Colonel Kovalenko's apartment on his motorcycle, he was hopeful that Sara was at least OK. He knew she was the toughest—physically, mentally, and emotionally—woman that he'd ever met, and he was thankful that God had put her in his path after the tragic loss of his first wife Faith, and children Kimberly and Jake Jr. He was even more thankful that God—and Faith, who had come to him in a dream—gave him the discernment to know that Sara was *the one* for the rest of his journey on planet earth.

***

Lying on her side, Sara stared at the dark cement wall next to the cot. She briefly looked up at the dark cross, barely visible on the wall above her. On this evening, she felt as hopeful as she'd ever felt during her almost four—*or is it five*—week ordeal. Her heart soared over the fact that Jake had been listening to her voice on the other end of the phone call earlier that day. She was also very thankful—and still couldn't believe that she got away with it—with slipping the words "peperoncino" and "bergamot" in her menu description.

For the pasta dish she described, the ideal—and original—red peppers to be used in the dish were the small red spicy ones...*from Calabria*. And the bergamot citrus, increasingly known throughout the world as a citrus with very healthy properties, was only grown in a microclimate along the coast of Calabria. For anybody who paid attention, they should have provided clues as to her general location. Both those words related to only one place on the planet: Calabria.

Her mentioning French Bordeaux, while it was indeed Jake's preferred wine, was intended as more of a distraction and to provide some levity to a very tense situation. She could just as well have mentioned a red Italian wine, like a *Vino Nobile di Montepulciano*, with its Tuscan *Sangiovese* grape, or an *Amarone* from the Veneto region. Jake liked those a lot, too, and he would have confirmed that. But she knew her mentioning of French wine would draw out ire from some and humor from others. That part had worked perfectly, as had the rest of her brief statement.

Dear Lord, she prayed. *Thank you for allowing Jake to hear my voice today. And thank you for the opportunity to say something which might—and I pray will—give Jake and the other listeners in Rome some sense of where I'm located. And thank you that my captors did not discover the hidden meaning nor punish me for what I said. And whatever is going on with Lia, please let it continue. Thank you, Lord. And please bless Lia. In Your Name, I pray, Amen.*

CHAPTER 72

Calabria!

IT WAS 4:14 A.M. JAKE TOSSED AND TURNED IN HIS BED. He was extremely grateful for Ukrainian Colonel Hennadiy Kovalenko and his gracious wife Mila, who had been hosting him for almost a month. Jake was thankful for the way the apartment was laid out, with his bedroom—and en-suite bathroom—on the opposite side of the three-bedroom apartment from the master bedroom.

When Jake moved in, Kovalenko told Jake, "You're in the mother-in-law suite. You can stay as long as you want. It will mean my mother-in-law cannot come and visit nor stay as long as *she* wants, and, by the Grace of God, that's fine with me."

Kovalenko winked at Jake, and Jake chuckled.

Jake tried to be as good a guest as possible. He always helped around the apartment, cooked his favorite meals, grilled an occasional steak, and kept the wine fridge and vodka freezer well-stocked with wine and Ukrainian vodka, which Jake easily found in Rome. But he felt it was time to move on.

The day prior had been an intense day. Jake was thankful to have heard Sara's voice on the phone. At first, he wasn't 100 percent sure it was her on the line. But then, when she answered a couple of questions that only she—and perhaps a couple of Jake's closest friends—would know the answer to, he was sure it was Sara.

Her description of Jake's favorite meal—a simple Italian dish of garlic, olive oil, and heat-inducing red peppers from *Calabria* mixed in with spaghetti—*was spot on*, he thought.

But the "bergamot pie" as a dessert? That was just plain weird.

Jake knew about bergamot citrus fruit because he and Sara both had a passion for lemons, as well as the *Limoncello "digestivo"* drink distilled from them. The first time and only time he'd heard about the bergamot citrus was when he and Sara had traveled down to Villa San Giovanni on the Calabrian coast before taking the ferry across the Straits of Messina. During that trip, they had driven through a bergamot citrus grove.

Jake's curious nature caused Jake to ask Sara about the lemons of Amalfi and the lemons that grew in a microclimate on the western side of Lake Garda, much farther to the north of the Amalfi coast, as well as much farther to the north from the citrus bergamot groves.

"I've never heard of bergamot citrus," said Jake to Sara after she first mentioned the light greenish citrus fruit.

"Well, you should get smart about it, Jake," Sara said. "Bergamot citrus is quite healthy, or so they say. It's supposed to be great for reducing cholesterol and a bunch of other stuff."

Later, Sara thoughtfully presented Jake with a book called *The Land Where the Lemons Grow: The Story of Italy and Its Citrus Fruit* (2014) by British author Helena Attlee. Jake was surprised that he could be so enthralled by a subject so simple as an Italian citrus fruit. But he was.

Jake learned from Attlee's book that the bergamot (citrus bergamia) "green gold" was, pound for pound, the most valuable citrus in the world. According to Helena Attlee, "It was the product of cross-pollination between a lemon tree and sour orange that occurred in Calabria in the mid-seventeenth century. It thrives *only* on a narrow strip of coastline that runs for less than fifty miles from San Giovanni on the Tyrrhenian Sea—and across from the Sicilian port of Messina—to Brancaleone on the coast of the Ionian Sea." If mainland Italy is a boot, then the bergamot growing area constitutes the tip of that boot. It is also the southernmost part of Calabria.

Lying in bed, Jake's rethinking of Sara's "strongest Italian pepper" and "bergamot pie" comments brought a vision and a connecting of the dots to his mind that caused him to bolt upright in his bed.

That's it! It's Calabria! If she's not near a Bergamot citrus grove, she must have been driven through one!

Jake's mind raced. He knew it was useless trying to sleep. He got up, grabbed his copy of *Jesus Calling* and the Good Book, and went quietly out to the kitchen to make a shot of espresso. He tried to settle his mind before tackling the day ahead.

✳✳✳

Hennadiy Kovalenko got up. He needed to get going earlier in the morning than his wife, Mila. When he came out to the kitchen, Jake asked Kovalenko if he could fire Kovalenko up a cup of cappuccino.

"Yes, sure, thank you so much, my friend," responded Kovalenko.

It didn't take long for Jake to froth some milk and add it to the steaming shot of double espresso, just like Kovalenko liked it.

Kovalenko sat down at the kitchen table, and Jake pushed the cappuccino across the table.

"Appreciate it," responded Kovalenko.

"My pleasure," said Jake.

Kovalenko sensed there was something on Jake's mind.

"What's up, Jake?" he asked.

"Hennadiy, you and Mila have been wonderfully gracious to me, especially during this rather trying time. I can't thank you enough. But I wanted to let you know it's time for me to move on."

"If I could ask...where to, Jake? Did you find a place? Do you feel safe enough to stay at an established address in Rome under your name?"

"Not exactly," answered Jake.

"Not exactly as in 'I haven't found a place' or not exactly as in 'I don't feel safe'"?

"Well...not exactly...to both."

Both men paused and looked at each other. Jake then looked at his espresso cup and back to the Ukrainian colonel.

"Hennadiy, I trust you like a brother. So here goes..."

"Likewise," responded Kovalenko. "Let me hear it."

"I'm 90 percent sure I know where Sara is, at least within a large area."

"How large?" asked Kovalenko.

"Like about a third the size of Calabria," said Jake. "I firmly believe she is being held in Calabria, and I'm quite certain I could eliminate the parts of the region that she is not in before I even get down there."

"And you know this because...?" asked Kovalenko.

Jake proceeded to tell Kovalenko about the proof of life call, what was said in that call, what the caller's accent was and what the Carbs had heard on a previous phone call...everything.

"Have you told the Carabinieri your thoughts of where she might be?'"

"They *must* know or at least have a good idea," replied Jake. "And if they don't, I would say Barney Fife would make a better law enforcement officer than them."

"Who is Barney Fife?" asked Hennadiy.

Jake chuckled.

"Let's just say he wasn't the brightest bulb in the building."

Kovalenko pictured the image and laughed.

"Well, in my experience, the Carabinieri have been pretty darn good," replied Kovalenko.

"And they definitely have been in mine, too," said Jake. "I really didn't mean that Barney Fife thing. I will tell the Carabinieri, but I'm not sure how quickly or how fully they will mobilize to find her. They have so many law enforcement irons on the fire right now. And we're still looking for a needle in a haystack, at least for now."

"Well, they probably need to know your thoughts," Hennadiy said. "So, back to my original question: what's your plan?"

"I'm going down to Calabria. And I'll be there until I find Sara—or the Carbs do—and rescue her."

Colonel Hennadiy Kovalenko sighed deeply and nodded.

"Can't say I wouldn't do the same thing, Jake. Who are you going down there with?"

"Nobody. It'll just be me."

Hennadiy Kovalenko took a long look at Jake.

"I don't think that's a good idea."

"Why not? I really appreciate you providing me a place to stay for as long as you have, but I'll go stir-crazy here now that I have at least an idea of where she is. My only mission in life is to find her...and bring her safely home, our home, wherever that might end up being."

"Well, I'm not going to let you do that alone."

Hennadiy Kovalenko thought of at least one other soldier—an American—who would not want Jake to go it alone, either.

"What do you mean?" asked Jake.

"Jake, I'm going with you, and I'll be with you for as long as I can. I'm going to take leave for fifteen days, maybe longer. Things are—thank God—quiet in the office right now. You and Sara saved Ukraine—and US sailors, and Italy, and probably Europe—from a crazy-ass oligarch who would have been worse than the guy sitting in the Kremlin right now, which is hard to imagine but highly probable. You and I need to talk more about what logistical help you might need, too. Trust me. Mila will fully support me in this. She is more of a fighter than I am."

Jake sat stunned.

"Now that you mention it, there a couple of items I—or we—could use, logistically speaking," he continued.

"We need at least one weapon, maybe two, now that you are on board. And night vision goggles, we could use some night vision goggles. And if we really want to be high-speed," added Jake. "Maybe a satellite phone. It's not a must-have, but I don't know how good the cell phone coverage down there is."

Colonel Hennadiy Kovalenko simply nodded.

"Got it," he said. "I'll do some checking around."

CHAPTER 73

More Intel

JAKE'S FIRST CALL THAT MORNING was not to the Carabinieri but an old friend from his previous time being stationed in Vicenza, Italy, with the 173d Airborne Brigade, Major General Michele Marcello Ranieri. Major General Michele Marcello Ranieri, an *Alpini*, or mountain infantry officer, now served on Italy's Defense Staff in Rome. He had once served as Italy's *Julia* Alpine Brigade commander as well as the commander of the international NATO-led Kosovo Force in Pristina, Kosovo.

Since their meeting on a training exercise conducted at the Alpine Training Center in the Dolomite mountains surrounding the mountain village of Brunico, the two officers remained in contact and kept up a steady correspondence. Jake's wife back then—Faith—had also hit it off well with the then-Italian major's American wife.

A thirty-something Italian Army major immediately opened the door to Major General Ranieri's outer office and led Fortina past the general's secretary and into the general's personal office.

"Can I get you anything, sir?" asked the major of Fortina. "Coffee, water?"

"No, thank you, major," replied Fortina.

After a warm reception from Major General Ranieri, Ranieri told Jake to "have a seat" on the brown leather couch. There was a large, dark brown coffee table in front of the couch. It was covered with several maps.

Ranieri took a seat by the recently retired US Army lieutenant colonel.

"This is the general area my battalion patrolled then, in November and December of 1990," said Ranieri, pointing to the map. "The Aspromonte area is where much of the kidnapping for ransom took place in the late 1970s, 1980s and early 1990s. Our national government was catching hell from the local Calabrian citizens, who felt the government in Rome was abandoning them. Feeling abandoned by the government has been a theme down there for decades . . . even centuries. That is one reason why the 'Ndrangheta Mafia has flourished there. While we were operating in Calabria, in the town of Polistena, the 'Ndrangheta tried to assassinate the local deputy mayor as punishment for spending the previous day with us, the Italian *Alpini* troops from the *Susa Alpini* battalion. There was no mayor in Polistena because he had already been taken out by the 'Ndrangheta."

Jake nodded, signaling his understanding.

"How is the terrain in Aspromonte?" asked Jake.

"It's rough. There is a lot of varying, thickly wooded terrain, with a lot of steep gullies and even steep drop-offs. I would not go walking around there at night. Another reason the area never got economically developed and remains largely impoverished to this day is because farming the land was next to impossible. It's good for grazing sheep, and that's about it. Therefore, most of the agriculture down there ended up along the coast."

Like the Bergamot citrus groves, thought Fortina.

"Anything I should know about the early spring weather?" asked Fortina.

"It's variable, meaning you can find yourself in a storm that you did not see coming. Washouts happen all the time. Closer to the coast, when I was leading a convoy down there in the Scilla area, our convoy got held up for a day because of a snowstorm that came out of nowhere. So, while in Aspromonte, since you are surrounded in three directions by sea, the weather can get nasty very quickly. And where you'll be going, it varies from 2,000—6,000 feet elevation. That's not super high, but it is high enough to create weather and movement challenges."

"OK, sir, *grazie*," said Jake.

Now, for the delicate question, thought Jake.

"How do I get the best intel possible about the lay of the land concerning the mafia down there?" asked Jake.

"Could you be more precise?" asked Ranieri.

"Yes, sir, I'll try. Let me be more direct. Do you remember discovering any remote 'Ndrangheta hiding places—buildings, caves, etc.—while the Susa alpine battalion was conducting patrolling operations there?"

The general got pensive for a moment, then he smiled.

"Yes, I do," replied Ranieri. "The Aspromonte National Park is roughly 250 square miles in size."

He pointed to the map at about a fifty square mile area in and around Aspromonte.

"This area is also part of the Aspromonte area. The terrain here is nasty and heavily overgrown," said Ranieri, again pointing to the map. "The locals we saw during our ten days there were mainly shepherds. They've probably been pushing their sheep over those hills and through those valleys for centuries. Besides the shepherds, we came across a rather suspect trio of guys, who we could do nothing about since we were not law enforcement officers, nor did we have any reason to question them."

Jake nodded his understanding.

"One final question, if I might ask, sir," said Jake.

"*Dimmi* (tell me)," said Ranieri, momentarily switching to Italian.

"I know it's a stretch," said Jake, "But is there anybody down there that I could talk to who is not in the pockets of the 'Ndrangheta? Somebody who might have noticed something new and unusual in the area?"

"Practically speaking? People who are not under the influence of the mafia are a small minority. That area has been saturated with mafia since at least the late 1800s or early 1900s. You never quite know who is and who isn't in the pockets of the mafia. You should just assume everybody is. But there is one thing you have going for you, Jake. You look like you could be a local. You are of Italian heritage, correct?"

"From my dad's side, yes, that is correct. He was part Sicilian. But my mom was Lebanese. My grandmother's family on my father's side was Calabrian, from Sant'Ippolito. My grandmother's family left Calabria and moved to Nebraska over a century ago."

"Your ability to blend in will help as you move around. But some locals will still know you are a stranger," said Ranieri.

"So, who can I talk to without having my tires flattened?" asked Jake, coming at the question one more time.

"If they are over seventy years old, you might be able to talk to someone, especially if you tell them you are an American soldier who is retracing your grandfather's service in Italy during World War II. Even the old-time mafia people still love the Americans—and allies—for liberating them from the Nazi occupation. You probably know that in Sicily, Lucky Luciano's connections with the mafia turned out to be a great source of local intelligence and support for the American and British-led forces that landed in Sicily."

"I *did* know about Lucky Luciano," said Jake.

"Are you Catholic, Jake?" continued Ranieri.

"I am," replied Fortina.

"And your Italian is very good, so you have that going for you, too," said Ranieri.

Ranieri again pointed to the map.

"There are churches here and here, and here is a famous—at least to the locals, good and criminal—Christian Sanctuary," said Ranieri. "The priests, as far as I know, are not corrupted. At least, that was true when I was there. And since many in the 'Ndrangheta claim to be devout Catholics, the mafia generally leaves the priests alone, although they did murder a priest near the Sanctuary of Polsi in June 1989. I believe that was just another reason the local population became inflamed against the 'Ndrangheta and why my battalion was sent down there some 17 months later. The priests *might* be able to help you get some more fidelity on local hideout locations. Sara's kidnapping was all over the news and social media...what was it, a few weeks ago?"

Jake nodded.

"Now, Jake, I have a question for you. Have you told the Carabinieri that you think Sara is down there?"

"I have, sir."

"OK, that's good," said Ranieri.

"But I didn't tell them I'd be personally mucking around down there," stated Jake.

"Well, you're a private citizen now, and you are married to an Italian. As far as I'm concerned, you can do whatever the hell you want, as long as it's within the limits of the law, of course."

General Ranieri smiled.

"Of course," replied Jake, smiling back at the general.

CHAPTER 74

Don't Ask

JAKE FORTINA FIRED UP THE DUCATI inside the basement parking garage.

I practically need earplugs to start this thing inside this echo chamber. He grimaced as the noise washed over him.

The thought that he was beginning his journey to find Sara put a smile on Jake's face.

He looked over at Hennadiy Kovalenko, seated in his Stornoway gray metallic, 2010 model Range Rover, with its supercharged 5.0-liter, V-8 engine. Kovalenko had convinced Jake that a second, off-road-capable vehicle would be needed as a trail vehicle rather than just the motorcycle. Jake was impressed by how well-maintained the 14-year-old vehicle was. And Kovalenko was impressed that Jake knew something about Range Rovers.

"The most dependable models were built between 2003 and 2012," Jake had said.

Kovalenko sealed the deal with Jake when he explained what the vehicle would mean logistically for their trip to Calabria, which, for now, was meant to last no more than two weeks for Kovalenko. While Jake had practically unlimited time, Kovalenko still had a high-profile—or, as Kovalenko preferred it for security reasons, low-profile—day job.

"We can carry more crap in this Range Rover, including a tent," said the Ukrainian colonel.

"Indeed, we can," Jake replied.

But what Kovalenko had not informed Jake of until this moment, just prior to their late afternoon departure, was that a third teammate had joined the potentially two-week expedition.

When Jake raised his hand to signal to Kovalenko that he was ready to depart the parking garage, Jake was stunned to see a passenger on the Range Rover's front seat.

The garage was sparsely lit, and with only a couple of garage ceiling lights glinting off the Range Rover's windshield, Jake couldn't see who it was. Because of the limited parking garage light and the vehicle's tinted windows, the only thing Jake could see was the dark outline of a human being, clearly seated in the passenger seat.

Jake shut off the motorcycle, dismounted it, and walked over to the passenger side of the Range Rover.

The passenger rolled down the window.

"Holy crap. What the hell are you doing here, Manny?" asked Jake, now smiling a big grin.

"I think it's pretty clear, boss," said Sergeant First Class Manny Alvarez. "I have a lot of respect for our Ukrainian friend being able to handle everything by himself, but you didn't think I'd let you go down there without me, did you?"

Jake stood stunned. He hadn't been at a loss for words like this in a long time.

Finally, some words came.

"Gosh, Manny, did your bride give you a kitchen pass for this little adventure?"

"Yep. Seems she likes you about as much as I do. How freakin' crazy is that?"

Jake looked at Kovalenko.

"Were you part of this deal, Hennadiy?" asked Jake, still quite surprised.

"Maybe," deadpanned Kovalenko.

Jake felt deep gratitude that Alvarez was there, in the flesh. He had known Manny Alvarez for well over ten years, and they had survived some tough scrapes in combat. The fact that Alvarez was willing to risk his life again—with and for Jake—sent Jake's heart soaring. Fortina was surprised at the moisture pooling in his eyes.

But feeling some responsibility for Alvarez and knowing little about how arduous or dangerous their trip might be to the middle of mafia country, Jake had to ask the question, although he knew it was pretty much rhetorical.

"Are you sure about this, Manny?"

"I'm more sure about this than *anything* I've been sure about. I'd be super pissed if you snuck down there without me."

Jake nodded his head.

"And Jake," chimed in Kovalenko. "There's more. Let's have a quick peek in the back. Sergeant Alvarez has, well, been a pretty darn good sergeant lately, haha."

"Lately?" responded Alvarez. "OK, I resemble that remark," he laughed.

Kovalenko popped open the Range Rover's back hatch, and the three soldiers, one retired and two still active, walked around the back.

Alvarez flipped up the tarp and rolled it back. Under the tarp was a tent. He rolled the tent back about halfway. Under the tent was a beat-up old toolbox and an M2A1, .50 caliber ammo storage box. Alvarez wiggled the toolbox out from under the tent. He opened it. Inside the toolbox were three Beretta 9 mm pistols, three sets of night vision goggles, and several boxes of 9 mm ammunition. Alvarez then pulled the ammo box toward them. Inside the .50 cal. box were a set of commercial binoculars and three small walkie-talkie radios. He informed Jake there was also one set of binoculars each under the driver's and passenger's seats.

Jake just shook his head. And then he shook his head some more.

"What, did you think you're the only American with good friends in Italy?" said Alvarez, laughing.

"I shouldn't ask, should I?" asked Jake.

"Nope, don't ask," replied Alvarez.

Alvarez shut the toolbox and ammo box, and Kovalenko and Jake helped him stow and cover the toolbox and ammo can with the tent and then the tent with the tarp. Kovalenko shut the back hatch.

"Let's go find Sara," said Kovalenko.

CHAPTER 75

He Never Existed

"WHAT DO WE STILL NEED THAT RUSSIAN SCUMBAG DOWN THERE FOR?" asked the *Crimine* board member, his question directed at Antonio Di Salva. "It's not like we don't have our own people already at the hideout and others who could do what he is doing...whatever the hell he's doing there now. And besides, I don't know if I feel too comfortable having a former Russian *delinquente* knowing about one of our old hiding places. We used to make millions of lire and euros from hiding people in Aspromonte. The Russian is a hired hand. Do we actually believe he is fully loyal to us?"

Di Salva had to admit if only to himself, *his Crimine colleague had a point.*

The *Capo Crimine*, who was glancing out the window to admire the early April spring day, raised his eyebrows at the word *loyalty*. Turning his attention back to the table, the *Capo* said nothing. Plain-spoken, he was deceptively wise, like an old fox. He preferred hearing everybody in the *Crimine* air their points out and hearing any arguments unfold before intervening or making a final decision. The top of the 'Ndrangheta pyramid was run much like the most effective commercial corporate boards in the world.

In 2021, *Forbes*, according to a report by Italian financial analysis firm *Demoskopika*, reported the 'Ndrangheta's net worth to be $72 billion. In 2013, EUROPOL, the European Union's (27 countries) chief law enforcement agency, estimated the group made about $44 billion annually. The 'Ndrangheta's illicit business activities included embezzling public funds, fraud (European Union subsidies and tax exemptions were favorite targets), and high-level corruption schemes, often involving politicians. Italy's parliament once estimated that 'Ndrangheta also controlled more than 80 percent of Europe's cocaine trade.

Having a Russian operating in their midst was just one of *Crimine's* several agenda items for the morning. Sara Simonetti's disappearance, the lack of information regarding her captors and their location, and the recent leak of those facts to the Italian media put her case back in the national media spotlight. So, the Russian's continued presence was brought to the *Crimine* for discussion and a decision instead of being handled at a lower level.

The *Capo Crimine* realized that if it was ever discovered by the Italian people that the 'Ndrangheta had ever mistreated—or worse, *murdered*—one of Italy's beloved, wholly uncorrupted, and high-profile Carabinieri officers, the 'Ndrangheta would pay dearly. While some Italian government officials looked the other way from the 'Ndrangheta's lucrative crimes, inflaming the Italian population against the 'Ndrangheta might change all that.

After all the *Crimine* members had spoken their piece, save the one who asked Di Salva the question about the Russian to begin with, the *Capo Crimine* spoke.

"The Russian is finished. As far as I'm concerned, he never existed. *Avete capito?*" ("Did you all understand?")

Heads around the table nodded.

The *Capo Crimine* locked eyes with the *Crimine* member who ran the 'Ndrangheta's "disciplinary operations." One of the most loyal and, at the same time, most ruthless members of the group, the man and his team of enforcers oversaw much of the mafia's dirty work, from warning—and scaring the hell out of—wayward mafia members to killing them and making them disappear in any number of ways.

It was clear the *Capo Crimine* wanted the Russian to disappear, as if "he never existed."

CHAPTER 76

Have A Nice Trip

JAKE WAS CRUISING AT 70 MILES PER HOUR when he saw the blue flashing light in his handle-bar-mounted rear-view mirror. He checked his speedometer again, although he knew he was traveling well under the autostrada speed limit of 130 kilometers (80.7 miles)-per-hour. He slowed down to 60 mph.

Did I miss one of those highway signs that indicated I had to drop my speed to 100 kph (60 mph)? He asked himself.

Rechecking his rearview mirror, he saw the answer. The *Guardia di Finanza* (in effect, Italy's customs police) patrol car was not pulling Jake over; it was interested in the gray Range Rover behind him. Jake observed the Range Rover pulling off to the side.

Fortunately, Jake and Colonel Kovalenko had already gone over such contingencies. If either the motorcycle or car got pulled over, the other conveyance would proceed to the next rest stop or exit, whichever came earlier. Once there, the vehicle would wait for a call from the stopped vehicle. They would then decide what actions they should take next.

Accordingly, Jake continued to a rest stop about six miles down the road.

Colonel Hennadiy Kovalenko slowly pulled the vehicle to the highway's narrow, tarmac shoulder. The trio had traveled almost ninety minutes since departing Rome, with Italy's third largest city, Naples, about another hour down the road.

Kovalenko could see the Italian customs officer get out of his car and begin approaching his driver's side window. Alvarez, from his passenger-side mirror, could also see another customs officer exit the passenger side of the patrol car. That officer, however, stayed outside his vehicle and stood next to the passenger door with—although not aiming it—both his hands on his weapon, about waist high. It looked like he was carrying a submachine gun with a leather shoulder strap.

Kovalenko duly rolled down his window. Both he and Alvarez reached for their wallets and pulled out—besides their driver's licenses—the most important document in their wallets: their Diplomatic Identification Card, issued by the Italian government. Within Italy, the cards were domestically every bit as respected as a black diplomatic passport when traveling abroad. If needed as backup, each had brought their diplomatic passports along as well.

"*Buona sera* (good evening) said Kovalenko, handing both Diplomatic ID cards and his driver's license to the officer.

"Buona sera," replied the thirty-something, gray uniformed and armed *Guardia di Finanza* officer.

The officer closely examined both cards, front and back. He looked past Kovalenko to corroborate Alvarez's identity with the photo on the ID card. It matched perfectly.

He promptly handed all three cards back to Kovalenko. The officer was not interested in asking for the vehicle's papers. He knew the two identification cards provided the officers enough immunity for him to not waste any more time with them. But he did have a couple of questions.

"Are you both working in Rome?" asked the officer.

"Yes, I work in my embassy there, and my American colleague works at his."

Alvarez nodded affirmatively, corroborating Kovalenko's perfectly accurate statement.

"Might you be heading down to the Post Exchange at the US Naval Base?" asked the officer. "I hear they have a very nice one down there."

Kovalenko and Alvarez just nodded, smiled, and laughed.

"We just might," said Alvarez.

What the officer said next pleasantly surprised—and almost shocked—Kovalenko and Alvarez.

"Well, I'm glad we are on the same team," said the Italian. "I hate that criminal Puchta and his pathetic minions. Have a nice trip, gentlemen."

"*Grazie*," said Kovalenko and Alvarez, almost simultaneously, before winking at each other.

The officer walked back to his vehicle. He realized he had misjudged the older model Range Rover and the passengers in it. He got into the Fiat patrol car and addressed his partner, who sat back with the submachine gun between his legs.

"Sometimes we find bandits, sometimes we find smugglers, sometimes we find human traffickers, and sometimes we even find mafia, but today I found a very pleasant Ukrainian military officer and an American sergeant. It made my day."

His partner nodded his head in approval.

CHAPTER 77

The Confession

AS THE TRIO CONTINUED SOUTH on the highway, Jake didn't know it, but Palmi, the town that the trio was bypassing and that they could see to the right, over by the coast, was a town where most of 'Ndrangheta's roots were established.

In 1888, a clerk of the local prefecture (an office with both law enforcement and judiciary powers) was slashed across the face as he came out of a theater. Police investigated and ended up rounding up 24 men, who by 1889 had all been arraigned. Several trials ensued.

In a June 1890 trial, a judge described a criminal "association" as having originated in Palmi's prisons. Once released from prison, the association's promoters "spread to other towns and villages where the association found fertile soil among the callow youth, old jailbirds, and especially goatherds." He also noted that the "Society" offered "a way to pasture animals illegally" and a way for goatherds to "impose themselves on landlords."

But Palmi was not Jake's objective. He wanted to be much closer to the Aspromonte area by the next morning, further inland from Palmi and the Tyrrhenian coast. Leaving the *autostrada* and turning inland just after 9:15 p.m., they had about 30 minutes of spring twilight left. They drove roughly six miles, where they found a two-track road leading away from the tarmac road into the foothills. They drove up and down the two-track until they were sure they were not near any houses or barking dogs. It did not take long before they found suitable parking spots back in the trees.

"What do you say, amigos?" asked Jake. "It's not glamping, but it looks like a secure spot."

"Agreed," said Alvarez. "The thick, low-standing pine trees provide good concealment from the road. If the good colonel is OK with it, I'm fine here."

"Done," responded Kovalenko.

They agreed each would pull three-hour guard shifts, staying awake in the Range Rover, while two others were sleeping in the tent. Over a nine-hour period, this would allow 6 hours of total sleep for each. Jake drew the short reed of grass, meaning he had to take the less favorable middle shift, the one which did not allow for six hours of continuous rest.

But in the early morning, with classic Alvarez resourcefulness, Alvarez broke out a Sterno can and, most importantly, a Bialetti aluminum espresso maker.

Jake and Kovalenko were thrilled.

"Hell, Manny, you even brought crème and sugar," said Jake. "Why am I not surprised."

The double espresso kickstarted the trio's day.

***

Back on the road, Jake loved the way the Ducati was performing as he drove farther and higher into the hills away from the Calabrian coastal road. Taking the less traveled road, he headed for the villages of Seminara and Delianouva before continuing east to San Luca (Saint Luke).

Jake kept pressure on the hand-controlled accelerator, and Kovalenko and Alvarez worked hard to stay behind him.

Eventually, after over two hours of travel, Jake and his two followers reached the village of San Luca, where they took a quick break. Jake hadn't ridden a motorcycle in so long that he was sore. Then, they drove another 45 minutes northwest from the village of San Luca. There, Jake pulled up to the medieval monastery and Sanctuary General Ranieri had pointed to. The almost 1000-year-old Sanctuary of the Madonna of *Polsi* was situated in a stunning gorge surrounded by verdant forests, rocky soil, and stunning outcroppings. Jake was awestruck by the mystical beauty and serenity of the Sanctuary's massive stone buildings and the white-stuccoed main church. At 2,850 feet of elevation, the Sanctuary was surrounded on its east side by mountains, including Montalto, Aspromonte's highest peak at 6,450 feet.

Jake had done his homework before leaving Rome. Jake knew the church and monastery were founded in 1144 by Roger II, a Norman King who somewhat amazingly unified Sicily under Christians, Jews, and the few Muslims remaining from the once-Muslim Emirate of Sicily (827–902). By 1091, Norman (Viking-descendant) tribes had conquered all of Sicily and southern mainland Italy, known in modern times as Calabria.

To this day, the Sanctuary holds a much-venerated statue of Madonna, carved from volcanic rock by a Sicilian artist circa 1560. Each year, on September 2, worshippers come from all over Calabria and eastern Sicily, making the Sanctuary an interesting if not peculiar mix of 'Ndrangheta Mafia members and the local, non-mafia-affiliated southern Italian and Sicilian faithful.

The 'Ndrangheta's affinity for the Sanctuary was first recorded in the reports of Carabinieri Captain Giuseppe Petella in 1903. Petella reported annual meetings between "several criminal societies" at the shrine. A former 'Ndrangheta member turned state witness (far rarer among the 'Ndrangheta than other Italian Mafia organizations), Cesare Polifroni, confessed that at the annual meetings, every boss "must give an account of all the activities carried out during the year...including kidnappings, homicides, etc."

In 1969, the police raided the mafia's so-called Montalto summit, held on the grounds of the Sanctuary. The Carabinieri raid netted more than 70 *'Ndranghetisti*, although some managed to escape. It was later discovered that mafia bosses from as far away as Canada and Australia regularly attended 'Ndrangheta meetings on the margins of the September 2 holy day at the Sanctuary.

Jake wasted no time in parking his motorcycle in a designated tourist parking area and in walking toward the main church, about 200 yards away. Kovalenko and Alvarez pulled the Range Rover into a parking space next to Jake's motorcycle, allowing them to keep an eye on the motorcycle as well as the Range Rover and, more importantly, its contents.

As he approached the monastery's church, Jake was intrigued. The tourists were relatively few, as the main visiting period, from late June through September, was more than a couple of months away. From mid-June through September, roughly 50,000 people converged on the remote holy place. The greatest concentration would arrive for the holy celebrations from August 31–September 2.

Jake entered the white-facade church's main doors. He paused to examine the church's cream white interior, estimating that it was probably built—or remodeled—in the late 1700s or early 1800s. He left the church's nave through a side door to seek out a priest.

It was not often that tourists sought out priests at the Sanctuary, although it did happen every so often. Most visitors were there to see the Madonna sculpture and the historically impressive stone structures. Those few visitors who did seek out a priest normally came to ask for God's blessings for a sick family member or themselves. Occasionally, the faithful would come in to ask a priest to hear their confession. That was Jake's approach.

Jake found a few side doors off a narrow, stone-covered hallway. As he looked through the first open door he encountered, Jake saw a priest in his robes, seated behind a small desk in what appeared to be the priest's cluttered and humble office. The priest was surprised to see Jake just walk right in.

"Father," said Jake in Italian. "I need some help. I would like to give my confession…but I also need some *help*."

The somewhat portly, fifty-something priest had ashy blond and gray hair and blue eyes. He looked quizzically at Jake. The priest detected a slight accent in Jake's Italian. But he also appreciated Jake's direct approach.

"Where are you from, *Signore*?" asked the priest.

"I just traveled down from Rome, sir," Jake replied.

"Well, you might *look* Italian, but you are obviously not from Rome," the priest commented.

"No, I'm not," responded Jake, realizing it was useless to lie to the man *and certainly not to a priest*, thought Jake.

"Where then?" asked the priest. "You sound like you might have a slightly northern Italian accent, but I don't think you're from the north, either. Your northern Italian accent seems to be mixed with another accent. You speak a very clear Italian but it's also a very peculiar sounding Italian."

The priest, who was of Irish origin, had been in Calabria for eight years and another 25 in central Italy. In his first 25 years as a parish priest, he had heard thousands of confessions. And being in a country where over 75 percent of the citizens claimed to be Catholic, he was completely OK with that. Besides, the local food and, more importantly, the wine were excellent.

"I'm from the *Stati Uniti* (United States)," replied Jake.

"Well, that's a very big place," said the priest. "My brother lives in New York. Where are you from? Texas? California?

And what's your name?"

"I'm from Michigan, and my name is Jake Fortina."

"Well, I got the Italian part right, didn't I?" said the priest, smiling.

"You did," Jake returned his smile.

"So, what do you do in life, Mister Fortina?" asked the priest.

"I am...or I *was*...a US Army officer until some weeks ago. I just retired."

The priest's eyes lit up.

"At what rank, if I might ask?"

"Lieutenant colonel," responded Jake.

Surprisingly—and somewhat embarrassingly for Jake and his humble disposition—the priest raised his right hand and saluted Jake.

Jake nodded and smiled.

Not a bad salute, thought Jake.

"Please sit down," said the priest, pointing at the single knobby wooden chair in front of his desk.

As Jake sat down, the priest reached under his desk.

"Well, it's a wee bit early," declared the priest. "But it's almost lunchtime."

As the priest's hand came from under the desk and back into view, Jake could see that it was holding an unlabeled, non-descript, corked, one-liter, brown glass bottle. He set the bottle on the desktop, reached into the lower right drawer of his desk, and pulled out two six-ounce clear glasses. They weren't wine glasses but rather were more like the glasses you might find in a hotel room...at the bathroom sink.

As the priest got up to lock the office door, Jake quickly glanced at this watch and saw that it was 11:25 a.m.

It's about an hour or two before any self-respecting southern Italian would have lunch, thought Jake, his eyes smiling.

The priest returned to his chair behind the desk, grabbed

the bottle, and poured red wine into both glasses, each to about two-thirds full.

"You are not allergic to red wine, are you?" asked the priest.

Jake laughed.

"Not at all, Father, not at all. You just noted that I *am* Italian, correct?"

The priest chortled. He raised his glass to eye level, and Jake mirrored him.

"From one soldier to another," said the priest.

"From one soldier to another," repeated Jake.

Both men took a drink of their wine. Jake was surprised at how good it tasted.

"Did you serve?" asked Jake.

"I did, and so did my grandfather," said the priest. "My grandfather landed at Anzio (Italy) with the First Battalion, Irish Guards, in January 1944, and he helped your Yankee forefathers liberate Rome on June 4, 1944. My grandfather then fought all the way up the peninsula. My interest in Italy came completely from him. As for me, I served for two years with the Royal Irish Rangers before they became part of the Royal Irish Regiment in 1992...when I joined the priesthood."

"Wow, I heard the Royal Irish Rangers were a pretty badass bunch," said Jake.

The priest smiled his broadest smile yet, showing his imperfect, wine-stained teeth.

"How about you, colonel? What's your story?" asked the priest.

"I'm just an old infantry officer who ended up in a military attaché assignment in Rome," said Jake.

The priest nodded, understanding that Jake did not want to—and probably couldn't—say more.

"What's your real reason for coming here?" asked the priest. "Somehow, I don't think you're here to give your confession. How can I help you?"

Jake took a deep breath and exhaled, looking into the priest's eyes. He proceeded to tell the priest of Sara's kidnapping and the real reason he was there: to find his wife.

The priest's countenance changed from curious to empathetic and serious.

"I see," he said. "I'm very sorry to hear that, my lad," he continued, even though he was only about a dozen years older than Jake.

"Listen," he said. "I wish I could tell you more, but the reality of the matter is, I just don't know much more than you do already. I know that just west and north of us, in the heart of Aspromonte…that place was a kidnapping haven for many years. The terrain is really, really rough there. It reminds me of what I once read about your area in America called Appalachia, with all its so-called hollers. That's what they're called, right? Hollers?"

The priest looked at Jake for affirmation.

"Yep, you got it," answered Jake. "Holler is correct."

"There seems to be a gorge or small valley every couple of hundred yards or so," continued the priest. "Most of that kidnapping for ransom business in Aspromonte ended in the late 1990s. Perhaps they are starting up again."

The priest paused. He became pensive and took another drink of his wine. He rubbed his chin.

"Listen," he said. "I have a good friend who runs the diocese in Oppido Mamertina. It's about two hours from here."

"I remember it. It's back the way I came. I saw signs of it on my way here," said Jake.

Jake did not know it, but the 5,500-population town was 'Ndrangheta central, with another town, Polistena—just to the north of Oppido Mamertina—equally mafia infested.

"Well, you need to go back there and talk to my friend, Bishop Rodrigo Catalan. He's a Spaniard, but he's been in Italy for the past 24 years. We studied together as young priests in the Vatican for a couple of years. He advanced through the ranks more rapidly than me," said the priest, laughing, "and for good reason. He's getting close to retirement, but he still has balls of steel and the faith of Saint Paul. The mafia can't touch him. And if they did, the Vatican—and the Carabinieri—would bring fire and brimstone on the mafia, and they know it."

Jake nodded, his heart becoming ever more grateful.

"What kind of car are you driving?" asked the priest.

"I'm riding a motorcycle," replied Jake.

"A motorcycle? Oh, right, I forgot, you're an infantry officer," said the priest, chuckling.

Jake laughed.

"It's a Ducati," replied Jake.

"Well, at least you are on a good Italian bike. Is anyone with you?"

"Yes, I have two friends with me in a separate vehicle, an older model Range Rover," answered Jake.

"Listen, Jake, it will not do for you and your buddies to go roaring into Oppido Mamertina together. I recommend—no, I demand—that you go into town alone. The fact that you are riding on an Italian motorcycle and look Italian will help. Be sure not to have one of your buddies riding on the back of it. That's how hits are carried out around here, with two guys on a motorcycle or a motor scooter. The back guy is always the shooter. If two of you go into town on that motorcycle, it will seriously raise eyebrows. Got it?"

"I understand," replied Jake.

"There is only one way for you to do this: do not stop anywhere in town and drive straight to the church. Drive straight out of town when you're done meeting with the bishop. Make sure you are not being followed. I will call you within two hours with further instructions once I speak with Bishop Catalan. I have his private cell phone number, and he always answers me as soon as he can. This visit might work for this afternoon, but it will likely have to wait until tomorrow or maybe the day after."

"Understood," replied Jake. "I'm deeply grateful."

CHAPTER 78

Thankful

LIA WAS DELIGHTED AS SHE CAREFULLY DESCENDED THE STEPS. Gio had told her that "the boys" were coming to take the Russian away. She did not know what the Russian's fate would be, although she suspected it would not be good. She had zero remorse for the Russian. But she felt delighted for her captive, knowing that Sara would no longer be taunted and tortured, mentally and physically.

Lia knew that she had crossed a mental and emotional line concerning Sara Simonetti. In the beginning, Lia was able to play tough with the Carabinieri officer. She realized she would even have done the unspeakable if the mafia *capos* had ordered it. But now, she felt different, and there was no going back.

But how is it that I like this person? Lia asked herself. *What the hell is wrong with me*?

Lia vaguely remembered her father talking about some hostage and captor "syndrome" from Scandinavia. She searched her mind to try to remember what her father had said.

I wonder if I have a similar syndrome? she asked herself.

The affair that launched the naming of the so-called Stockholm Syndrome Lia was trying to recall began on August 23, 1973, when an escaped Swedish convict walked into *Sveriges Kreditbank*, situated on the *Norrmalmstorg* Square in Stockholm, Sweden. The man held up the bank and took three female hostages, with a fourth male later discovered to be hidden in a stockroom. A hostage crisis ensued. The bank robber insisted that the police bring the robber's famous—or, more accurately, infamous—accomplice (who, as a serial bank robber, was a near-celebrity in Sweden) from prison to join him, and the police complied. By day two of the six-day crisis, the four hostages grew sympathetic to the plight of their two captors.

"I fully trust Clark (the accomplice) and the robber," said Kristin Enmark, one of the hostages. "I am not desperate. They haven't done a thing to us. On the contrary, they have been very nice. But you know…what I am scared of is that the police will attack and cause us to die."

By day three, the hostages reported from inside the bank that the hostages had formed a "bond of friendship" with their captors. The entire affair was filmed live, making it the first crime in Sweden to be covered by live television. The crisis ended on day six when police were able to complete the drilling of holes through the bank's ceiling and force tear gas into the bank. The captors gave up, and the hostages were allowed out of the bank first. In a scene that suggests life is stranger than fiction, some of the hostages hugged and kissed their captors, and in one case, a hostage asked her captor to write to her.

Lia, most decidedly, did not have Stockholm syndrome, but she wondered if she might have the opposite side of the same "syndrome."

"Good morning, *Signora*," said Lia.

"Good morning, Lia," responded Sara.

Sara was stunned at what Lia was carrying on a plastic cafeteria tray as she came through the cell door: two slices of olive oil-coated bread, an apple, and two hard-boiled eggs.

Sara looked at the tray, a tear forming in her eye.

"I thought you could use some protein," said Lia.

"*Mille grazie,*" said Sara.

"How are you feeling today?" asked Lia.

"I could use a good run," said Sara, chuckling, realizing it was the first time she had chuckled and almost laughed out loud since before she had found out about Captain Bondanella's death on the outskirts of Rome. "But I'm thankful."

"Thankful for what, Sara?" asked Lia.

"Thankful to be alive, thankful that my child seems to be doing well, and I'm thankful for you, Lia."

Lia was now the one who was stunned. Lia had never told Sara her name, but as Lia thought about it for a moment, she realized Sara must have heard her name on their first day traveling to the hideout or perhaps after the scuffle with the Russian.

I have never heard anyone say, "I'm thankful for you," not even my own family members, thought Lia.

CHAPTER 79

Stubborn

JAKE MANEUVERED THE DUCATI ALONG THE SP2 (*strada provinciale* or provincial road). The narrow tarmac road—winding through the steep, rocky, and intermittently forested terrain, without road markers between the two lanes—was barely wide enough for two cars. In the narrower spots, especially around the hairpin corners and switchbacks, oncoming cars had to slow down to about five or ten mph before passing each other. Fortunately, Jake had only come upon two cars in the last ten miles of the trip from the Sanctuary.

Jake turned off the tarmac road and onto a gravel road. In the Range Rover, Kovalenko and Alvarez were right behind him. Within two hundred yards, Jake drove the motorcycle off the gravel road to the exact spot—adjacent to an olive grove—where the Irish priest told him to park the Range Rover before continuing to Oppido Mamertina on the motorcycle. The spot was on the property of a small olive grove and chicken farm owned by a rare local resident who had not sold his soul to the 'Ndrangheta.

"The man is a devout and true friend of the Catholic Church," the Irish priest had said.

The trio was six miles from Oppido Mamertina.

"Well, that was fun," said Alvarez as he got out of the Range Rover to stretch his legs. "For a minute there, with this crazy terrain, I thought we were back in Afghanistan."

Jake nodded his head and smiled.

"OK, gents, this is where you guys need to hang tight until I come back. Try to stay out of trouble, will ya?" said Jake.

"I think *you're* the one who needs to stay out of trouble," Kovalenko shot back.

"I'll do my best," said Jake. "I'll be pulling out of here in about fifteen minutes. As we discussed, I'll drive into town and straight to the church. I don't expect to be at the church for longer than thirty minutes. They'll be expecting me. I'll have my phone with me, but who knows how coverage will be there or here. If I'm not back in ninety minutes, do NOT send the dogs for me. I don't want you guys getting caught in an ambush or some kind of trap."

Alvarez checked his phone.

"I show two bars. Whoops, I now show one. The coverage looks spotty here."

"Ok, that's it then. If you can't reach me, don't come for me. Get out of dodge and head home," implored Jake.

"What do you think the chances of us heading home are, boss?" asked Alvarez.

Jake shook his head.

"Manny, listen…" replied Jake, before Kovalenko interrupted him.

"He's right, Jake," interjected Kovalenko. "There is no way in hell we're leaving you behind. Besides, you should know us better than that."

A brief silence descended upon the group.

"We came here with you, and we're *leaving* here with *you*… sir," said Alvarez, breaking the silence. "I seem to remember a certain Green Beret captain having said something like that to a bunch of soldiers a long time ago in a faraway place."

More silence.

"OK, OK. Roger that," replied Jake, nodding.

"You guys are a helluva lot more *stubborn* than I thought," added Jake. "If I would have known you were this damn stubborn, I would have rethought this whole deal."

Jake smiled, and his two battle buddies smiled back.

***

Jake entered the outskirts of the 5,500-inhabitant town of Oppido Mamertina. It was 3:25 p.m., and the warm Calabrian sun was still high. Jake's destination was *La Cattedrale di Santa Maria Assunta* (the Cathedral of the Assumption of Saint Mary). It was one of several cathedrals of a similar name in Italy, including locations in Florence and Vicenza.

As Jake made his way through the narrow streets to the church, he saw a middle-aged woman dressed in black mourning clothes and then another older woman who was also in black. Other than a few parked cars and one small farm tractor, the streets were bare of activity. It was siesta time, and most local shops—a few bakeries, butcher shops, houseware establishments, and bars—would not reopen until 4:30 or 5 p.m.

This place feels like it hasn't changed since the 1950s, thought Jake.

Rare were the stone-walled and stucco street-front homes and shops—one attached to the other—that were not gray or light brown from decades and even centuries of weathering and decay.

These are not the colorful building facades of Amalfi, Peschiera-del-Garda, or Portofino, thought Jake.

The town's origins went much farther back than the 1950s, with the Greeks first having settled in the area in the fourth century BC. The first recorded mention of the town as a fortress was in 1040, during the Byzantine Era. The town's claim to fame, some 20 years after its existence was first recorded, was for its prolonged resistance against the conqueror Roger I ("the Norman"), to whom it finally fell in 1056.

Jake headed toward the church plaza. It was easy to find because it was the cultural center of the town, where a weekly outdoor market was held. Its roughly five-story clock tower was only slightly higher than the church itself, and both Catholic edifices were higher than any other building in the town.

Easing the motorcycle across the sun-splashed plaza, he parked it in the limited parking spaces to the left of the church's front entrance. He dismounted the Ducati and walked up to the massive, 12-foot-high, double-wooden doors that were part of the two-story building that extended from the church's left side. Inside the church's extension building were the bishop's living quarters and office, the attending priests' quarters, and offices for a few support staff.

Jake pushed the black doorbell button located on the right side of the big doors. He could barely hear the bell buzzing through the thick doors. Jake heard some metal jiggling and heavy metal clunking. The door to the right was pulled back, opening inward about a foot.

"*Buongiorno*," said a white-haired monsignor, peering through the narrow open space.

"*Buongiorno*," replied Jake. "I'm here to see Bishop Catalan. My name is..."

"Yes, I know who you are," interrupted the monsignor. "Please come in."

The monsignor stepped back, opened the door another foot wider, and said, "*Prego* (please)."

Jake walked in, and the monsignor shut and locked the door behind him.

"Come with me," said the ramrod straight 59-year-old monsignor, wearing his gray priest's clergy shirt with white collar.

He led Jake almost the full length of the high-ceilinged

and stone-floored hallway. Along the way, Jake noted that the walls were covered in oil portraits of former bishops dating back to the early 1800s. The monsignor stopped at the last door on the right.

The monsignor lightly tapped on the robust office doorframe and said, "*Permesso* (with your permission)," slightly raising his voice.

Jake understood this was the courteous Italian way to announce your presence in private locations—including homes—where others might be present.

Jake followed the monsignor into the large, high-ceilinged office, where a civilian man with a white long-sleeved shirt and black pants was standing next to the seated bishop.

The bishop nodded to the monsignor, and the monsignor left the office.

Jake approached the elderly man, whom Jake estimated to be around 70. The man had chalk-white hair, dark eyes, and a healthy-looking, if slightly red, tan, evidently from overexposure to the sun. Jake had been around people of high authority—senior general officers, ambassadors, foreign ministers, and even a couple of heads of state—but he had never felt a presence of authority like this.

Jake extended his hand to shake. Jake felt encouraged when the bishop responded to Jake's courteous gesture by nodding, smiling, and—still seated—putting out his right hand.

"I'm Jake Fortina, Your Excellency," said Jake, bending and shaking the man's hand.

"So I've heard," said the man in perfect American English. "Excuse me for not standing up, but I sort of overdid it while hiking recently. Please have a seat."

"Thank you, sir," replied Jake.

"Can I offer you a Coca-Cola?" asked the bishop.

Jake smiled. He'd never once been offered a Coke in Europe, let alone Italy. He felt like the man was anxious to be hospitable, and Jake responded accordingly.

"That is very kind, sir...Your Excellency, thank you," replied Jake.

The bishop nodded to his attendant, who looked at Jake.

"With ice, sir?" asked the attendant.

"Sure, that would be great, thank you."

Within two minutes, the attendant was back with two glasses filled with Coca-Cola, each with a slice of lemon in it.

The bishop smiled.

"The lemon is from our nearby lemon groves," said Bishop Catalan. "And I can have rum added to it if you'd like."

"No, thank you, bishop," responded Jake. "This is wonderful."

The bishop gestured toward his attendant, who left the room and shut the massive wooden, 220-year-old office door behind him.

Jake took a drink of the Coke. He was surprised at how refreshing it was with the local lemon slice.

"Sir, your English...it's *very* good," said Jake.

"Thank you," replied Bishop Catalan. "Before I joined the priesthood, two of my buddies and I bought an old station wagon outside of New York City and traveled across your beautiful country, taking over three months to do it. We saw a lot of the sights: the Empire State Building, Niagara Falls, the Grand Canyon, Utah's national parks, the California Redwoods, San Francisco, Los Angeles, and *a lot* of places in between. We went from Catholic parish to parish, painting parish living quarters, fixing fences, laying concrete, refinishing pews, trimming trees, whatever quick work we could find for a few bucks, some hot meals, and a few nights of good rest. It was amazing. I learned a lot about how culturally varied and vast your geographically blessed country is. When our trip was done, we sold the car in LA and almost got what we paid for it."

The bishop smiled a big smile, and so did Jake.

"I bet that trip was really something, sir," said Jake.

"It was," said the bishop. He paused before continuing. "Listen, Jake. My dear Irish friend told me what you are up to. I think you are crazy. But I fully understand your motivation. You must know that you're taking a huge risk that could cost you your life."

Jake nodded.

"I do know that," replied Jake.

"Good," replied bishop.

On the small round walnut table—a bit larger than a nightstand—between their plush, nineteenth-century wood and cloth chairs, was a one-page, 1:50,000 scale black and white copy of a map covering most of Aspromonte.

The bishop picked up the paper, leaned toward Jake, and pointed to the map.

"There are buildings here, here, and here," said the bishop. "They belong—or at least they used to belong—to the 'Ndrangheta. But then again, almost everything around here has the 'Ndrangheta's stamp on it. Everything...but this diocese."

The bishop had penciled *X*s on the buildings' locations. He then highlighted each X with a yellow highlighter.

Jake's eyebrows were raised.

"I know what you're thinking," said the bishop. "How do I know about those buildings? Right?"

"Well..." Jake hesitated while he began to formulate an answer, and the bishop interrupted him.

"It's OK, I understand," said the bishop. "Do you remember Pope John Paul II?"

"I certainly do," said Jake, referring to the Polish pontiff and the first non-Italian to be elected Pope in four and half centuries.

"Well, he loved the outdoors. Within one year after I was

ordained, the Italian bishop who ordained me in the Vatican—and who loved that I spoke fluent Spanish, excellent English, and very good Italian—found a way for me to do a sort of internship, although it was not called that back then. It was basically an administrative position on the Pope's staff, intended to assist the Pope whenever he traveled. That was over thirty years ago, 13 years before Pope John Paul II died. Even in his early seventies, the Pope was a real outdoorsman, and he was as fit as a fiddle. He loved to hike, and at times, I was one of the *blessed* people who got to go with him."

"I have hiked all over Aspromonte.," continued the bishop. "It's difficult because the terrain can be unforgiving if you venture in the wrong places and don't know where the sudden cliffs are, but I learned a lot in my 25 years of hiking in Calabria. Of course, I never went alone, and the mafia wouldn't dare touch me."

Jake's respect for the bishop's grit and courage soared.

"Listen," continued the bishop, "I will retire next year. But before I do, I don't want to ever read or hear in the news that you have been seriously hurt or, worse, have gone missing. Understand?"

"Yes, sir, I understand," replied Jake.

"Then go with God," said the bishop.

CHAPTER 80

Anybody Home?

JAKE, COLONEL KOVALENKO, AND SERGEANT FIRST CLASS ALVAREZ were encouraged. They had found the first of three structures the bishop had pointed out on the simple map. The three soldiers were lying in the increasingly damp grass since the sun had set about two hours earlier. Alvarez and Jake were wearing the old US Army Battle Dress Uniforms (BDU) brought along by Alvarez. The uniforms were devoid of any patches or attachments. BDUs were officially in service from the early 1980s until being phased out in 2008 when the army's new daily-use uniform became the digital Universal Camouflage Pattern uniform. However, given the Calabrian forests and terrain, the BDU's camouflage pattern worked the best. Kovalenko was wearing his country's version of the Air Force Field Uniform. All three were also wearing night vision goggles.

"It's been going on three hours since we've been here," whispered Jake from their elevated perch about 80 yards from the decaying white concrete building.

"We've seen nothing...no activity, no light emanating from the shutters...nothing."

"Roger that," replied Alvarez. "I say we check out that two-track road that leads up to it for recent vehicle tracks. If we see no tire tracks or other tracks, we can be pretty sure there is nobody inside."

"Concur," said Kovalenko. "But should we also maybe check out the building to be completely sure?"

"I think that makes good sense," whispered Jake.

The three men started moving down the slight incline toward the building, hand-carrying their pistols. Larger, fourteen-inch diameter leafy trees were intermixed with saplings, and there was intermittent brush and deadfall.

Kovalenko stepped on a big, two-inch thick branch that was suspended from a fallen tree before the trio had gone even ten yards. It made a loud "crack" sound, echoing through the trees and increasingly damp night.

Jake raised his right hand to signal his two comrades to stop and then, just to be sure, said "freeze" with a voice slightly above a whisper and within earshot of Alvarez and Kovalenko.

All three men stood like statues in the blackness. Jake and Alvarez listened for a full minute. No sounds. That was good because it meant the sound had not alerted anybody—not even dogs—in the nearby vicinity, including at the stone building.

Jake eased back to within a couple of feet of Kovalenko and put his hand on Kovalenko's shoulder.

"Hey, Hennadiy," said Jake, "I know you're a badass fighter pilot, but do you think we might be able to move through this forest without sounding like a herd of elephants?"

Alvarez grinned widely.

"It's been a minute or two since I did my escape and survival training," said the Ukrainian colonel, "but I hear you. I will try."

Jake raised his left hand up near Kovalenko's face, giving the colonel a "thumbs up" that Kovalenko could see through his night vision goggles.

Jake turned toward the building and raised his right hand—as if he was taking an oath—and moved it in a slightly forward motion. The trio continued.

Jake and Alvarez arrived at the narrow two-track road at

about the same time and about four yards from each other. Kovalenko was a few steps back.

Through their NVGs, both Jake and Alvarez observed the trail and then got down on one knee to feel the road's surface. It was heavily overgrown with weeds and even a few half-inch tree saplings. There was no evidence of tire or human tracks.

Jake stood up and signaled to both men to follow him up to the house.

Jake signaled to Kovalenko to move up right behind him—and Alvarez instinctively did the same, signaling Kovalenko to bring up the rear. The trio moved from the side of the building to its front.

As Jake moved forward, he could see the two large wooden front doors with a hasp lock running between them. But there was only a rusty nail securing the lock. There was no padlock.

Jake gently took out the nail, grabbed the metal hasp, and then pulled the door open.

The door's rusted hinges made a loud creaking noise.

Those things are in serious need of some oil, thought Alvarez.

Jake entered the damp and dusty space first, and the other two followed. The floor was covered in dirt. Overhead were several rafters and several more spider webs. Jake noted some rickety-looking steps in the corner. He signaled to the two men to wait as he stepped toward the stairs.

He realized with the first step on the stairs that they were so rotted his foot might go through the wood at any moment. He had to see the upstairs though, just to be doubly sure that Sara was not up there, and he could fully eliminate this place as her holding place.

Putting much of his weight on the railings to take the weight off the steps, he finally reached the opening to the upstairs. He put his gloved hand on an old wooden door, about six inches open, and pushed it back.

He stepped into the concrete-floored second-story room. Besides some empty old wine bottles, there was a single old wooden chair near the shuttered window and nothing else in the dusty and musty space. Well, at least there were no other solid objects. But there was something on the wall.

A swastika about a foot high was engraved into the concrete. Beside it were the words, in about four-inch-tall letters, "Heil Hitler!"

Heading back for the door and the steps, Jake realized that while the 'Ndrangheta *might* have used this place to hide hostages, the German Wehrmacht soldiers who were in the area through the mid-winter of 1944 had *definitely* been here.

And, most importantly, he thought, *Sara is not here, nor is there any evidence she was held here.*

Jake mentally checked the first of the three buildings off his list.

CHAPTER 81

Jackpot?

THE SHEPHERD WAS MOVING HIS FLOCK along as quickly as it would go, just off the side of the gravel road.

He is moving them to fresh pastures, thought Jake as he slowly eased the Ducati past the sheep while giving them plenty of room and showing respect to the shepherd, his energetic dog, and his forty or so bleating companions.

A biblical verse popped into Jake's brain. He had just read it that morning. It was from the book of John, Chapter 10, verses 27–28: "My sheep hear My voice, and I know them, and they follow Me. And I give them eternal life, and they shall never perish; neither shall anyone snatch them out of My hand."

As the Range Rover moved by the shepherd, Manny Alvarez got a good look at him. Alvarez's observance and sensing skills had not declined since he had departed the US Army Special Forces as a medic some six years prior.

He looks to be about 18, maybe 20, he thought.

Alvarez observed that the young man was wearing a weather-beaten brown hat. It was much like the old, olive green "boonie" hats US Army Green Berets wore in Vietnam—and was being reintroduced to some Army units in 2024—or that might be seen almost any time in the Australian outback. The shepherd was carrying a black backpack and was wearing well-worn but modern hiking shoes with thick soles. He also carried about a six-foot-high wooden staff, useful for navigating difficult terrain.

That's standard equipment for a shepherd, chuckled Alvarez.

Other than a quick glance, the shepherd paid neither Jake nor the Range Rover much mind. Tourists, mainly curious Germans and Brits, occasionally ventured or stumbled into this area, with their geographical or historical curiosity and their noses the only things leading them.

The tourists were told—or had heard—that "as long as you don't get in their way, the mafia will pretty much leave you alone." And that was *pretty much* true.

"It's a *maremmano-abruzzese*," said Kovalenko.

"Excuse me?" asked Alvarez, not sure what Kovalenko had said.

"The dog," replied Kovalenko, a dog lover. "It's from Italy, from the Maremma, or southwestern Tuscany, and Abruzzo areas. That breed, also called the Maremma sheepdog, is nicknamed the 'Wolf Crusher.' They date back to Roman times. Wolves don't stand a chance against them."

Alvarez nodded his head and took a good look at the large, roughly eighty to ninety-pound sheepdog.

"He does look pretty powerful," said Alvarez.

Manny considered asking the shepherd where a certain dwelling might be that the trio had been looking for. He and Jake felt strongly they were within a half-mile of it, thinking they had perhaps just missed a hard-to-see turnoff or trail.

Is this kid part of the local mafia? Alvarez asked himself.

He decided not to ask the kid about the dwelling, *which must be nearby*, Alvarez thought.

In fact, the kid was not part of the 'local mafia,' which was a rarity but not impossible for people from these parts. The teenager's father had been killed by the 'Ndrangheta when he was three years old, and the young man's faithful grandmother had raised—and prayed—the kid into decency. The shepherd knew that sheepherding was not going to be for his entire life.

With movie star looks, the athletically fit *Calabrese* had met a Dutch girl while walking on one of Calabria's nearby beaches some two weeks prior. He had told the pretty blond, blue-eyed girl—who said she was in Italy "to learn some Italian"—that he worked in a local hospital and that he was about to attend university farther north, in Bologna, in September. Both were lies, but the kid knew he'd fallen hard for the Dutch girl, and anyway, he wanted a new and different life.

She, on the other hand, had found temporary seasonal work at the four-star international Gardenia Hotel located near the beach, just south of Reggio Calabria. Her intentions were nothing more than to have a spring fling with the attractive and perpetually bronzed Calabrian, and if it lasted through the summer, she had no intentions of allowing it to get serious before she returned to Amsterdam in the fall.

***

The trio parked their vehicles in a heavy pine tree stand, well off the gravel road and well secluded from passersby on the road. Jake suggested that they travel "by foot express" because they had not managed to find the building while traveling on the motorcycle or in the Range Rover.

They were searching for the second of the three dwellings that Bishop Catalan had pointed out. Jake recommended they wait for nightfall and use their night vision goggles to traverse the challenging, thickly wooded terrain in the direction they thought the secluded building should be.

As night fell, the men rechecked their water, shoulder holsters and pistols, ammo, night vision goggles, extra batteries, beef jerky and trail mix, and rucksacks for some extra layers for when the night temperatures dropped into the low 50s or high 40s.

"Manny, let's move in a triangle formation, with me on point, and you taking the right flank and rear, with Colonel Kovalenko on the left rear and covering the left flank. Remember to frequently check behind us," Jake said to both of his companions. "Let's keep about 10 to 12 meters (about 35 to 40 feet) between us. Don't ever let the distance get any more than that because we don't want to get separated. If we come upon some thick stuff, let's close it up to two to three meters between each of us. Any questions? Hennadiy, are you OK with this?"

Jake knew that Alvarez understood exactly how to move in a reduced and simple tactical formation like this, but he wanted to be sure that the former Ukrainian Air Force pilot fully understood.

Kovalenko gave Jake a single thumbs up and replied with a confident, if slightly accented, "Roger."

"Good," replied Jake.

***

At full dark, they began their movement through an area with large deciduous trees and a fairly bare, uncluttered ground beneath them. Jake moved with stealth, exaggerating the way he picked up his feet and gently placing each step back down again, trying to almost feel through the soles of his shoes what was beneath each step.

The team moved slowly but steadily and even more slowly as they went through new terrain, still with trees but now with thicker undergrowth. Jake motioned to the duo behind him to get closer. After about 200 yards of advancing on a slight downslope, Jake raised his right hand. He almost didn't have to. Immediately after the trailing duo saw Jake's hand go up, signaling the two to stop, Alvarez and Kovalenko saw the same thing Jake did.

The three men froze in place. Jake reached for his night vision goggle tubes and adjusted their binocular focus.

Manny got us some good gear here, thought Jake.

Alvarez and Kovalenko were doing the same thing.

Jake and his two teammates wanted to be sure of what they were looking at.

Off in the distance, they could see a faint light emanating from what they thought was a single small window about eight or ten feet off the ground. Above that, the two-story building seemed to have some shutters, with a bit of light leaking out from the sides of the shutters.

Jake could also tell that the wooded area they were in only had maybe 20 yards to go before it ended and opened out to a clearing. The building they were looking at was maybe 70 yards or so across the clearing, barely set back into some trees, with the side of the house they were looking at on the clearing's edge.

"We need a better look," said Jake, thinking he'd leave the two men there and then do a recon of the other side of the building.

"I'll do it," replied Alvarez, already quietly moving off to his right.

"Manny!" whispered Jake as quietly but forcefully as he could, hoping to get Alvarez to stop.

Alvarez did not hesitate. He'd heard Jake's whisper but had no intention of responding.

Jake shook his head but remained quiet. The fact was Jake totally trusted Alvarez to get the job done.

Jake moved over to Kovalenko and motioned to him to get down. He then whispered to Kovalenko, "You observe this area," while pointing to a 180-degree swath of forest and clearing running from Kovalenko's left front to his left rear.

"I'll take this side," said Jake, sitting down in the dirt with a tree to his back. The two men were no more than six feet apart, each facing in opposite directions, much like mature deer or elk do when they stop to bed down.

Alvarez continued to move counterclockwise around the clearing, always keeping about 15 yards of trees between him and the open clearing. He had learned as a teenaged hunter that clearings are great hunting spots for deer, and after he joined the Green Berets, this was driven home about humans, too. A clearing, much like a road or a dry riverbed, is a dangerous area for an infantryman. By staying at least 15 or 20 yards or so back from the clearing, he knew his odds of being spotted went down dramatically, while his odds of surviving went up by a similar amount.

It's highly unlikely that anybody has NVGs out here, he thought, *but you can never be too sure.*

Still inside the trees and about 50 yards from the back of the building, while it was at a bit of an angle, Alvarez could see the small opening high up on the first floor.

It seems to have a bar or two running vertically through it, he thought, his heart rate increasing, *but I'm not sure. We'll have to wait for confirmation in the morning. But those, for sure, are window shutters above the opening.*

Alvarez continued on his way, needing to get a better look.

So far, thankfully, no barking dogs, he thought, knowing barking dogs were more than a nuisance when trying to do a good reconnaissance of a place, day or night.

Slowly moving with all due stealth and keeping about 40 yards from the building, he moved around to the building's front side or back side from where Jake and Kovalenko observed the building. There, he saw a Jeep SUV parked about 10 feet from the building. Looking at the building's front façade, he saw a single wooden entrance door with no windows on that side of the first floor. There was a shuttered window on the second floor, smaller than the shuttered one on the backside.

Seeing the car, he wanted to locate the road leading up to the building. Taking no more than another fifteen steps, he found a simple, narrow, two-track, muddy road cutting its way through the thick forest to his right.

He continued his movement, not retracing his steps but beginning to complete a full, counterclockwise circle from where he first left his two buddies.

And then he heard the sounds. At first, he thought the animals were running straight for him. He quickly drew his Beretta 9 mm pistol and sent up a flash prayer, hoping not to have to use his sidearm. A gunshot would certainly alert whoever was inside the building. He quickly searched the ground for something to throw at the wild boar sow headed in his direction. Nothing useful was there.

Thinking he might have to pull the trigger, the sow and the three squealing piglets behind her were about 20 yards away and charging toward him. At about 15 yards from Alvarez—just before Alvarez squeezed the trigger—they veered off at a 45-degree angle. Moving as fast as they could, they headed past the house and in the general direction of Kovalenko's position. The piglets were falling behind their mama. In the next instant, Alvarez saw the wolf. It was gaining on the piglets.

In a split second, the 36-inch-high, deceptively agile, and surprisingly quick 110-pound wild boar turned around. The wolf, at roughly 26 inches high and 50 pounds lighter, stopped. The entire scene was unfolding about 35 yards from Alvarez. Alvarez stood as close to a 16-inch-thick beech tree as possible. He knew that if the wind conditions were right, the preoccupied animals might never observe him. At the same time, he knew at that distance that whatever was about to happen, he had a good chance of walking away unscathed.

The wolf made a pass at one of the piglets. That was a bad decision without four or five other wolves to help him. The protective wild boar immediately attacked the wolf, driving its tusks and sharp teeth into one of the wolf's shoulders while ripping about a four-inch piece of fur and flesh from just below the wolf's shoulder. The wolf screamed a chilling, high-pitched scream-bark that echoed through the forest.

Alvarez heard the house's shutter windows open. Suddenly, light spilled out from the house's second-floor window into the forest. It was the Russian, nervously peering out into the darkness.

"What the hell was that?" he said, looking at Gio and Lia, still seated at the kitchen table.

"What? Has the Ruskey never heard of wolves in the wild before?" replied Gio, chuckling and shaking his head.

Lia laughed out loud.

Alvarez, having put the tree—about 30 to 40 yards from the building—between him and the open window, heard the Russian yell back to Gio and Lia but could not make out Gio's response.

In the next instant, the wolf, who had not yet retreated and whose hunger was overcoming its pain, stood firm. With her piglets whimpering behind her, the boar made another lunge at the wolf, almost missing it but butting the wolf's wounded shoulder with her hard snout. The wolf yelped and turned away, limping and whimpering into the darkness.

The wild boar did not hesitate to turn around and lead her squealing threesome through the forest in the general direction of Kovalenko. Within 50 yards, the boar picked up Kovalenko's scent and veered sharply to the right, avoiding and bypassing Kovalenko by a similar distance.

The Russian shut the shutters and returned to the kitchen and adjacent living area.

"I didn't know Italy had wolves," said Ivan.

"They are in many places in Italy, but especially in Calabria," replied Gio.

Alvarez waited until he could no longer hear the wild pigs and then waited another two minutes.

He continued to move counterclockwise around the clearing toward Kovalenko's position. Alvarez keyed his walkie-talkie to let Kovalenko know he was approaching.

"I'm inbound," whispered Alvarez, wanting to make sure Kovalenko did not mistake him for someone else.

Alvarez's transmission woke Kovalenko up. He'd just dozed off no more than a minute prior. Kovalenko realized he'd dozed off. Taking a second to remember where he was at, he was not quite sure who it was that was approaching him. His night vision goggles soon assured him that it was indeed Alvarez approaching.

As Alvarez slowly but deliberately stepped forward in the darkness, Jake moved over to Kovalenko. Both men were now standing, waiting for Alvarez to take his last few steps. Alvarez and Jake knew that sound always carried farther at night.

Alvarez finally got within touching distance of Kovalenko and Jake.

"Well, that was *fun*," deadpanned Alvarez in a whisper.

"We could hear it all the way from here," said Jake.

"We thought we might have to come get you," added Jake, smiling.

Alvarez laid out the entire scene to his two battle buddies.

"I can't be sure," concluded Alvarez. "With some daylight, we should know for sure. But I believe there are bars in that small window down there. And there are at least two people in that building. I think we might have hit the jackpot."

Jake's heart soared. But he was also anxious.

If Sara was in there, he thought, *what kind of shape would she be in? What must we do to ensure we get Sara safely out of there?*

CHAPTER 82

Bars

JAKE LOOKED AT HIS ANDROID GPS BLACK WRISTWATCH. On this emerging spring day, the sun would rise in another 27 minutes, at 6:19 a.m. Some ambient gray light was already appearing in the forest. Jake loved that Alvarez was firing up some espresso. It would go well with the granola bars and dates Jake had brought along for breakfast, originally intended for just him and Kovalenko but now to be shared among the three of them.

The previous night, they had decided their only option was to sleep under the stars. They moved upslope away from the clearing about thirty yards before Jake and Alvarez broke out some old Vietnam-era, camouflaged army poncho liners. They provided a surprising amount of heat, given their light weight. Colonel Kovalenko had simply pulled another layer out of his backpack. All three used their backpacks as pillows. They could no longer see the house, but that also meant nobody in the house could see them.

As the temperatures were expected to hit highs of 78F in southern Italy, Kovalenko decided to remove his additional layer and stick it back in his backpack. In a few minutes, the rising sun would be fully visible, and it would begin to evaporate the night's dew on the grass and weeds around them.

"For the best observation points, we'll need to low crawl back down to our original positions from last night," said Jake.

We'll stay no more than ten yards apart from each other. Your fields of observation will be the same. Hennadiy, you have our left flank and left rear from six o'clock to ten o'clock. Manny, you've got two o'clock to six o'clock on our right, and I'll take ten o'clock to two o'clock, with the house at twelve o'clock. If you see anybody approaching, don't challenge the person unless it's clear that we've been compromised."

Both men nodded their understanding.

"Our mission today is to find out as much as we can about what's going on in that house and in the end, determine if Sara is in there. It's one of the three buildings the bishop suspected, and we've eliminated the first one. But still, just because Manny observed life in there, we can't automatically assume Sara's in there, too."

"Roger all," replied Alvarez.

Kovalenko nodded and then simply said, "Got it," before asking, "but what if she is in there, Jake?"

"Then we do what I said we would," replied Jake. "We step back, and I'll call Colonel Ricci in Rome. I trust him. Until we know what the lay of the land is in there, let alone that Sara is in there, we can't do much. We don't have the forces nor the firepower, and if she is in there, I don't want to put Sara in danger by just stumbling in there."

CHAPTER 83

Shots Fired

LYING ON HIS STOMACH AND PROPPED UP on his elbows, Jake held his binoculars steady. He could clearly make out the three black objects in the window. There was no doubt about it: there were three vertical bars in the small window on the first floor.

Could Sara be there? he again asked himself.

"You were right about those bars," said Jake. "I can see them, Manny. There is no doubt. Now, the question is, who, if anyone, is behind them?"

"Yep, I can see them, too, boss," replied Alvarez.

"Our mission remains the same," said Jake. "But we have to get more intel on who is going in and out of that place and why they are there in the first place. It might take days."

"We have the time, Jake," Kovalenko reassured him. "We have the time for you and Sara."

Jake gave Kovalenko, who was also in the prone position, a thumbs up and a big smile.

It did not take "days," however, for a new development.

"Gents," whispered Alvarez about forty-five minutes later, "there is a vehicle driving up to the building. Looks like a mid-sized silver sedan."

Alvarez, who was the farthest to the right of the three, could just barely see part of the area behind the building, on the right side as the three faced the building. He got maybe a three-second glance at the car before it disappeared directly behind the building.

"We need to work around to the back of the building to get a better look at that car," said Jake. "I'll do it."

"No, sir," replied Alvarez. "I already know the lay of the land down there. If I can recon it at night, I sure as hell can recon it by day."

"Are you sure, Manny?" asked Jake, knowing it was a futile and rhetorical question.

"*Cento percento* (one hundred percent)," replied Alvarez in Italian.

Alvarez got up and immediately began moving toward the building.

Several minutes later, as Alvarez was working his way around the right of the clearing and back to the building, Jake and Kovalenko saw the second-floor window shutters swing wide open. Peering through their binoculars, they were surprised at what they saw in the room.

A woman? thought both near simultaneously.

***

On the other side of the building, the Russian looked out the window toward the two-track road. He'd heard the car driving up. He was close to panicking, thinking he had more time.

As the car drove up to the building, the car's passenger-side mafia man told the driver, "Don't draw your weapon until we get upstairs. If he hesitates to comply with our orders, we will kill him right then and there."

No sooner had he said that when he looked up and saw the Russian in the window, looking down at the car and the two mafia men seated in the front and approaching the building.

Their orders had been clear, "take him across the border." They understood that was code for killing him and dumping his body in one of the remote caves in Aspromonte, where, according to locals, only hardened 'Ndrangheta criminals ever dared to venture.

The night before, thinking the Russian had gone to bed, Gio mentioned to Lia in the kitchen area that "they're coming to get the Ruskey tomorrow." Ivan had his ear to the bedroom door as he did most every night before he went to bed in the room shared with Gio. All night, from the moment he'd heard that, Ivan had been planning his getaway on foot. He believed taking his chances with Calabrian wolves was safer than hanging around for whatever fate awaited him at the hands of the mafia soldiers on the way to get him.

The Russian left the window, went to his bedroom, and grabbed his pistol from between his mattress and the metal-framed bed springs. He slipped the pistol under his belt in the small of his back and made sure his long-sleeved black cotton shirt was pulled out of his pants and covering his backside.

As the two physically imposing mafia soldiers got out of the car, they looked back at the house window. The Russian was no longer there. They were told by Gio "to just come on in" when they arrived.

The first mafia soldier said, "Wait. It's been a long trip. I gotta take a leak."

He walked over to the oak tree not far from the building and relieved himself. He returned to his partner and said a simple *andiamo* (let's go).

The first mafia man entered through the house's old wooden door with his partner close behind him. He found the steps to the right, grabbed the rickety railing, and began climbing.

Ivan, at the top of the stairs, grabbed his pistol from the

small of his back. He waited for the second man to be on the steps. Assured the second man was also on the stairs, he turned the corner, glanced downstairs, and raised his pistol. Both men were holding the railing of the steep stairs, with the first man about to look up. The second man was looking down at the heels of the man in front of him. Ivan shot the second man—still looking down—in the crown of his head. As he tumbled backward, Ivan aimed at the first man, whose terrorized eyes were now locked with Ivan's. The mafia man highest on the steps struggled to draw his weapon from his shoulder holster as Ivan pulled the trigger, taking off the side of the man's cranium from an eight-foot distance.

Ivan immediately turned toward the kitchen. Gio, sitting unarmed, bolted off his chair to see what happened. Ivan shot him in the neck and face. Gio died instantly, crumpling to the floor. Lia started for her bedroom. Ivan screamed at her and told her to put her hands up. In lifesaving compliance, she stopped, her arms above her head.

"Put your hands behind your back," directed Ivan.

Lia again complied.

"Don't make another move, or I'll blow the back of your head off," said Ivan.

He placed handcuffs on Lia, who would now be his hostage.

Jake, Alvarez, and Kovalenko heard the sounds echoing out of the concrete building and across the clearing. They were unmistakable.

If Sara is in there...is she alive? Jake wondered in growing fear. *Dear God, let her be alive.*

Alvarez kept moving toward the house, wisely skirting the clearing all the way, but now moving much faster, practically bounding from tree to tree.

Ivan took Lia by the arm and led her down the stairs and past the two dead bodies, grotesquely crumpled at the bottom of the steps.

"Stand here and don't move," he said to Lia, leaving her at the door's exit.

Ivan, recognizing the driver, searched the pockets of the man lying near Lia's feet and took the car keys out of his pocket. The Russian placed the keys in his pocket and headed to the jail cell. He turned the corner toward the cell. Intent on seeking revenge for the "indignities" Sara had caused him, the Russian started to raise his pistol toward a terrified Sara. She was unflinchingly standing near the back wall of the cell's wall; her side turned toward the Russian in a brave effort to make a smaller target.

At that instant, Lia tried to kick the front door open, succeeding on the second try. She got about ten feet out of the building before Ivan shouted, "Stop!" and fired a warning shot through the doorframe. The shot almost hit Lia.

Lia stopped. Her diversion had worked—at least for the moment—in keeping the Russian from shooting Sara.

Alvarez, now about 50 yards behind a tree with a good view of the back of the building, could not tell if Lia—dark-complected like Sara but shorter—might be Sara.

After all, *she's been held captive for several weeks*, thought Alvarez. *She might look a little different at this distance.*

Alvarez could see that the Russian had grabbed the woman by the arm and was moving her toward the car. Alvarez keyed his radio and told Jake what he was seeing.

"They're trying to make a break for it in the car," said Alvarez. "He's got a woman with him! She looks like Sara…but I *cannot* confirm it is Sara. I will try to delay them. Get to your bike, sir, and maybe you can cut them off or catch up with them before they get too far!"

His combat leadership decisiveness kicking in, Jake told Kovalenko, "Go provide backup for Manny. He needs your help. And don't get shot!"

Jake bolted in the direction of his motorcycle. The former high school two-sport athlete and West Point boxer knew that he needed to cover over 200 yards in the fastest run of his life. He sprinted as hard as he could, avoiding all obstacles—dead logs on the forest surface, brush, saplings, and the dreaded "wait a minute" vines growing in the thicker areas—like an American football running back picking his holes and seeking daylight through which to run. Within a half-minute, the 43-year-old's lungs and legs were on fire, but adrenaline and thoughts of Sara took over.

As the Russian shoved Lia into the back of the car, Alvarez fired his first shots, trying to hit the vehicle's front tire. But he knew he had to be extra cautious because if his aim was off, the woman now in the back seat could take a bullet.

The Russian immediately got down on the ground and, lying next to the car, returned fire. Manny kept the tree between him and the Russian. Lia lay down on her side in the back seat, trying to make herself a smaller target while adding a little protection with the shut car door between her and the shooter from the tree.

Alvarez fired another shot, then waited. The Russian reached up from the ground to the driver's side door and quickly crawled into the front seat. Keeping his head down, he pulled the keys from his pocket and started the car, quickly slamming it in reverse.

Alvarez fired another two shots, being sure not to hit the car. Aiming *at* the car was now too dangerous. He simply wanted to give the driver something to think about and possibly delay him further.

Alvarez radioed Jake. "They're on the move in a silver sedan."

Now, within 20 yards of the Ducati, the radio transmission spurred Jake faster.

Quickly backing out, the Russian pulled a 180-degree buttonhook maneuver in the car and bumpily headed down the two-track road and into the thick forest.

Jake hopped on the Ducati, quickly throwing on his helmet without fastening the strap, and started the engine. In Jake's mind, every second counted.

"I'm on the bike and on the move!" Jake radioed to Alvarez and Kovalenko.

CHAPTER 84

Divine Intervention?

KOVALENKO CAUGHT UP WITH ALVAREZ IN THE FOREST. The getaway sedan had only departed seconds prior.

"Let's check inside," said Alvarez. "I will lead the way."

Alvarez moved in short spurts from tree to tree and, within seconds, reached the side of the building. He quickly moved around to the open door. He'd assessed that while an adversary might still be in the building, he also figured that after all the shooting, the odds for that were low. Kovalenko was right behind him.

Meanwhile, the Russian drove the sedan as quickly as it would go down the narrow mud-puddle-pocked two-track road, knowing that a crash would ruin his plans of escaping with a hostage who might later bail him out.

Jake steered the Ducati down the gravel road, which ran parallel to the two-track road with about 250 yards between them. Both Jake and the Russian traveled south. Jake sensed he needed to take the first right he came upon, as that was in the general direction of the road connecting to the turnoff and back to the house.

At the house, Alvarez and Kovalenko kept their weapons drawn and at the ready as they entered the house. They immediately stepped over the two dead mafia members, crumpled half on the last three stairs of the staircase and half in the hallway leading from the front door. Alvarez checked each for a pulse. Nothing. Alvarez proceeded cautiously up the blood-splattered staircase, trying to keep the old wooden stairs from creaking, but it was impossible. Kovalenko followed.

Hearing the two men climb the stairs and having heard the gunfire outside earlier, Sara wasn't sure if the newcomers she heard on the stairs were more mafia types or someone else. She decided to keep quiet and pray fervently.

After traveling for a half-mile on the two-track road, the Russian came to a T and took a right, now traveling on a slightly wider, rarely grated, dusty road.

A minute later, Jake also took a right and headed west on the very same road as the Russian. Jake didn't know it, but he was about a half-mile behind the Russian and Lia, headed west. Jake accelerated the Ducati, traveling as fast and as safely as he could.

Back in the house, Alvarez and Kovalenko crested the steps and turned toward the open living area. Alvarez needed to only take four steps when he saw Gio lying face down in a pool of his blood. Again, Alvarez checked for a pulse. The man was dead. Alvarez and Kovalenko quickly cleared both bedrooms and then looked out the window to the clearing. Nobody was there. They headed back for the stairs to see what was behind the small, barred window they had spotted earlier in the morning.

Jake saw the dust trail from the Russian's car ahead of him and knew he was getting close. And then, there it was, through the intermittently dissipating dust cloud: the silver Fiat sedan, bumping along the dirt road. The Russian spotted Jake in his rearview mirror and sensed trouble.

And then, the Russian saw the sheep ahead of him at about the same time Jake did. Slowing down and approaching the herd of sheep even more slowly, the Russian began honking his horn as often and as loud as he could. The horn honking had little to no effect. The sheep were not bothered by the vehicle's sounds. The Russian stopped the car. He had to. The sheep were jammed on the narrowly confined road, with a gradual slope up to the left and a very steep and dangerous slope—almost a sheer drop off—to the right.

Knowing the danger, especially off to the right, the road is exactly where the shepherd wanted his sheep to be. The sheep's safety was the shepherd's first and overwhelming priority.

The upward slope to the left was too steep for the old Fiat sedan to traverse. There was nowhere to go for the Russian but straight ahead. Looking in his rearview mirror, the Russian could see the Ducati less than 100 yards away and closing. The Russian thought if he drove over one or two sheep, the others would be terrorized enough to move up to higher ground. He crushed one bleating sheep under the vehicle and then another.

The shepherd's dog was barking as if it had lost its mind.

The shepherd turned around and couldn't believe what he was seeing. He reached for his waist-holstered pistol and fired a warning shot in the direction of the sedan.

"*Che cazzo stai facendo!*" yelled the shepherd.

The Russian, realizing the futility of continuing forward, threw the vehicle's transmission into park, got out of the vehicle, opened the rear passenger door, grabbed Lia, and jerked her out of the car with him. He slowly walked her backward up the wooded slope while keeping his eyes on the shepherd. He held the still-handcuffed Lia around the neck with his left forearm and his pistol in his right hand. The Russian was facing the shepherd, about twenty-five yards to his front left, and quickly shifted his gaze to the right, to Jake, who had dismounted the Ducati and was about thirty-five yards from the Russian.

"You both just keep going, and she will not get hurt," said

the Russian in Italian.

Jake could now see that the woman, who had clearly been forcefully taken, was not Sara. He was confused and disappointed.

And then Jake's radio crackled.

"Jake, we have Sara!" Alvarez's voice yelled through the walkie-talkie. "She's safe! And the vehicle you are hunting for is being driven by a Russian psycho who has taken a friend of Sara's!"

Jake's heart leaped with joy that Sara was safe, but he instantly realized he needed to resolve the crisis unfolding in front of him.

The man holding Lia kept backing slowly up the hill.

Jake knew his best option was to distract the man while thinking of his next course of action.

Jake knew maybe five words of Russian, and he was about to use one, hoping to throw the man off balance.

"*Nyet* (no)!" he yelled as loudly as he could. The sound of the Russian word for "no" put the Russian back on his heels. He figured the man who had been on the Ducati was just another mafia man coming to kill him.

The shepherd gave a low-volume command—almost a whisper—to the sheepdog, and the dog moved farther up the slope, slightly to the left of the Russian's peripheral vision. The Russian was focused on Jake.

"Why don't we do *this*?" asked Jake, "You let her go, and we let you go. You know she's only going to be a burden to you, anyway. Right? You'll be forced to move much slower with her constantly at your side."

Calculating Jake's offer, the Russian hesitated. What Jake said made sense. Moving through the rough Calabrian hills, she would only be a liability.

"So, what do you say? You release her, and we're good," added Jake.

There is no way I'm letting that bastard just walk away, thought the shepherd.

"How do I know you won't follow?" asked the Russian.

The shepherd gave another one-word, soto-voiced command and a head nod to his wolf-slaying dog.

By the time Jake had finished slowly saying, "Now, why would I want to follow you? What I want is...," the Maremma sheepdog, just out of the Russian's peripheral vision, exploded across the thirty feet between him and the Russian. The Russian didn't know what hit him.

The dog took a powerful vice-like bite out of the man just above his left hip. The searing pain almost caused the Russian to black out. The pistol came out of his right hand, and his hold on Lia's neck fell away. The Russian helplessly dropped to his knees and then to his right side. Lia immediately grabbed the pistol and, facing the downed Russian, took several steps backward down the incline. The dog ripped into the man's left forearm, and the shepherd gave the dog another single word, Calabrian-accented, Italian command. The dog returned to the shepherd and took up a seated position next to his master. The dog—ready to spring into action again if his master so commanded—continued to observe the whimpering and crying man on the ground.

The Russian started gasping from pain from the serious bite wound to the left of his hip. Two inches higher, and the bite would have punctured his spleen. As it was, the dog's teeth had penetrated the man's small intestine and barely missed his stomach. The bite to his left forearm was extremely painful.

"Are you OK?" asked Jake of Lia.

"Couldn't be better," said Lia, visibly shaking and still holding the Russian's pistol and pointing it at him.

Jake approached the Russian and examined him. The shepherd commanded his dog to tend to the sheep, and the shepherd also walked over to the Russian.

Jake's medical training as a US Army Combat Lifesaver, which he had volunteered for as a lieutenant when on his first army assignment with the 173d Airborne Brigade in Vicenza, Italy, kicked in.

"He should survive," said Jake to Lia and the shepherd, "but that wound to his side will need to be kept closed and as clean as possible until he gets competent medical help. He's not losing a lot of blood, so that is good. Those bites on his arm will need to be cleaned and patched up, too."

"I couldn't care less if he doesn't make it," said Lia. "He's an animal, not a human. That dog is more of a human than that sick Ruskey son-of-a-bitch."

"I don't know what your laws are in Italy," said Jake, "but where I come from and where I was trained, I have to do my best to treat this man...or make sure he is treated by someone else."

"Well, you are not only in Italy," said Lia, disgusted. "You are in Calabria. And *our* laws are *different*."

The shepherd smiled but stood motionless and silent. He understood Lia, but he also somehow understood the American, too. He could have commanded the dog to kill the Russian, but he didn't.

Jake took off his camouflage shirt, wrapping it gently around the man's open flesh wound and stomach, tying the sleeves together to secure it in place.

"If you want to live," he said to the Russian, "you need to keep constant pressure on the wound."

"Are you the American who is married to Sara?" asked Lia. "The one who was in the news a few weeks back, after we...uh, after she...got snatched?"

"Yes, I am," responded Jake.

"Well, you married a tough lady," said Lia. "You should be proud of her."

Lia walked back to the vehicle and grabbed one of her tennis shoes that had come off when the Russian yanked her out of the back of the sedan. She put the shoe on, made her way through the bleating sheep on the road, and kept walking.

I wonder if Jake knows she is pregnant, thought Lia, headed into the Calabrian hills that she knew so well.

"Sir, are you *OK*?" crackled Jake's radio.

"I'm fine, Manny," said Jake. "What about Sara? Please put her on."

Jake heard some ruffling background sounds as Alvarez passed the radio to Sara.

"Jake!" exclaimed Sara.

"Hi, beautiful," said Jake, "how are you?"

"Now? Couldn't be better!" she responded. "*Ti amo!*"

"*Ti amo molto di piu*! (I love you much more!)" replied Jake.

Both were crying tears of joy.

"We will get you out of there as soon as we can," said Jake to Sara.

Jake explained the plan to her. Jake would call Colonel Ricci and explain everything to him. Sara was to stay at the house with Alvarez and Kovalenko until the Carabinieri got there to hear everyone's account of the preceding events. Jake would request two helicopters. Jake would pass the GPS coordinates for the building to Colonel Ricci and explain to him that a helicopter could easily land in the adjacent field. He would then recommend they get Sara to the regional hospital in Reggio Calabria as soon as possible and have her checked out. Jake would ask Colonel Ricci to order a second medevac to get the Russian to a hospital as well. Jake would stay with the Russian until he was medevacked and then head for the hideout as soon as that task was complete.

"Also, Sara, I recommend you use Manny's cell phone and call General Comitini's office yourself and let him know you're fine. You are fine, aren't you, *Cara Mia*?" asked Jake a second time.

"Hearing your voice, I'm better than fine," Sara replied.

Jake could hear the relief and love in her voice. His eyes continued to stream. Taking a bracing breath, he continued, "OK, if you haven't left the hideout by then, I'll go straight back there and fly with you to the hospital. If you leave before I get out of here, I'll meet you at the hospital."

Sara, ever the Carabinieri officer, considered Jake's plan… and agreed with it.

As Jake waited for Colonel Ricci to answer his phone call, Jake looked at the shepherd, his dog, and the sheep. Two words came into Jake's mind: *Divine Intervention*.

Thank you, he thought, looking to the heavens above.

CHAPTER 85

A Celebrity

JAKE WALKED THROUGH THE AUTOMATIC SLIDING GLASS DOORS of Reggio Calabria's *Riuniti* ("Reunited") Hospital and approached the front desk. The attractive, *olivastra*-complected forty-something nurse behind the counter looked up from her computer terminal.

"How can I help you, sir?" she asked.

"I'm here to see Sara Simonetti," answered Jake.

"What is your relation to her?" asked the lady.

"I'm her husband," responded Jake.

"May I see your identification cards?" she asked.

Jake reached into his wallet and pulled out his Italian driver's license and his US military retired ID card.

"Oh, you mean Carabinieri Lieutenant Colonel Sara Simonetti."

The lady smiled.

"Yes, that's her," Jake responded.

Jake could see three other women, two seated and one standing behind the counter, turn their heads toward Jake.

"She's only been here a little over an hour, and she is already a celebrity," said the lady.

Another nurse at the adjacent computer terminal smiled approvingly and nodded her head.

Jake smiled, too.

"She's up on the third floor, in the maternity ward," replied the nurse.

"Did you say *maternity ward?*" asked Jake.

"Yes, in—room 3B201."

Jake's mind spun, unsure what that meant.

"Please take only the number two elevator," added the nurse.

Jake took the number two elevator to the third floor. He did not know it, but because of the special patient on the third floor, the other elevator was programmed not to stop on the third floor. Only the number two elevator did that. As Jake exited the elevator, there was a Carabinieri guard seated on the opposite wall. The officer stood up and asked Jake for his ID. Jake again pulled out both ID cards and told him he was there for Sara Simonetti.

The guard smiled broadly and gave Jake an enthusiastic handshake, wanting to kiss Jake on his cheek.

"So, you are the *American*! It's so nice to meet you, *signore*!"

The Carabinieri corporal handed the ID cards back to Jake.

"She's just down the hall, last door on the right."

"Nice to meet you, too," replied Jake.

Jake turned and headed down the hallway, only to see another Carabinieri officer outside the door.

The officer whom Jake had just met nodded vigorously to the officer down the hall, meaning Jake had been cleared to enter the room where Sara was.

Jake slowly turned to enter the room. Sara, lying in her bed, was talking to a female doctor who had just completed an ultrasound on Sara five minutes earlier. The two ladies were in animated, pleasant conversation.

Sara turned her head toward the door and saw her handsome man standing in the doorframe, in jeans and a black t-shirt. She held out her arms, the tears flowing unbidden down her glowing cheeks.

The doctor—her face beaming—stepped back and looked at Jake.

Jake walked quickly across the room to Sara's bedside. He bent over at the waist and hugged Sara where she lay, back against the elevated bed. They cried and hugged for a long time.

"Everything is fine!" said Sara finally, giggling through her tears. "We should know if it's a girl or boy in about three to four weeks!"

CHAPTER 86

Three Months After Aspromonte: "Finito"

LIA LOOKED AT HER FAMILY ALBUM. In her grandmother's home, Lia realized she had reached the end of the line in working for the 'Ndrangheta. Due to Sara Simonetti's positive comments about her treatment from Lia—"they were perhaps even lifesaving, for me and my unborn child," Sara had told investigators—there would be no warrants for Lia's arrest.

It must be that the Carabinieri have "bigger fish to fry" than some low-level mafia functionary, thought Lia.

Lia became resolute in her plan. *She would help her grandmother around the house for another six months, for a modest monthly stipend and free room and board, before seeking employment elsewhere, maybe in northern Italy, or maybe even in Germany,* she dreamed. A waitressing job seemed like a perfectly good new place to start, no matter where that was.

Ho finito (I have finished), she thought, *with this warped way of life.*

Lia's heart had been forever softened by Sara Simonetti, whom she greatly admired.

***

Nikolai, "the Torturer"—a.k.a. Ivan—who had tortured civilians in Syria; who had gruesomely tortured a hapless and unfortunate Myanmar Army colonel on behalf of "the Wolf" and his deputy, Boris Stepanov, both now in prison, and who was sickly perverted in wanting to torture and abuse Sara Simonetti as well, was stunned at the short jail sentence. A mere five years was all the judge meted out to him.

What Ivan didn't realize—or couldn't recall—was that during his first week in the hospital when the Russian criminal was at times delirious with fever from his infected wounds, he had told everything he knew to his Carabinieri interrogators. It was all they needed to hear.

"You tell us everything, and we'll get you the best drugs available," said one of his interrogators, "and, if you behave in this hospital, we might even be able to get you a very reduced jail sentence."

Ivan told them *almost* everything, including how he got hired by the 'Ndrangheta, as well as providing additional incriminating evidence against his former boss, Boris Stepanov, and how Ivan had killed the three mafia men, including Gio, at the hideout. The Carabinieri got everything on tape. There was one thing the Carabinieri strongly suspected: Nikolai was a marked man. And they were not wrong.

What Ivan didn't realize when he received his sentence—and not even his defense lawyer told him—was that he was being sent to Italy's infamous *Badu 'e Carros* prison near the town of Nuoro, on the Italian island of Sardinia. The prison held two significant populations: terrorists—domestic and international—who had committed their terror and crimes against the state of Italy, and former mafia members from all three of Italy's prominent mafia organizations, including 'Ndrangheta.

Within two weeks of entering the prison, Ivan was found hanging in his prison cell by a simple but sufficiently long "Made in Italy" men's belt. He died naked and severely mutilated.

CHAPTER 87

Five Months After Aspromonte: Rome

THE SHEPHERD LOOKED AND FELT UNCOMFORTABLE in his new dark blue suit, with expensive brown leather shoes. His grandmother had purchased the ensemble and insisted the shepherd wear it for the big occasion.

Being escorted by a young Carabinieri officer to the large room where the event was about to take place, the shepherd was curious about some of the young female Carabinieri officers who gave the young Calabrian man a second look. The shepherd wondered, *does my suit fit OK? Why are they smiling at me like that?*

The fit of his suit, of course, was not what the ladies were looking at. The young man, at 6 feet tall, with a dark southern Italian complexion and black curly locks, was strikingly handsome.

A female Carabinieri officer in her twenties stood outside the large meeting room, greeting people and handing out the programs for the ceremony that was about to happen inside.

The young, bold Carabinieri officer, with blue eyes and dark blond hair, was instantly smitten by the handsome, unassuming man with the elderly lady as they approached. She chose her words carefully.

"Could I ask your name, sir?" She inquired of the shepherd.

"Yes, Ma'am," said the shepherd. "My name is Marco Marino. I was invited to..."

The young lady cut him off.

"I know who you are," said the beaming Carabinieri officer, her knees almost buckling.

"We have been waiting for you. My name is Marina. Here is the program for today's ceremonies. And who is the lovely lady beside you?" she asked.

"She is my *nonna*," responded Marino.

The lady also handed Marino's grandmother a program.

"Please step inside," she said to the shepherd and his grandmother. "The ceremony will begin in about seven minutes."

As they walked into the spacious room, with his grandmother proudly wearing her Sunday best, the shepherd didn't see any faces he recognized. And then, as if out of nowhere, he felt a tap on the shoulder.

"Great to see you again, my friend," said the American in Italian. He also wore a fine dark blue suit, but he looked far more comfortable and confident in it. "I hope you are well. Who is this beautiful lady next to you?"

"She's my *nonna*," said the shepherd, "and if it wasn't for her, I probably would have ended up like that Russian."

Jake smiled and shook the lady's hand. Tears welled up in her eyes from what her grandson had just said. The American introduced his wife Sara to the shepherd and his grandmother. The shepherd was stunned by the elegant woman's grace, beauty, and charm. In her third trimester, the woman still looked fashionable in her stylish maternity dress.

Also present for the ceremony, to be led by a Carabinieri three-star general, were US Army Sergeant First Class Manuel "Manny" Alvarez and Ukrainian Air Force Colonel Hennadiy Kovalenko. They were both in their formal military uniforms, with Alvarez wearing the more formal Army Blue Service Uniform (often referred to as "blues"). Alvarez's wife, Cristina, proudly sat in the audience, as did Colonel Kovalenko's wife, Mila.

A young Carabinieri major, who was serving as the three-star general's aid, asked the audience to be seated. He then introduced the general, who lauded the significance of the "valorous actions" of the four honorees present, now standing on a small stage—flanked by the Italian *tricolore* (tricolor) national flag and the general's three-star flag—in the large conference room: one honoree from Italy, one from Ukraine, and two from the United States.

Before presenting each man his award, the general also mentioned a certain sheepdog. And to the sound of warm applause, gave the shepherd a Carabinieri Certificate of Appreciation for his loyal dog.

One by one, the major read the citations for the valorous actions of each honoree in the room. He began with the shepherd and concluded with Lieutenant Colonel (Ret.) Jake Fortina. In each case, he read their names and then the award to be received.

"The brave shepherd, Marco Marino, who stood calm in the face of great danger and aided in the apprehension of the Russian criminal, thereby saving the life of Lieutenant Colonel (Ret.) Jake Fortina, is awarded the Order of Merit of the Italian Republic, in the rank of Knight."

"Colonel Hennadiy Kovalenko, for his participation in the efforts to find Lieutenant Colonel Sara Simonetti-Fortina and bravery in the face of danger, is awarded the Order of Merit of the Italian Republic, in the rank of Officer."

"Sergeant First Class Alvarez of the US Army, who twice volunteered to recon the house and who also engaged the Russian criminal with his weapon, 'thereby slowing the criminal's departure from the hideout,' is awarded the Order of Merit of the Italian Republic, in the rank of Commander."

"Lieutenant Colonel Jake Fortina, for leading the effort to

find his wife, Lieutenant Colonel Sara Simonetti-Fortina, and for organizing the medical evacuation efforts of the Russian and his Carabinieri wife, is awarded the Order of Merit of the Italian Republic, in the rank of Commander."

The room erupted in applause.

Three months later, Marco Marino was offered the opportunity to enter the ranks of the Carabinieri. He accepted the opportunity without hesitation. As to the Dutch girl who jilted him at the end of the previous summer, he completely forgot about her. A beautiful young Italian Carabinieri lady from Lucca became the love of his life.

CHAPTER 88

Nine Months After Aspromonte: The Baptism

"IN THE NAME OF THE FATHER, OF THE SON, AND THE HOLY GHOST," said the Catholic priest as he sprinkled holy water on the baby boy's forehead. Sara cradled and looked at her newly christened son, Giacomo Giorgio Fortina.

Sara had chosen the first name Giacomo—and Jake had agreed—because while also meaning "James" in English, Giacomo meant Jacob or "Jake" in Hebrew. The Giorgio name was to honor Sara's father, a Carabinieri captain who died at the hands of a Sicilian *mafioso* when Sara was just four years old.

Sara looked up at Jake with a full heart. Love filled Jake's eyes. She looked around and smiled at each of their friends, gathered in a semi-circle around the baptismal font at the private ceremony in the church in Vicenza. It was the same church where she and Jake married.

Sergeant First Class Manny Alvarez stood with his lovely wife, Cristina. The decade-long friendship between Alvarez and Jake had extended to their wives after Manny and Cristina's marriage in this same church.

Colonel Hennadiy Kovalenko and his wife Mila were there, too. Some two-plus years prior, Kovalenko and Fortina supported each other with invaluable intelligence about the Russian oligarch, Anatoly Roman Volkov, a.k.a. the "Wolf," as well as what was going on inside the Kremlin. More recently, the

Kovalenkos had taken Jake in when he most needed personal security and a place to which he could clandestinely escape.

The Carabinieri officer, Colonel Ricci, was also there, as were Jake's friends from nearby *Peschiera-del-Garda*, the Bovos.

After the baptism, the entourage left the church. Jake held his dear son, Giacomo. He and Sara smiled at each other. They were en route to a nearby *taverna* for what would become a long Italian lunch. They knew their future—and that of Giacomo—was more than bright.

ACKNOWLEDGMENTS

The author wishes to acknowledge the superb reviews of the manuscript by Lieutenant General (Italian Army, Ret) Gianni Marizza and Major General (Italian Carabinieri, Ret) Sebastiano Comitini.

The author also acknowledges Rachael Rhine Milliard's brilliant collaboration in editing, designing the book cover, and preparing *Change of Mission* for publication.

ABOUT THE AUTHOR

RALPH R. "RICK" STEINKE is the award-winning author of *Next Mission: US Defense Attaché to France* (2019; a revised version to be republished in 2025 or 2026), a memoir selected as a finalist for the Indie Excellence Awards and Honorable Mention for the Readers' Favorites Book Awards. He is also the author of the *Major Jake Fortina* series, including *Major Jake Fortina and the Tier One Threat* (2022) and *Jake Fortina and the Roman Conspiracy* (2023). Both books have received recognition, individually and as a series, with the Chanticleer International Book Awards in the Global Thriller category. *Roman Conspiracy* won the First and Grand Prizes in the Chanticleer Global Thriller category.

Steinke has spent a lifetime in US national security roles, including twenty-eight years in the US Army and fourteen in the Department of Defense. His official duties have taken him from the US Military Academy at West Point to over thirty countries on the Eurasian landmass, including Afghanistan and Ukraine.

While serving as a US Army exchange officer with the *Susa Alpini* (Alpine Infantry) Battalion in Pinerolo, Italy, Steinke deployed to Italy's Calabria region in November and December 1990. That deployment—directed by the Italian government—was in support of Italian local citizens who were besieged with crimes and kidnappings by the 'Ndrangheta Mafia.

Steinke holds master's degrees in West European studies and Diplomacy from Indiana and Norwich Universities, respectively, as well as post-graduation certificates in National and International Security Affairs from Harvard and Stanford Universities. His personal passions include faith, family, fly fishing, and travel.